TO THE BONE

DAVID WOLF BOOK 7

JEFF CARSON

CROSS ATLANTIC PUBLISHING

DAVID WOLF SERIES IN ORDER

Gut Decision (A David Wolf Short Story)– Sign up for the new release newsletter at http://www.jeffcarson.co/p/newsletter.html and receive a complimentary copy.

Click Here to instantly add Audible Narration of To The Bone,
and keep the story going wherever you go.

CHAPTER 1

THE GIRL STOOD at the side of the dirt road, rooting around inside her trunk. As she looked up at Wolf's approaching vehicle, he recognized her immediately.

She must have recognized him too, because her first reaction was to step back and drop her jaw.

Skidding to a halt, Wolf rolled down his window just as a cloud of dust engulfed them both.

"Hi, Cassidy," he said, peering through the choking dirt.

"Hi, Mr. Wolf."

Her pristine red German sedan was tilted to the rear passenger side.

"Flat tire?"

"Yes," she said, waving a slender hand in front of her face.

"Sorry." He squinted as a hot blast of air came in the window. "Let me pull over. I'll give you a hand."

"Okay, thanks," she said with a mixture of relief and what sounded like dread in her voice.

He pulled behind her car and shut off the engine. As he stepped out onto the shoulder, the weeds snapped and crunched under his old leather work boot, flushing out some grasshoppers that scattered like popping popcorn. Their cracking wings and the burbling Chautauqua River below on the opposite side of the road were the only sounds.

It was only 9 a.m. and the early August sun was cooking the back of his neck.

The wind cleared the dust and Cassidy Frost stood with her hands in the pockets of her frayed jean shorts, which were barely more than a bikini bottom in Wolf's estimation.

He knew Cassidy Frost, had known her well for the past seven months, because she was dating his fifteen-year-old son, Jack. She was just older than Jack, two months into her sixteenth year, and with a driver's license; and since Jack was living with Wolf, and still without a driver's license, Cassidy had been burning a lot of gas, driving up and down this road lately.

But today? He hadn't expected to see her today.

Her eyes were wild-looking, adrenaline still pumping through her veins from the tire, and she stutter-stepped forward with an outstretched hand.

He nodded and took her thin, dainty hand, which tensed into a firm shake.

She really was quite beautiful. Her large blue eyes always reminded Wolf of his late ex-wife, Sarah. And then there was the straw-blonde hair streaming across her face. The resemblance was uncanny, and he knew it was more than coincidence that Jack was drawn to this girl who looked like his mother.

Skid marks had gouged the gravel just a few yards from where she'd pulled over. It was clear she'd been traveling just above unsafe speed when the blowout had happened, and now the adrenaline-powered look in her eye made sense.

"You all right?"

She nodded.

"You have a spare, right?"

"Yeah, it's in the trunk."

He walked to the open trunk. Inside, a piece of carpeted plastic had been pulled away, revealing a thin spare tire and a cheap, insufficient-looking jack. Next to the compartment, a sleeping bag was pushed into the corner, and next to that was a duffle bag, dusty with a piece of pine bark clinging to the fabric.

Pretending not to see those two items, he pulled out the tire and jack.

"I was trying to call for help,"—she held out her phone—"but there's no service here."

"There's never any service all the way down this road until you hit our house."

He wondered where Cassidy's tent was.

"I'm going to help you do this, all right?" he said. "Every sixteen-year-old needs to learn how to change a tire."

She smiled sheepishly and put her phone in her back pocket. "I know. My dad keeps saying the same thing."

Wolf helped her set up the jack, remove the tire, and put on the spare. She was a quick study, asking intelligent questions, all in all diving into the whole thing with a commendable attitude.

But his mind reeled as he watched the sixteen-year-old girl tighten the last lug nut.

Just a sleeping bag and a duffle bag. Where was her tent?

"Mr. Wolf?"

"Yeah?"

"I ... was asking, what next?"

"Oh, yeah." He showed her how to lower the car safely and stow the damaged tire and jack—once again playing the unobservant idiot with the camping gear as he pushed down the trunk with a thump.

"Take it into Mitch's tire shop as soon as you can," he said, keeping his hand on the warm paint of the trunk.

They stared at one another for a few seconds.

"And, Cassidy?"

Cassidy swallowed. Her face dropped and her lip quivered involuntarily as she looked into Wolf's eyes. "Yes?"

"Were you camping with Jack last night?"

Her eyes welled up with astonishing speed.

"What's the matter?"

"You think I'm some sort of slut. I know it."

His mouth dropped open and his face went red hot.

"I see it. I know you do."

He felt like he was being punched repeatedly in the stomach. "Cassidy, I don't think that."

She was openly weeping now, tears splashing in the dust.

He reached out a stiff arm and patted her shoulder, unsure of what else to do. "No. I don't think that."

"I hope you're telling the truth." She looked up with desperate eyes and sniffed.

It was the truth. He often questioned where the second half of her outfits had gone, but he'd known a lot of sluts in his day, and Cassidy Frost was not one of them. Her parents were good people and he knew they were good parents, and she was a good kid. And if Jack and Cassidy were now ... ugh ... "I just saw your sleeping bag. Jack didn't tell me you were included in the group of his friends going camping."

Her eyes narrowed for a second and then she looked away, and Wolf knew at that moment there was no "group of his friends."

"Take the tire into Mitch's tire place. You know it?"

She nodded.

"Tell him I sent you. Or tell him your dad sent you, I guess. He knows your dad too. But get it taken care of. You don't want to get another flat tire and be stranded in the middle of nowhere with no way out."

She nodded and stared up at him, and then her lip started

quivering again.

"That would suck," he said with a smile.

She burst into her own smile. "Yeah, it would."

He saw a perfect moment of escape so he backed away. "Okay. See you around. Drive careful. Drive slow."

"I will. Thanks, Mr. Wolf."

She wiped her nose and climbed in the car, started it, and drove away back toward town.

He watched her trail of dust disappear around the bend, and then sat behind the wheel with a sigh.

"What the hell ..." he murmured to himself as he fired up the engine.

He drove at a steady clip up the meandering Chautauqua River toward his house, seeing little of the road ahead of him. It was times like these that he missed Sarah the most. Not that he thought she would know what to do in this situation. In fact, he could picture Sarah's eyes darkening with a distant gaze, and her jaw screwing shut at the news that her son may have just spent the night with a girl.

He smiled at the thought as he drove up the hill to the headgate of his ranch. He missed having a partner, a teammate, to work these things through with. But she was gone. The problem was all his to bear now.

Nate Watson was at his house already, parked in front and standing on the circle drive next to the tall lanky figure of Jack. Jet, a retired German shepherd police dog that Jack had adopted six months ago, wandered next to the barn with his nose on the ground.

Wolf came to a stop behind Nate's full-sized pickup truck, which was branded with a Watson Geological Services Inc. decal that included a professional-looking logo.

"There he is," Nate said with a smile.

Jet lifted a leg against the barn and stared into the woods, and Jack waved and kicked at a weed.

"Sorry I'm late," Wolf said, closing his door. "I had to help a motorist with a flat tire. Hey, Jack. You're home early."

Jack nodded, offering no further explanation.

"I thought you weren't coming back from the trip until tomorrow morning. Heck, you made a big enough deal about it."

Jack shrugged, still averting his gaze. "Mitch Henderson drove, remember? His mom called and wanted him home for some emergency."

"Really? What emergency?"

"Psh, I don't know."

"I hope it's not serious."

His son shrugged and pointed into the distance. "Nate says you guys are cutting trees because there's a fire up north?"

Wolf nodded.

Jack squirmed under his gaze and took a theatric breath. "Well, all right. I'm going to go inside."

Wolf nodded.

Jack loped away on his stick legs toward the house, picking up his camping gear on the way and dumping it by the kitchen door.

Nate Watson stepped forward and clamped his hand on Wolf's.

With each pump of his friend's hand, Wolf was reeled out of his dark mood. "Hey."

"What was that about?" Nate asked in a low voice.

Nate was a thick stump of a man. Standing at five foot seven, he was at least two hundred pounds, with a thick chest and an inverted delta-shaped torso, like the men Wolf had served with as an army ranger.

Nate's blond hair was shaved to the scalp nowadays, hidden under a sweated-out Colorado School of Mines hat—both ways of coping with the growing bald spot on the top of his head.

The two men had grown up playing football together. The field was where they had bonded, with Wolf at quarterback and Nate at running back, with Nate always there to block for Wolf, always there to throw a bail-out pass to when there were no other options.

Through the years, despite the occasional missed blocks and footballs that had hit him in the back of the helmet, Nate had always been the most reliable man Wolf had ever known. And true to undying form, Nate was here now.

"I just saw his girlfriend. She blew a tire down the road and I helped her change it. He was camping with her, not his friends."

Nate nodded and gazed into the distance. "Yeah, I know. I was here when she dropped him off."

Wolf narrowed his eyes.

"I was going to tell you."

Like the other people Wolf chose to surround himself with, Nate was a reliable man, but he was also a man that liked to sugarcoat things. He also had the habit of omitting information if he deemed it would cause someone unneeded stress.

Wolf shook his head. "No, you weren't."

Nate ignored him and turned to the north. "So, you're freaked about this new fire, huh? I thought you and Jack already had a hundred feet of defensible space cleared around this joint."

A horrific smell swirled around them for a few seconds and then dispersed on the wind.

Nate wrinkled his nose. "What the hell is that?"

Jet sat a few yards away with a leather glove in his mouth. He dropped it and backed up, looking proud of his find.

Wolf bent over and picked it up. "I lost that glove months ago. Good job, boy."

Jet's tail swished and thumped on the crispy grass.

"That's cool that he finds things," Nate said, "but what's wrong with his ass?"

"Let me guess," Wolf raised his voice toward Jack, who was back outside, picking up his tent, "you forgot to give him the medicine before you went camping."

Jack stared at the sky in thought.

"Why don't you go get it?" Wolf said.

Jack looked at him.

"What?"

"I don't know where it is."

"Maybe Cassidy can give you a ride to refill the prescription today."

Jack nodded and disappeared back inside.

Six months ago, Wolf had gotten a call from a friend in the Vail Police Department asking whether he was interested in adopting a retired German shepherd police dog named Jet. Wolf had looked at the implications of taking in the dog, and knew he wouldn't have time to take care of it with his job, so he'd said no.

Overhearing Wolf talk about it the next day, Jack had told him categorically that he wanted it.

With Jack losing his mother almost a year ago, and the depression, anxiety, and anger that followed finally showing signs of lifting, there was no way Wolf was going to say no to his son. So he called his friend back and said yes.

When they'd driven up to meet the dog, Wolf had been impressed. Jet was massive, which had concerned him at first because, like other German shepherd police dogs, Jet had been taught various commands such as *Fass!*, which was German for attack. But the dog's demeanor had been calm and stoic, like a wise old man who'd seen plenty of battle and saw little that surprised him now.

During the visit, they'd learned of Jet's nine-year career

with the Vail County Police Department as a tracking dog, busting countless smugglers and criminals along the I-70 corridor over the years. In the end, they'd been charmed by the dog and brought him home.

On many occasions since, Wolf had seen the animal's intelligence, and his bursts of impressive speed and strength. But Jet was quick to tire and getting on in age, there was no doubting that.

Along with fatigue and a passion for finding things that his human master might find useful or illegal, Jet had developed a bacterial overgrowth in his small intestine, common with German shepherds, and now, unless Jet kept up with a regimen of pills from the veterinarian, he tended to live up to his name— jetting hot air from his backside

Nate cleared his throat and slapped Wolf on the shoulder. "The fire?"

"Yeah. Have you heard about it?"

"The brush fire north of Cave Creek? I heard about it from you this morning."

"Right. Well, I had Jeff Adkins up here the other day and he was saying I should clear those trees on the southwest corner."

Jeff Adkins was the local fire chief and he had been doing house calls, making sure everyone was ready if and when a fire hit.

Nate put his hands on his hips and looked to the southwest. "They haven't been touched by the beetles."

"They haven't, but everything else out there has."

The forest to the south howled as a hot blast of wind blew through the trees.

It had been one of the driest summers on record, and after a hundred years of fire suppression coupled with the widespread pine-beetle infestation of the Rocky Mountains and Mountain West, huge tracts of forest that had once been green and thriving were now rust-colored, dead, and hollowed out by the voracious bugs.

At least half of the trees visible to the south and west of Wolf's property had been hit.

"And that fire to the north has you spooked, and you want to make sure you're prepared if some jackass tosses a cigarette butt out the window on Williams Pass," Nate said.

"You know me well, my friend."

While the acreage to the south and west was thick forest, the trees on the east mountainside behind Wolf's house had been charred and scarred from an explosion years ago, and now saplings grew where the new gaps had been made. As for the reconstruction of his house, it had been long, and Wolf had lived in a half-shell of a house with no running water through one cold winter. He'd likened the experience to living in a shallow cave and he wanted none of that again.

"There're seven to cut," Wolf said, pointing.

"Piece of cake." Nate picked up the plastic case at his feet. "I've got my Stihl. Yours probably won't start, so, you just want me to go ahead?"

Wolf ignored him and went to the barn to retrieve his own chainsaw, knowing full well that Nate was probably right and it was going to take some doing to get the finicky motor of his much older saw to turn over.

Jack came back outside staring at his phone, and stumbled at the bottom of the stairs.

Probably getting a text message from Cassidy explaining that their little jig was up, Wolf mused. Or one of the million other things he did on that phone every day.

"Dad." Jack put the phone to his ear.

Wolf slowed to a stop at his son's excited tone.

"What's up?"

"Cassidy?" Jack held up a finger to Wolf. "Why? ... okay,

okay." Jack stepped up and thrust the phone at Wolf. "It's Cassidy. She wants to talk to you."

Wolf raised both his hands like Jack had a pistol pointed at his face. "Jack, tell her we'll talk later. After you and I have a talk."

"Dad." Jack put the phone against his body and covered it with his other hand. "I've never heard her so freaked out. Something happened. She said something about how she couldn't call 911 on her phone."

He thrust the cell out again and Wolf took it.

"Hello?"

"Mr. Wolf! My—"

There was scratching and then silence.

"Cassidy?"

No answer.

Nate and Jack stared in mute curiosity.

"Cassidy? Can you hear me?" Wolf's curiosity was piqued. The few words he heard definitely sounded spooked.

"Mr. Wolf? Can you hear me?"

"Yes. What is it?"

"My dad's been shot. He's been shot. Can you hear me? I can't call 911 on my—"

Silence again.

"Is he hurt?"

No answer. Damn it. Damn the cell service. And what a question, Wolf thought. Of course he was hurt. He was shot.

"Cassidy? Is he okay?"

"No."

The simple answer, the clarity and desperation in her voice, made Wolf's insides sink.

"Go to the Sheriff's Station, Cassidy. Go there now."

CHAPTER 2

WOLF STOOD ALONE in front of the Frost residence next to Ryan Frost's corpse. The driveway was the size of a baseball infield and about the same dirt consistency. Surrounded by trees and sheltered from the wind, it radiated heat like a skillet, and with the sun blowtorching the back of his neck he felt like a piece of sizzling bacon.

"DOA," Wolf said into his cell phone.

"Shit." Sheriff MacLean's voice was crisp in Wolf's ear.

A swarm of flies had set in on the body and they bumped against Wolf's jeans. He ignored them and kept rooted to his spot. "I see two sets of footprints behind the body. No brass on the ground. Shot in the back of the head. Looks like an execution-style murder."

"Ah, Christ, that's all we need right now. That pile-up in Cave Creek, and now a murder? It's like death came into town ..."

Wolf pulled the phone away from his ear and eyed the ground. Cassidy had left for the station after her call to Wolf, and since he'd gone straight to her home he hadn't gotten the full story from her. The dirt beneath his feet told him plain enough, though. Small footprints, deck shoes, trailed up to Ryan Frost's body and skidded to a stop. Wolf imagined Cassidy driving up, wondering what her father was doing as she slowed, the panic as she parked and got out of the car, the disbelief when her father wouldn't answer her, the realization as she got close enough to see the blood ... he shivered and blinked the thought out of his mind.

MacLean's monologue came from his phone speaker, but he ignored it, opting to concentrate on the weight of the department-issue Glock in his sweating palm. Twisting, though not moving his feet, he scanned the woods again.

Cassidy had come and gone unharmed, which meant it was likely the culprit was long gone. But the dead body at his feet had his senses on edge. There was no doubt Ryan Frost had been killed in cold blood. Half the man's face had been deformed by the bullet exiting his cheek. Then there was another blossom of red in the center of his back. Some psycho could have driven away, parked somewhere a couple of miles out and hiked his way back through the forest to see the ensuing police action. It happened all the time in cities—murderers returning to the scene of the crime.

"Wolf! You there? Damn cell phones."

Wolf raised the phone to his ear. "Yeah, I'm here." At the same moment, he noticed the front door to the house had been left open.

"Are you listening?"

"I've gotta go."

He pocketed the phone without ending the call and ran to the edge of the house. The front door bumped shut, then rebounded open, seeming to be driven by the wind.

"Sheriff's Department! Come out with your hands where I can see them!"

Once again, the house breathed through the front entrance.

The door was made of solid wood, adorned with softly glowing frosted glass. Nothing moved behind the windows as far as he could tell.

Sweat slid down his temple and he wiped it away. He caught movement in the corner of his eye and aimed his gun.

A chipmunk stared back at him, twitched his tail, and scurried out of sight beneath a downed log.

He stepped up onto the concrete porch and, ducking low on one knee, he pushed open the door and aimed his pistol.

The door opened noiselessly all the way in a one-hundred-and-eighty-degree swing and bumped against the wall.

"Sheriff's Department!"

The only answer was a soft, pulsing high-hat with a steady bass pattern emanating from somewhere inside.

With a final scan of the woods, he slid into the house, gun barrel first. He ignored the floor-to-ceiling windows displaying the majestic views of the green-sloped ski resort and town below as he swept through the main floor.

The kitchen was all stainless steel and shiny rock, with no one inside it. As he entered a home office, he faintly registered the giant boulder in the middle of the carpeted space and the walls of dark-wood shelves stocked with countless hardback books. He could stand and gawk at the impressive interior of the house later. At the moment, they were distractions that could get him killed. He moved on and through the four bedrooms upstairs. Each had crisply made beds, including Cassidy's room.

Making his way back downstairs and down a long hall, he reached a lone closed door and opened it, revealing a darkened garage. He snapped on the light and pointed his gun. No one was inside, but Wolf straightened and leaned back at the sight of what was. Two shiny black Land Rovers, a Mr. and Mrs. pair, were parked on the left, and to the right was a collection of what looked like ancient bones.

Hundreds of them. There was blue masking tape on the smooth concrete floor separating specimens from other specimens, and within each of the cordoned-off areas were neat arrays of bones, claws, skulls, and tusks. Some were recognizable: a triceratops skull, a mammoth tusk. Others were just lumps of dirty rock to Wolf's untrained eye.

He closed his mouth and backed into the house again. Shutting the door, he moved down the hallway, back the way he'd come.

Toward the music.

It came from downstairs, he realized, so he walked over rustic wood floors in the main great room to the edge of a wide staircase leading down.

"Sheriff's Department!"

He aimed his gun down the steps and crept closer. A flashbang grenade as a precursor would have done nicely right about now, he thought. In fact, he was not about to go down without one. His six tours of experience in the army had instilled him with a healthy dose of paranoia.

The faint sound of an approaching siren floated in through the open front door.

There. He crouched and stepped back when he saw movement downstairs—a piece of blue fabric that had come into view and then disappeared.

He backed up another step and crouched to get a better look, but the angle between the ceiling downstairs and the stairway was too small.

The sirens were louder now.

Natural light lit the downstairs level, streaming in through windows that probably matched the enormity of the ones upstairs. He made a quick decision—bolting out the front door and taking a right.

He moved along the bright front of the house to the south

side and paused. Pistol ready, he turned the corner, and saw it was clear. He stalked his way down the slope, sliding on dried pine needles, to the rear of the house.

Wind chimes clanged, dangling from the underside of the rear deck. Trees on the slope below howled and creaked.

He stopped and peeked around the corner. No one. Edging his way to the first window, he peered inside and saw the blue fabric again, which was now clearly a hanging drape fluttering on the wind streaming through an open sliding glass door.

The music was louder now, a steady urban beat playing through tiny top-of-the-line speakers mounted in the corners on the underside of the deck.

Inside he saw the recreation room he had heard plenty about from Jack on many occasions. There was a pool table, a pinball machine, two couches, and a large flat-screen television. Framed European landscapes hung on the walls.

He stood for a full minute, looking inside the window. All the while sirens grew in volume over the howling wind until they were right outside the front of the house.

Still, there was no movement inside. Nobody fleeing out the back door next to him.

His phone vibrated in his pocket.

He answered. "Yeah."

"Where are you?" Deputy Tom Rachette said. "Why aren't you on your radio?"

"I shut it off. I'm at the rear of the house. I want you to stay out front. I'll be right there."

"Are you inside?"

"I'm going to come out the front door. If there's someone else in here I'll probably flush them out."

He pocketed his phone and walked to the sliding screen door. Covering his hand with his shirt so he would preserve fingerprints, he slid the door open and walked inside.

The music was louder still in here, and he walked to the stereo and poked the power button with his knuckle, plunging the room into silence.

Once again, he stood motionless, listening to the wind outside and the clanging of window coverings throughout the basement. They were the sounds of a hastily abandoned house —a house whose owner had stepped out with every intention of returning, but got sidetracked with a gunshot to the head and back, and never returned.

After a quick sweep of the downstairs, he returned to check the upper floors before emerging through the front door.

Deputies Heather Patterson and Tom Rachette were behind the hood of their SUV with pistols trained on him as he walked outside.

They relaxed and pointed their guns skyward.

"All clear." Wolf's voice echoed through the trees, joining the sound of another approaching siren. He took his radio from his duty belt, turned it on, and pushed the button. "I'm looking at a pistol discarded right here in the bush next to the front porch."

He stepped off the cement porch and down the walkway to the beginning of the dirt. "I see four sets of footprints here. They go all the way to the body. And you can see Cassidy's prints there. And mine."

Patterson scribbled in her notebook.

"Off to your left"—Wolf pointed—"I saw fresh vehicle tracks."

He stepped back to the porch and walked along the front of the house, then skirted the trees and returned to his deputies. "Looks like two gunshot wounds. One to the head, one to the back. No brass."

Rachette eyed Ryan Frost's body. "Anything else?"

Wolf clipped the radio back on his duty belt as he neared them. "Probably a lot else. A bunch of bones in the garage."

"Bones in the garage?" Rachette's eyes were wide with alarm.

"Like fossils. Animal bones."

"Oh."

The revving engine and roaring tires of the second department SUV drew their gazes down the dirt road. The driver kept his foot on the gas until the last second, at which point he mashed the brake and began a long slide that ended with a rocking vehicle buried in an explosion of dust.

"Easy, Turbo," Rachette said. "My God, this guy."

Deputy Patterson had ignored the chaos behind her and stood rock still, looking at Ryan Frost's corpse. Her Colorado sky-blue eyes were hard, unblinking, all business and forensic science. She pulled a stray strand of her shoulder-length auburn hair behind her ear and looked at Wolf for the first time. "Ryan Frost you said? This was Cassidy's father? Jack's girlfriend?"

He nodded.

"Geez."

Rachette pulled off his SBCSD ball cap, revealing a brand-new buzz cut of his blond hair underneath. Wiping his forehead, he said, "Damn. It's hotter than Satan's nacho farts out here." He pushed his tongue against a wad of chewing tobacco in his lip and spat on the ground.

Patterson twisted her face. "Why don't you show a little respect?" She gestured to Frost's body and then to Wolf.

Rachette shrugged and looked at Wolf. "What?"

"That's Jack's girlfriend's father."

Rachette mouthed the words silently, and then looked at Wolf. "Shit, sorry. Man, I didn't know that."

Deputies Barker and Hernandez thumped their car doors shut and emerged from the cloud of dust.

Deputy Greg Barker was in front as was his alpha nature, trotting at three quarters of a sprint. At six foot one, he was muscular with freckled white skin and red hair and moved like a track star. "Sorry, sir, we were up at mile marker 137 for the 10-32. Five cars."

"So I heard," Wolf said. "You guys got here fast."

Deputy Jon Hernandez approached with thumbs hooked on his belt, his eyes fixed behind them at Ryan Frost's body. He let out a whistle through his teeth, mumbled a quick sentence in Spanish, and crossed himself.

Soft from eating his wife's meals, but certainly fit enough to make Wolf's squad, Hernandez was short, an inch taller than Rachette, but had a large personality that everyone had warmed to. Everyone save Barker. Warm feelings and Barker never fit well together.

Barker stood shaking his head, hands on his hips as he craned his neck to see behind Wolf. His blue eyes were wide and his chest heaved. "Damn."

Wolf looked back at the swirl of shoe prints in the dirt, and a thought knocked the wind out him. He remembered that one of the shoe prints behind the body had been about Wolf's size and with a diamond tread pattern that resembled Converse All Stars. Many young people wore that shoe, and said person with large footprints would have been tall. Wolf knew a tall young person intimately. Did Jack have Converse All Stars?

"Sir?" Patterson asked.

"Boss?" Rachette asked. "What's the matter?"

"Let's get to work. Patterson, get the camera and start processing the body. Hernandez and Barker, I want you two inside. Is Lorber on his way?"

She nodded. "Yep. He and his team will be a few minutes."

"Rachette, secure the scene. Set up the tape a good hundred yards up the road. I don't want ..." Wolf let his sentence die at the sound of popping tires. A truck was easing down the road toward them.

"Who's that?" Hernandez asked.

Wolf shielded his eyes and stepped toward it. "I don't know."

The truck rumbled at an idle, the tires crackling as it approached at no more than a few miles an hour.

When Wolf put his hand on his pistol, the truck skidded to a stop. He pulled the pistol and held it pointing at the ground in front of him.

With the glare, it was impossible for Wolf to see through the windshield, but whoever was inside was no dummy. Two arms thrust out the open driver's window, palms out.

"Don't shoot!" a voice said, barely audible behind the diesel engine. One hand disappeared and the engine shut off. The truck rocked in place, and then the open hand appeared again. "Don't shoot!"

Wolf stepped sideways to the edge of the woods to get a view inside the driver's window, keeping his pistol at the ready.

The man fumbled with the door, trying to open it from the outside. It was locked so he had to reach back inside to unlock it.

The door opened and bounced on its hinges.

Wolf saw a shiny leather loafer first, and then the driver stumbled out from behind the truck door. In that moment, he also saw that the passenger seat and the rest of the extended cab appeared to be empty.

"Hi," the man said with a disarming smile. "Scott Levenworth. Please don't shoot me."

The man was in his early fifties. His hair was wavy gray, full and swept back like he was sitting in a wind tunnel set on low speed. He wore a snap-button cowboy shirt rolled to the elbows, revealing tanned arms. His fingers were adorned with multiple rings. A gold watch circled one wrist, a gold bracelet the other.

His teeth gleamed in the sun like they were under a black light. "Can I put my hands down now, Deputy?"

Wolf twirled his finger. "What are you doing here, Mr. Levenworth?"

The man closed his door and put both hands on the hood of his pickup.

Wolf frisked him quickly and thoroughly, checking the waistline, which was wrapped with a handmade leather belt and large buckle. The man's cologne was thick.

"You can turn around." Wolf holstered his gun and backed up.

Scott Levenworth had lost his smile and gained a puzzled look. He kept glancing toward Wolf's squad of detectives, who stood staring back at the new visitor.

"My God," Levenworth said. "They killed him?"

CHAPTER 3

WOLF STARED AT THE MAN, waiting for more words that never came.

"Who's they?" he asked.

The man said nothing, still staring at the corpse down the road.

"Who?" Wolf raised his voice a little.

Levenworth blinked and snapped to attention. "What?"

"You said 'they' killed him. Who are 'they'?"

The man's eyes were drawn to the corpse, which seemed to override his ability to speak.

"Sir, why don't you start by showing me your driver's license?"

The man dug out his wallet and produced his ID, an Arizona driver's license that confirmed the name he'd given. Then he produced a business card that had a raised gold symbol —an eagle clutching arrows and an olive branch in its claws, which Wolf recognized as the Great Seal of the United States. The black writing said *Scott Levenworth, United States Senator, Arizona.*

"Senator?" Wolf asked.

Senator Levenworth nodded absently.

Wolf stepped between the senator and the view of the body, and Levenworth focused on him as if for the first time.

"What are you doing here, Senator?"

"I'm here to pick up the bones I bought from Ryan Frost."

Wolf remembered the scene inside the garage. "The bones?"

"The fossils."

"And what kind of fossils are we talking about here?"

"Dinosaur fossils."

Things were coming back to Wolf about the activities of Ryan Frost. Cassidy had once come to dinner with Jack at the house, and she'd mentioned that her father was "into" fossils. Wolf hadn't known at the time that being *into* fossils meant he was selling them.

"Ryan Frost ran a business selling fossils?"

Levenworth raised his eyebrows and nodded. "He's a big deal in the fossil trade world."

"Really."

He'd apparently appeared confused because Levenworth said, "The company is called Ancient Acquisitions. He's kind of a legend in some circles. A broker who sources bones for buyers. Has a fancy website. Booths at all the big trade shows. But I think he does everything out of his home here. As far as I know, he's a one-man operation."

Wolf nodded again. "You said ... you asked if they'd killed him when you drove up. Please, tell me who you're referring to."

"I guess I meant the sellers of the bones. Frost is the broker. I'm the end buyer."

"The sellers?"

Senator Levenworth stared at the ground in deep thought. His breathing became shallow.

"Senator."

"It makes sense. They wanted all the money up front."

Levenworth shook his head. "They probably took the money. Hell, they probably kept the bones. Gah! Dammit. I knew I shouldn't have ..." Levenworth turned and rubbed his face.

Wolf thought again about the small set of footprints that ran up to Ryan Frost's body. He remembered Cassidy's shaky voice on the phone.

"Senator, I need you to start making sense."

"Yeah, sorry. I gave Ryan Frost a million dollars last week."

Wolf raised an eyebrow. "I didn't know it was possible to even get that kind of cash in this day and age."

Levenworth chuckled. "It's tricky from a bank, but I didn't get it from a bank. I had it."

They locked eyes for a few seconds, listening to the howling treetops and the ticking pickup truck.

"I need you to come down to the station and tell us everything."

Levenworth looked back toward the house. "Yeah. Okay, sure."

"Barker," Wolf said into the radio.

"Sir."

"Please come over here."

Barker strode over, his small eyes volleying between Wolf and the senator as he neared. "Sir?"

"This is Senator Levenworth. He's here because he had a business transaction scheduled with Ryan Frost. Please escort him to the station—"

"I know where it is, Deputy," Levenworth said.

Wolf turned to Levenworth. "Still, I would like my deputy to escort you. I'll be in shortly. At that time, I'd like to take your statement personally."

Levenworth's eyes narrowed, as if he rarely took orders from anyone and didn't like it. Then, with a strained smile, he said, "Yeah. Okay."

CHAPTER 4

AN HOUR AND A HALF LATER, Wolf pulled into the Sluice–
Byron County building's parking lot and shut off the engine. He
stepped out onto the asphalt, which gave off so much heat he
felt it on his chin.

He could scarcely remember feeling so hot in the Rocky
Mountains of Colorado. This was a place that fogged breath
most mornings, even in mid-August, and now it felt like the
deserts of Arizona.

Stepping through the automatic doors and into the building
was like moving into a walk-in refrigerator. He weaved his way
through the shiny halls and past the administrative offices,
passing men and women he'd never met but knew by sight.
There was a lot of that in Rocky Points nowadays. The locals
had been overrun by neighbors to the south. That went for here
in the building, the Sheriff's Department upstairs, the bars and
taverns in town, and everything else in between.

The town was still Rocky Points, getting a modern update in
most places, but still quaint despite a few more people. It was
easy enough for Wolf to get used to. But the county building
was something else altogether. Because besides the onset of

hypothermia, whenever Wolf entered the place he also felt like he was entering a city. The fast pace, the suits and ties, the politics, and the bureaucracy were overbearing.

He walked past the elevator and the terrazzo stairway that led to the Sheriff's Department and went to the front reception area.

Jack, Cassidy, and Nate were sat in chairs in a nook near the windows. Jet was lying on his side next to Cassidy's chair, his chest heaving as he slept.

Jack stared at a muted television playing baseball highlights while Cassidy sat next to him, staring through the carpet.

Tammy stayed in her chair behind the reception counter, nodding greeting to Wolf with a reassuring close of her eyes. Wolf had spoken to her earlier for an update and she'd assured him she'd do all she could to keep Cassidy comfortable.

Nate rose from his chair and walked over. "Hey."

"How's she doing?"

"She's in bad shape."

Cassidy turned at Wolf with an unblinking, haunted gaze. By the looks of her sunken red eyes, she was cried out and numb.

"What about her mother? Have you asked where she is?"

Nate nodded. "I talked to her earlier on Cassidy's phone. She's sitting at the airport in Sacramento. She was at some health-food conference."

Cassidy's mother was the owner of Mountain Organics Market, which was commonly referred to as "MOM's" by the locals.

"She said her flight comes in tonight to DIA. It was the earliest one she could get. I wrote down the flight number." Nate dug in his pocket and produced a wadded piece of paper and handed it to him.

"Thanks."

"Ryan took her to Denver to catch the flight yesterday and was supposed to go pick her up from the airport tomorrow night, so she has no ride back."

Wolf nodded. "I'll go get her."

Nate stared at him and shook his head. "I don't know how you do this shit." He glanced over his shoulder at Cassidy. "You got any leads on who did this? We gotta be on the lookout for some psycho running around? My house is less than a mile from theirs."

"We're not sure yet, but it looks work-related. I'd keep the gun handy, that's for sure."

Jack had his arm around Cassidy now. The situation was too much for two kids their age, Wolf thought.

He slid his gaze to Jack's shoes, which were of the low-top hiking type with athletic tread on bottom. Perfect for camping, he supposed. He couldn't recall what Jack had been wearing earlier in the day.

Now that he was staring at his son in the flesh, though, he realized that Jack didn't wear Converse shoes. Never had. Even during his skateboard years. He remembered the old pair of Vans that had disintegrated on Jack's feet, and then —yes—it had been another pair of Vans that he'd wanted after that, and Wolf had bought them. It had been a whole thing with Sarah about who was going to go with Jack to buy them that day.

Vans had a universal tread pattern as well, but they were tiny diamonds, or crisscrossing lines, or ... hexagons? Octagons? Whatever the pattern, it was completely different to the one he'd seen next to Ryan Frost's dead body.

Why was he still convincing himself?

Wolf looked at Nate and realized his friend had been talking. "What's that?"

"I said her brother is on his way up from Blue Mesa Reservoir. I can take them all to my house when he shows. This is no place for them to be hanging out all day."

"Did they take her statement?"

Nate nodded. "Yeah, Munford took it. I was there."

Wolf took his hat off and walked to Cassidy. "Hey, Cassidy."

She stared up with hopeless glassy eyes.

Jet stretched and groaned, then resumed his deep sleep.

"I'm sorry, Cassidy," he said.

She swallowed and blinked.

"I just wanted you to know that I'll go pick up your mother from the airport tonight."

She nodded.

"I hear your brother is on his way. When he gets here, Nate has offered to put you guys up for the night, or however long you need. He has plenty of room at his house."

Nate nodded and sat down. "We talked about it."

Cassidy sniffed, closed her eyes, and leaned on Jack's shoulder. And then it looked like she went instantly to sleep.

CHAPTER 5

WOLF MADE his way to the third floor via the stairs and walked down the long hallway, not bothering to stop at his own office, which was one of a string of four along the west side of the building.

With a good view of Main Street below, and plenty of space, his personal room was a dramatic improvement over his last office, but he spent little time there. Just like the rest of the building, the space made him want to be *out*.

The Sheriff's Office stood on the west side of the cathedral-like squad room at the end of the hall. A large cube made of glass that butted up against the exterior windows, the Sheriff's Office's architectural design apparently had a psychology behind it. MacLean seemed to embrace it, keeping the blinds open to impress upon his deputies that he was an accessible leader, transparent in his actions. Or so Wolf had heard him declare once to a county-council member.

Not now, though. Right now, the wooden blinds were closed. Over the chatter and bustle of deputies, Wolf heard the bellow of MacLean's laugh and someone else inside coughing as if choking on liquid.

He walked to the heavy wood door and knocked just below the gold plaque that said *Sheriff William MacLean.*

The knob twisted and MacLean peered out. "Oh, there you are."

He pulled open the door and walked back to his desk. "Come in."

Wolf followed him in and closed the door behind him.

Senator Levenworth sat across the desk from MacLean, sipping a cup of coffee. Next to him, Deputy Barker sat with crossed legs, smothering a smile against his own cup of steaming liquid.

Barker's smile vanished, and he stood and took position standing next to Wolf.

"Take a seat with us," MacLean said, landing in his own leather chair, which hissed underneath him.

"No thanks. I'll stand."

"You mind freshening this?" Senator Levenworth held up his empty cup. It was unclear whom he spoke to.

Wolf and Barker stared at it for a second, and then Barker stepped forward and grabbed it.

"I'll take that, Deputy," Wolf said.

Barker paused. "Wh—? Are you sure?"

Wolf grabbed it from Barker's hand and left the office.

"Two sugars, please," Levenworth said before the door clacked shut.

Wolf went out to the squad room and walked to the kitchenette counter area where the coffee maker was. He swirled the meager contents of the beaker and poured it into a Styrofoam cup, filling it a third of the way.

"Sir."

He turned and leaned back at the closeness of the voice. Deputy Barker had followed him out.

"Hey," Wolf said. He reached over to the tap and turned on

the hot water.

"Sir, I feel I need to fill you in on who Senator Levenworth is."

The water was scalding in less than five seconds, which was a nice modern feature of the brand-new county building.

"Looks like he's a friend of yours," Wolf said, filling the rest of the cup with the water.

Barker blushed and then frowned. "Uh ... you're just going to fill up the cup with water?"

"No." Wolf ripped two packets of sugar and poured them in.

Barker grabbed a red plastic stirrer and held it out.

Wolf ignored it and walked past him.

Barker stepped next to him. "He's the chairman of the Appropriations Committee for the Senate. Or the Senate Appropriations Committee, or whatever it's called."

Wolf slowed. "So what?"

"So ... that's the committee that basically controls the federal money. And he's the head honcho."

Wolf blinked.

"I'm just saying. We need to be delicate with this guy."

"Thanks for the heads-up."

"Yes, sir."

He reached MacLean's office with Barker in tow.

"Here you go," Wolf handed the cup to Levenworth.

The senator furrowed his brow and swirled the contents of the cup.

"Here you go, sir." Barker held out the red stirrer.

"Thank you, Greg."

Wolf cleared his throat. "I'm not sure what you've already told the sheriff and Deputy Barker here, but—"

"Everything." Levenworth took a sip of his cup.

"But I'm the chief detective of this department, and I'd like to hear it all again. Let's start with where you were last night."

Levenworth took his time with another sip of coffee water, then smacked his lips and frowned, like it was the worst-tasting thing he'd ever had. "Like I told the sheriff, who has since confirmed, I was at my residence in DC. I had a committee meeting yesterday. I flew in to Eagle Airport this morning and drove down to Rocky Points immediately after landing. You can confirm with the aviation company, the pilots, the stewardess ... especially the stewardess"—he bounced his eyebrows—"you can confirm with the Senate Appropriations Committee members. That enough?"

MacLean leaned forward in his chair. "Detective Wolf, I have let our esteemed senator know that we're in no doubt of his whereabouts, but we're checking on it."

Wolf nodded. "Can you discuss this deal, this fossil deal, in a little more detail, please?"

"I purchased some fossils from Mr. Frost. I was here to collect my bones."

"And take them where?"

"To my home in Flagstaff."

"In the back of ... whose truck is it that you're driving?"

"My own. I keep it at my Beaver Creek residence."

"Okay." Wolf nodded. "These bones cost you a million dollars. You were just going to put them in the uncovered bed of your pickup truck?"

"They're encased in casting material. The drive wouldn't hurt them any."

"Ah." Wolf took off his hat and scratched his hair. "I'm still confused about the terms of this deal. I don't see how you could just give Ryan Frost a million dollars and trust him to deliver on his end of the bargain. Wouldn't you rather use some sort of escrow service, or something? A non-cash mode of payment? To get some sort of guarantee you wouldn't get ripped off in the end?"

Levenworth smiled and stared at Wolf for a beat. "It was the terms the seller wanted. If I hadn't done it, there're a hundred other people who would've."

"Really? A hundred other people could come up with a million dollars in cash?"

Levenworth shrugged. "Who's to say?"

"And you said you 'had' this money."

"Meaning it was not a withdrawal from my bank. I had the reserves in my own private vault at home."

Wolf pulled the corners of his mouth down and nodded. "Was that part of the terms? That the money would not have a Treasury Department trace attached to it?"

Levenworth smiled. "Do I need to get my lawyer in here, Sheriff?"

"No," MacLean said. "I don' think that's necessary at all. Do you, Detective Wolf?"

Wolf held up a hand. "So you trusted Ryan Frost with this money?"

"Yes."

"But you had to trust the seller to deliver on his end."

Levenworth shrugged. "I trusted Ryan Frost. The digger? He sent photo proof of everything. All the merchandise was accounted for in photographs. I had no reason to doubt Frost. He was my escrow service. The guy's foundation is his word."

"Can I see these photographs?"

Levenworth pulled out his phone and pecked at the screen. "I've already sent these photographs to your sheriff."

"I've sent them on to you already, Dave," MacLean said.

Wolf nodded.

Levenworth stood up and came next to Wolf, shoulder to shoulder, angling the screen so he could see.

"You can see here—these are at the dig site."

The first picture was an exposed bone, looking like it had

been dug out but not yet removed from where it had been discovered. It was stone-colored with a web of surface cracks, and had two bulbous mounds on either end. Next to it was a tape measure pulled out and laid down on the ground.

"A leg bone?" Wolf asked. He'd seen plenty X-rays of his own leg in the past year. "A femur?"

"Very good. The femur."

Wolf shifted his weight, feeling a dull ache in his right leg—a nagging symptom from the cracked femur he'd suffered during his fall at Cold Lake.

Levenworth swiped to the next photo, which showed a group of smaller bones laid on a dirty drop cloth.

"Proximal phalanges, middle phalanges ... hand bones. You can see the claws."

He swiped through them faster without pausing. "Like I said, you guys have all these photos now."

"Wait, stop. Could you please go back to that last one?"

Levenworth swiped back. "One of the ribs."

Wolf was more concerned with the footprint in the dirt next to it. It had the identical diamond pattern from the crime scene.

"Thanks," Wolf said, stepping back.

Levenworth sat down.

"Do you know where these bones were ... exhumed?"

"Somewhere in northwest Colorado. That's all I know."

Wolf narrowed his eyes. "Is this a legitimate deal?"

Levenworth's eyes went cold.

"It's a valid question, Senator. You say the bones are from northwestern Colorado. Last time I checked, the majority of land up there where they were pulling out dinosaur fossils was a place called Dinosaur National Monument. I would say it's gotta be against some federal laws to dig up a fossil specimen from there and sell it."

"It was found on private property. Well outside the boundaries of the National Monument."

"I thought you said they were exhumed 'somewhere in northwest Colorado,' and that's all you knew."

MacLean started rubbing his eyes.

Levenworth gave a conceding hand gesture and nod. "Yes, okay. I was told it was private property, away from the Monument. Clearly, with the nature of my job I was concerned about that. Ryan Frost gave me his word. He said he had proof and he could provide it if need be."

"And he didn't show you this proof?"

"He's a broker. He takes a ten to twenty percent cut of the purchase price. I understood his motives to keep the location secret and I didn't press. Like I say, I trusted him, but I guess he didn't trust me. Didn't want me going straight to the seller and cutting him out. But that's just good business."

Wolf let the information settle in his brain for a few seconds. "And, if I may ask, what's in it for you? A centerpiece in your living room?"

Levenworth chuckled and splayed his hands, like he'd been waiting for someone to ask him the question. "In 2010, a female Allosaurus fragilis that a team found in Wyoming was sold at auction in Paris for $1.8 million."

MacLean whistled and leaned back in his chair.

"That specimen was considered to be seventy percent complete." Levenworth twisted a ring on his finger. "This one is seventy-five. At least. And larger."

MacLean chuckled softly. "That sounds like a payday."

Levenworth sipped his coffee and shrugged.

"Back to the terms of the deal," Wolf said. "You were supposed to pick up the bones this morning. When were the bones supposed to be delivered?"

"Frost told me they were going to be delivered yesterday—

Sunday. Hence my timeframe of flying in and picking them up this morning."

"Who else knew about this deal?"

Levenworth pulled down the corners of his mouth. "Hell, I don't know. I assume the seller had a team. You don't just dig up a specimen like that alone. Let's see, then, maybe Frost's wife? Anyone else he told ... his family? I haven't told anyone else, except for my wife and a contact I have at the auction house in Paris ... but I really didn't get into the specifics of what I had with that contact, other than letting him know I was going to be bringing something big. You know, whet his appetite."

"You tell any friends in DC?"

He laughed. "Friends? Ha!"

MacLean hissed a laugh through his teeth.

"No, I didn't tell anyone in Washington. I've learned to keep my personal affairs private with those jackals." He smiled at MacLean—just like a jackal, Wolf thought.

"Anything that struck you as odd about the deal? I mean, other than having to put up a million cash, unsecured?"

Levenworth eyed Wolf for a second, like he was trying to figure out whether Wolf was needling him, then said, "I guess the secretive nature of the whole find was odd to me. I swear, I really *was* vigilant in making sure the bones came from private property. Because usually, in the fossil circles, a find like this becomes big news fast. People often like to shout from the highest mountain about what they've found, especially if they're looking to sell it. I mean, why not call in the newspapers, get some news crews in there? Get some buzz going? It did strike me as odd." He shrugged.

After a few seconds of silence, MacLean slapped a rhythm on his desk. "Well? I think you've been a great help, sir. We thank you."

"And we'd appreciate it if you stayed available," Wolf said.

Levenworth nodded. "I'm going to stick around for a few days, see how this pans out."

Wolf nodded. "There is one more thing, Senator."

"What's that?"

"It looks like the worst-case scenario happened with your money. I'm sorry, but we didn't find it."

The senator looked unfazed. "I'm not interested in the money."

Wolf nodded. "I understand. We didn't find the bones either."

This news clearly shook the senator.

"I'm sorry."

Levenworth recovered with a convincing smile. "Well, I hear you're the best. I have no doubt you'll find them."

Wolf nodded. "I have no doubt I'll find the killers either."

Levenworth hesitated, and then nodded with closed eyes. "Of course, of course."

Wolf walked out the door and left it open behind him.

Barker's squeaking shoes trailed behind Wolf into the squad room.

"What's next?" Barker asked.

Wolf turned around and eyed Barker. The sergeant deputy was the seniormost ranking deputy on Wolf's squad, appointed to the team by MacLean without any input from Wolf.

Wolf still remembered meeting Deputy Greg Barker for the first time. It had been down in Byron County, when it was still the stand-alone Byron County and not merged with Sluice. Barker had been on crime-scene log duty, standing with his clipboard, a satisfied grin on his beady-eyed face when Wolf had needed to leave and an ambulance had locked him into his parking spot.

The image of Barker's pleasure at Wolf's misfortune—however temporary and dumb the misfortune had been—was locked in his mind. In that single shit-eating grin, Wolf had read the man like a *Where's Waldo?* book. The man was a climber—ready to step on anyone in the process to get where he wanted to go.

"What is it, sir?" Barker asked, his face twisted in what looked like mock confusion.

Wolf had a suspicion his detective was thinking about that exact same moment now too.

"Nothing."

MacLean stepped out of his office, shut the door behind him, and waved Wolf to the windows. "I need to speak to you."

Barker took the hint and meandered away through the squad room desks.

Wolf and MacLean stepped to the windows overlooking Main Street three stories down.

The stop sign swayed in the wind below. People on the sidewalks leaned into the raging air. The pine trees bent and thrashed.

"Damn, something's rolling in," MacLean said.

Wolf said nothing.

MacLean put a hand on Wolf's shoulder and squeezed. "I know this is a particularly tough one. Cassidy's dad and all."

Wolf nodded.

"I saw her and Jack downstairs. Did you see them?"

"Yeah."

They stared outside for a few seconds, and then MacLean looked back at his office. Senator Levenworth was apparently staying a while longer.

"I know what you're going to tell me," Wolf said.

"Oh, really?"

"Yeah. You've got your nose so far up the senator's ass it's not hard to figure out."

MacLean squared off. "One of these days you're going to

learn some respect. Just because you've been sheriff once doesn't mean you are now."

"The bones weren't there," Wolf said. "And even if we find them during this investigation, they're going to be held in evidence for a long time."

MacLean stood silent.

Wolf looked over his shoulder toward the office. "This guy's a crook. He's paying with untraceable bills, all cash? He knows the source of these bones is suspect. And you're going to help him get his hands on them?"

MacLean made a wishy-washy gesture but said nothing.

"You really think this guy can help you with re-election in three years?"

MacLean snorted. "You think he can't? You're lucky I took this job. You wouldn't last a single term."

There was movement and sound on the street below. A young man, early twenties, was marching away from a vehicle that had been parked across the street—illegally. Another man of the same age had gotten out of the passenger side and was jogging after him.

A muffled honk filtered through the glass as a car stopped just short of hitting the lead kid, who didn't flinch or bother looking.

"I gotta go," Wolf said.

"Listen." MacLean grabbed his shoulder. "I just ... want to make sure you're taking front and center on this."

Wolf glanced over into the squad room, catching Deputy Barker studying their conversation. "What? You don't want to put your man Barker on this?"

MacLean looked down and hitched up his pants.

"Detective Wolf, please come to reception. Detective Wolf," Tammy's voice said over the speaker system.

Wolf left down the hall.

CHAPTER 6

"DETECTIVE WOLF, please come to reception. Detective Wolf," Tammy said again, this time with a tinge of impatience.

Wolf upped his pace and skipped a stair between steps. As he reached the stairwell door to the first floor, he could already hear the furious barking.

Launching into the hall, Wolf sprinted to the lobby.

Amid shouts and squeaking shoes, and Jet barking on the perimeter, a swarm of men were tangled in a standing wrestling match. Cassidy's brother had arrived.

"Hey!" Wolf shouted.

Jet flung saliva into the air from his bared fangs as he barked.

"Jet! Heel!"

Jet went quiet, backed up, and sat.

Wolf sprinted to the center of the chaos, peeling Jack and Nate's arms off. Jack saw Wolf and backed away, but Nate stayed in close.

Amid the sweat and adrenaline, the stench of alcohol was strong.

Keegan Frost's eyes were wild, his lips drooling, teeth bared.

"What the fuck did you say?" he yelled at Nate.

Nate shook his head and backed away, slapping at Keegan's hand to let go of his T-shirt.

"Stop it, Keegan!" Cassidy screamed at the top of her lungs.

The room went silent at the ear-splitting outburst.

Keegan looked like he'd been punched between the eyes. He swallowed and panted, staring at his little sister.

"Stop," she said.

"Is it true?" Keegan asked her.

Cassidy stepped to her brother and hugged him.

"Is it true?" The young man stood motionless, staring past them all for a few seconds, and then he dropped his head, his body racking with sobs.

Wolf locked eyes with the second man who had come in with Keegan. He looked early twenties, straight out of a sleeping bag and into the car for a few hours—and he seemed dumb-struck. His pupils were pinpricks, eyes frozen open.

Wolf walked to him, grabbed the sides of his head with both hands and pulled him close, taking a big sniff of his breath. "You been drinking?"

"Last night," the kid said.

"And him?" Wolf thumbed toward Keegan.

"Last night."

Must have been some kegger.

"Where?"

"Blue Mesa. The reservoir."

"Where do you live?"

"Off fifth. Fifth and Wildflower."

"Walk home."

Wolf walked up behind Keegan and squeezed his front pockets. "Give me your keys."

Keegan let go of his sister and twisted violently, just missing Wolf with a flying elbow.

Wolf locked one of Keegan's muscular arms behind his back and pushed him into the corner.

Keegan fought but Wolf had him solidly. He put his lips to Keegan's ear. "You need to calm down and give me your keys. You're in the Sheriff's Department and reek of beer. Now I said I want your keys. Got that?"

Keegan's body slackened and he nodded. "Yeah, okay."

Wolf held tight for another few seconds and then let go.

They bounced apart, and Keegan faced him and wiped his lips. He dug into his pocket and tossed Wolf the keys.

Wolf caught them and flung them at Nate in one motion. "Can you move that to a proper spot?"

Nate wiped his nose and nodded. "Yeah."

Keegan looked like the fight had left him now, and he searched the room for his sister again. Without another word, he stumbled to her and hugged her tight.

Nate was about to leave, then hesitated and walked to Wolf. "You all right?"

"Yeah, you?"

Nate nodded.

"You going to talk to him? Take some sort of statement?" Nate asked.

"Not right now."

"Okay. I'm going to take them to my house. And you don't have to worry about Jack. I'll take him to my place and give him a ride home if he needs it."

"Thanks."

"And you?"

Wolf shrugged. "I'll go pick up Trudy Frost and get back to work on this thing."

They stared one another down for a few seconds. Nate broke first and looked at his feet, scratching his chin. A classic I-want-to-say-something Nate gesture.

"What?"

"I could take Jet ... but ..."

Wolf waited for the rest of the sentence, then understood. "But Kenny's allergic." Kenny was the youngest of Nate's three sons, and the allergy was no joke. "Okay."

"I could just put him outside. It would be no trouble."

Wolf shook his head. "No, I'll keep him here and take him back to my house later."

"You sure?" Nate asked.

"Let's go, Jet." Wolf looked around the room.

Jet was already by the bank of elevators, sitting patiently.

"Huh." Wolf raised his eyebrows. "I'll talk to you soon."

CHAPTER 7

"Jeffrey Green, professor of paleontology at the University of Utah." Patterson's high-pitched voice echoed through the amphitheater squad room. "He was using his university email account to communicate with Frost."

Wolf stood at the front of the situation room. The polar-opposite of the tiny one he'd been used to for over a decade, this room could seat sixty, with rows that climbed up at a twenty-degree angle. He also knew that the room could fill up to capacity and beyond, because twice he'd spoken to the entire department, and both times the room had been packed like the ski-resort parking lot on New Year's Eve. Both times he'd felt out of sorts in front of such a crowd, but today there were only a few of them. The only discomfort he felt now was in his nose from the smell billowing out of Jet.

He walked to the bank of windows and pulled up the blinds. The panoramic view of the mountains to the east was brightly lit by the late-afternoon sun. He opened two windows a foot and took a greedy inhale of the fresh, pine-scented air.

Patterson clicked the mouse on her laptop and a website for

the University of Utah's paleontology department flashed on the giant screen at the front of the room.

After a few more clicks, a bio revealed itself on the projector screen. The heading said *Professor Jeffrey Green, PhD*.

In the photo, Green wore round, black-framed glasses that hid the color of his eyes behind glare. His mouth was small and his smile puckered, only a few crooked upper teeth showing. His greasy black hair contrast starkly with his white skin, and was combed straight to the side to try and cover a prominent bald spot on the top of his small head.

"Harry Potter did not age well," Rachette said.

Hernandez and Lorber laughed, and Rachette leaned back in his chair with a satisfied smile.

Patterson clicked again and an email came up. "According to this email, Green was due to deliver the bones to Ryan Frost last night at 8 p.m."

Hernandez's mustache stretched in a smile and he turned to Rachette. "She's such a smart woman. If you could cook like my wife, then you would be fighting me off."

"Down, boy," Rachette said.

Jet lifted his head off the floor and gave a curious grunt.

"Not you. You stop farting," Rachette said. "My God, what is Jack feeding this animal?"

"It's a common gastro-intestinal disorder with German shepherds," Dr. Lorber said. "Especially those that have gotten on in age. You need to put him on, and keep him on, proper medicine."

"Thanks, everyone," Wolf said aloud. "Can we get started?"

"We have fourteen exchanges back and forth between Green and Ryan Frost," Patterson said.

"Professor Green?" MacLean descended the center aisle with Undersheriff Wilson behind him. When he reached the front of the room, he wrinkled his nose and sat down, eyeing Rachette suspiciously.

Wilson nodded to Wolf and Patterson and sat quietly with a notepad and paper.

"It's the dog," Rachette said.

"Who's Professor Green?" MacLean asked.

"He works at the University of Utah," Patterson repeated. "He's been there eleven years according to his bio, and he teaches a few classes in the paleontology department on Jurassic fauna."

"Jurassic fauna?" MacLean asked. "Animals?"

She nodded.

"Why don't they just say that?" MacLean asked.

Rachette nodded. "That's what I told her."

MacLean ignored Rachette and blinked.

"When ... we found out it was Professor Green," Patterson said, "I took the liberty of checking his financial records, and according to his credit-card statements he rented a UrMover truck from Windfield, Colorado, two days ago—Saturday afternoon—at 12:25 p.m."

"Windfield is south of Dinosaur National Monument," Rachette said. "I've been there."

"And?" MacLean asked.

Rachette cleared his throat. "And there's a dinosaur quarry there."

MacLean grunted.

"All right," Wolf said. "So Green presumably exhumed the bones from his dig, which is somewhere near Windfield, Colorado, loaded them up and brought them down to Rocky Points, where he was to deliver them to Ryan Frost, who procured the sale with Senator Levenworth. Has anyone called the university? Talked to the paleontology department to track Green down?"

Rachette raised a hand. "I called and got nowhere. Everything's closed on Sundays. But we have Green's cell number. I called twice and it seems like he has his phone switched off. I didn't leave any messages at the university or with Green."

"I'll take over on the calls," Wolf said.

"I'll call the locals," MacLean said, referring to the local law enforcement in Windfield.

"Keep me in on that," Wolf said.

MacLean widened his eyes. "Yes, sir."

"Let's get back to the crime scene," Wolf said.

Lorber leaned forward. "We have two slugs inside Ryan Frost. Both .38 special. And no brass at the scene, so a revolver. But there's more. Hernandez and Rachette?"

"The nearest neighbor," Rachette said, "is a guy named Sam Tinniker. You know him?"

"He drives ski-resort shuttles," Wilson said.

"And he lives down the hill from Frost," Rachette said. "He says he heard three gunshots at 8:15 p.m. at dusk. He swears he heard three."

"But Ryan Frost only sustained two gunshot wounds," Lorber said.

Wolf nodded.

"'The gunshots were like pop-pop ...'" Rachette was reading from his notepad. "'And then a minute passed, then there was another shot.' That's what our witness said. He says it was strange to hear three shots like that, because usually Frost is, quote, 'blasting off a lot more rounds when he's practicing shooting.'"

"And the other neighbors?" Wolf asked.

"They didn't hear anything," Hernandez said.

Lorber crossed one long leg over the other. "Judging by the proximity of the shots fired into Frost, I'm going to venture that the third shot didn't miss."

"Then where did it go?" Wolf asked.

Lorber splayed his hands.

"Obviously, we need to search for that bullet. Fingerprints?"

Lorber looked at Dr. Blank, the assistant medical examiner.

Blank shook his head.

"The only ones that are coming up are Frost and his family's," Patterson said.

"And the pistol in the bushes?" Wolf asked.

"Kimber TLE II .45 cal," Hernandez said. "Registered to Ryan Frost. No shots fired. Only prints on the gun are his."

"What about the tire tracks and footprints?" Wolf asked.

Patterson clicked her computer a few times and pulled up a file with photographs in it.

A picture came up on the screen with an imprint of a tire-tread pattern clearly visible in fine dirt. "This tread is our UrMover truck. Tread pattern matches that on the UrMover Moving truck, according to the file we received from the rental agency." Patterson was clicking through the photos continuously now. "The tracks that come after it are from a full-sized pickup truck with Goodyear P265/70R17-model tires."

"That's specific," Wolf said.

"Yes. But the bad news is that many American-made trucks from 2009 to the present have this exact tire model on them straight out of the factory. That includes Chevy, Ram, GMC, and Ford. In fact, half the vehicles in this department have the same tires as our SUV, but sixteen- instead of seventeen-inch. The only thing we can gather is that we're looking at a full-sized American-model pickup."

"Why not a Toyota?" MacLean asked. "Nissan?"

"Because of the wheel spacing."

"And the shoe prints?" Wolf asked.

Lorber stood up from the chair, and the vision of a giant climbing out of a clown car came to Wolf's mind. The Sluice-

Byron county medical examiner stood six foot seven inches tall, four inches taller than Wolf, but weighed at least twenty pounds less. A former hippie that had kept the hair as a memento, Lorber stroked his pony tail with one bony hand and pointed at Patterson with the other. "Patty, hit me with the folder I sent you."

Patterson clicked and a picture of the driveway came up on the big screen. The photo had been taken with a wide-angle lens to get the entire space in the frame.

Lorber produced a laser pointer and swirled a green dot around Ryan Frost's body. "Here we have Frost, and around him we have *five* sets of footprints we're worried about, and one set we're not, which was Sheriff ... uh, sorry, Detective Wolf's. Next."

Patterson took her cue and clicked the button.

"Here's a photo of Cassidy Frost's shoe prints. Clearly her prints were left last, as they go on top of the other four in question. It jives with her story that she found her father this morning, and, besides, we've established that Cassidy was out camping with Jack Wolf,"—he looked at Wolf over his frameless spectacles—"your son, last night. Jack also confirmed this in his statement to Deputy Munford."

Wolf felt heat rising in his face, and when Lorber stared at him for a few seconds Wolf raised an eyebrow.

"Right ... so that leaves—next—the other four sets of footprints around the body and the rest of the crime scene. Next."

A picture of the ground, filtered digitally with some effects to highlight the footprints, appeared. "We have two sets of prints—Converse All Stars, size sixteen, and work boots of unknown brand, size approximately ten or eleven, walking behind two more sets."

"Christ," MacLean said. "My head's going to explode."

Lorber stopped and stared at MacLean. "I don't ..."

Patterson cleared her throat. "The prints tell us a story: Two men escorted Ryan Frost and *someone else* from the front door to the spot we found Frost's body. We're assuming this someone else with Frost was Professor Green, because of the emails. We know the two in question escorted them because their footprints go over the top of Frost's and whoever else was next to him."

MacLean twirled an impatient finger. "I get it."

Lorber nodded. "Yes. Right. Thank you, Patty. Next."

A hissing sound, like a deflating tire, pierced the air.

Jet lurched awake from a deep sleep, licked his teeth, and then dropped his head to the floor again.

"My God," MacLean said. "I tell you what, give me the short version, or a gas mask."

Lorber backed away from Jet and nodded for Patterson to take over.

Patterson scrunched her nose and clicked the mouse, bringing up some more pictures of treads and shoe prints. "Basically, the story goes like this. One man drove in with the UrMover rental truck—a box truck we're assuming was rented by Green from Windfield.

"One set of footprints comes out of the rental truck, and a *different* set, the Converse All Stars, goes back in and drives it away. Following the rental truck into the driveway was a full-sized pickup truck." She clicked further. "Converse All Star and Work Boot got out of the pickup that followed. We're reasonably certain that Work Boot got out of the full-sized pickup from the passenger side, then left *driving* the full-sized pickup truck."

Wolf nodded, seeing what she was getting at. "And let me guess, Converse All Star leaves driving the UrMover truck instead of the pickup truck."

"Exactly," Patterson said.

"So, we think Green drove the moving truck in to deliver

the bones," Wolf said, "and it looks like two people followed him in and got out of their truck."

"Yes," said Lorber. "But the delivery doesn't happen. Because there's a shitload of bones in the garage." He pointed to Patterson.

Patterson clicked and a picture of the garage interior came up.

Lorber swirled his laser pointer on the screen. "But no Allosaurus fragilis. No delivery."

Patterson clicked her mouse again.

A picture of an empty space on the smooth concrete floor of the garage came up. It was cordoned off with blue masking tape and had a sign that said *Allosaurus fragilis—Levenworth.*

"And," Patterson raised a finger, "that brings me to the most interesting transaction on Green's credit card. He bought a plane ticket to Buenos Aires, Argentina, scheduled to depart DIA this morning at 8:27 a.m. Guess who was not on the flight?"

"Green," Wolf said.

Patterson nodded. "And like we said, he hasn't returned the moving truck."

Silence descended on the room.

Lorber folded his arms. "So he's probably toast, too. These two guys knock on the door with gun raised, force Frost and Green out of the front door by gunpoint. Frost was no dummy, was packing heat, but he didn't have it drawn and the two culprits made him take it out of his waistband. Had him chuck it in the bushes. Shows that Frost didn't suspect danger until they pointed their gun. Might be a clue right there. They might've known who was at the door. Didn't consider them dangerous."

Patterson nodded. "Two shots for Frost, one for Green. They take the cash. They take the bones. They ... go somewhere."

"And where's Green's body?" MacLean asked.

Patterson shrugged. "Back of the pickup? Back of the moving truck?"

"Makes sense," Rachette said. "Green missed his flight. The rental truck hasn't been returned."

Lorber folded his long arms and widened his stance. "We've gotta find Green's dig team. Senator Levenworth was right—he had to have had a dig team. And this whole trip to Argentina is fishy. Points to motive."

"How?" MacLean asked.

"Think about it," Lorber said. "The dig team had to be in on the bones sale, right?"

"And Green buys a ticket to Argentina," Patterson said. "Due to take off this morning. He'd already decided to take the money and run."

Rachette shook his head. "That makes no sense. How big and heavy is a million bucks in hundred-dollar bills? Like half a dump-truck full?"

Patterson pulled up Google and typed in the question.

"20.4 pounds in bundles of hundreds."

"Still risky taking it on a plane," Rachette said. "You'd have to check it in luggage, and hope some airport worker doesn't steal it. Then hope you don't get searched in customs when you land."

Lorber nodded. "Let's say he's willing to take that risk."

"A big risk," Rachette said.

Lorber ignored him. "But the dig team figures out what he's going to do. Maybe they come across his plane ticket to Argentina or whatever. They follow him down here and get the money, and off him."

"And Ryan Frost," Wolf said.

They descended into silence again.

"And leave a whole hell of a lot of prints and tracks," Hernandez said.

Lorber raised a stick finger. "But no trace evidence. No fingerprints. No hair."

Patterson clicked her mouse and a photo of the UrMover box truck came up. "Basic white paint. This is a ten-foot model."

It was scratched and dinged to hell on the sides. There was a black-and-white logo with a guy winking and giving a thumbs-up. Underneath it said UrMover Moving, Windfield, CO, with a listed phone number.

"I've called up north to Brushing PD and Summit County," Barker said in a voice louder than needed. "The truck hasn't come up on their radar."

"And south?" MacLean pressed him.

"Same thing. Nothing found south of Williams Pass. Ashland PD said no. We've got a BOLO out everywhere."

Wolf nodded at Patterson. "You have the credit-card trans-actions for Green. I take it he didn't purchase gas in the last twenty-four hours."

Patterson shook her head.

Wolf split two fingers and pointed at Patterson and Rachette. "You two head out right now and get to the gas stations down south. Retrieve footage."

Patterson paused for a second, glanced at her watch, then nodded and stood up.

Rachette frowned and looked up at her, like she had agreed to kill someone without an argument.

"Wait," Wolf said, "I forgot. It's Sunday night. You have something going on, don't you?"

"Uh, yeah," Rachette said, "if you count a bridal shower as something important."

"It's no problem," she said. "This is more important. They'll understand."

The room fell still and silent.

Wolf pointed at Hernandez and Barker. "You two go instead."

"How far south?" Hernandez asked.

"Those UrMover trucks come full to the rim with gas," Wolf said. "We know Green didn't fill up from Windfield down to here, he wouldn't have needed to. Figure out the distance it could have driven to on the remaining gas and check all those stations within that circle radius.

"We'll do what we can tonight. Rachette, you take the local stations. Hernandez and Barker head south. Then we'll start north bright and early tomorrow morning. It's been a long day, and it's looking like it's going to be a long one tomorrow."

"Who's going to check out this dig team?" Rachette asked.

"I am." Wolf walked up the aisle of the room. "Jet, come."

"Alone?" Rachette asked.

"I'll have local support." He nodded at MacLean to follow him.

MacLean stood up and walked after him. "Where are you going now?"

"To the airport to pick up Ryan Frost's wife."

"DIA?"

"Yep."

MacLean followed silently through the doors into the squad room.

"Can you do me a favor?" Wolf asked.

"Shoot."

"Watch Jet while I'm gone."

"No."

Wolf stopped and turned, and Jet did the same.

"Have you smelled him? I'm not putting that bag of methane with legs in my office." MacLean looked around the squad room. "Have one of these grunts do it."

"I'll put him in my office. Nate Watson is dropping off some medication down at the lobby to help his gas. I need you to give it to Jet. It's important. If his bloating gets out of control he could die."

MacLean rubbed his silver goatee and stared at Jet. "Fine."

Jet raised an eyebrow.

"How do I give it to him?"

"Shove it in some food." Wolf pulled out his wallet. "Piece of cake."

"Where's the food?"

Wolf handed him a ten-dollar bill. "At the store."

CHAPTER 8

WOLF STEPPED into his office with Jet on his heels. The metal and wood furniture shone in the afternoon light like a nuclear detonation, so he went to the windows and cranked the blinds.

A brochure sat conspicuously on the desk. He picked it up and leafed through it.

"Who in the hell?" Wolf said under his breath. He dropped it in the trash, sat in the leather chair, and closed his eyes. The seat material beneath him was slippery and smelled like industrial cleaning agents, just like the rest of the building.

His phone chimed and vibrated in his pocket.

Margaret Hitchens.

He stared at the screen for the duration of the call and set his phone down—now the brochure made perfect sense. If ever there were a time to avoid a Margaret Hitchens call, it was now. The owner of the largest real-estate brokerage in the county, Margaret Hitchens was a hard-nosed motherly figure in Wolf's life, even more so now that Wolf had lost Sarah.

Clearly, she felt duty bound to make sure Wolf was on a proper path of healing, and it was getting on his nerves.

Margaret had foregone leaving a message, and the phone

began its vibrating and chiming all over again. She was going to call until he picked up. Every once in a while, she did that. A week ago, out of curiosity, he'd let her call six times in a row before he'd finally answered.

He poked the screen and brought the phone to his ear. "Hey, Margaret."

"Hi, David," she said in that smug, knowing tone of hers that she had no clue she used.

"I'm in a meeting. I can't talk right now."

"Bullshit. I just talked to my niece and she said you just walked into your office with Jet."

He needed to go over some phone call rules of engagement with Patterson. "You're so resourceful."

"That's the understatement of the year. Did you get the brochure I left on your desk yesterday?"

Wolf leaned over and looked in the trash. The brochure was gone.

He frowned, wondering for a second whether he'd gone crazy, and then he saw Jet. The dog sat staring at Wolf, the brochure in his mouth. He stepped to Wolf and dropped it at his feet.

Wolf stared at the brochure, now crumpled and covered with slobber, and shook his head at Jet.

"You're working with her?" Wolf asked.

Jet tilted his head.

"What?" Margaret asked.

"Nothing." Wolf threw the brochure back in the trash.

"And what do you think?"

Wolf said nothing.

"David, you remember what brought Sarah back from the brink of depression?"

He stood and peeked through the blinds.

"Are you there?"

"Yeah. Please, go ahead," Wolf said.

She huffed into the phone. "Those community meetings in that brochure—they're what brought her back into your life before she died. Do you remember?"

Wolf said nothing.

"Shit, Sarah's parents are up in Vail all the time now. They're checked out. It's tough raising a kid all by yourself. Even though you guys weren't technically together, you used to be able to talk to Sarah about all the stuff that happened with Jack—the scraped knees, girls ... whatever."

The overnight camping trips.

Wolf sat down. "You haven't heard about Cassidy?"

"No. What?"

"Her father was killed."

She sucked in a sharp breath. "My God. How?"

"Shot."

"Murdered?"

"Yeah."

She went silent.

"So I have quite a bit on my plate at the moment. Besides, I don't think that type of thing is for me."

"That type of thing is not for you?" She stuttered a line of incomplete cuss words. "Happiness is not for you? Being able to communicate your feelings and get help from real people who've gone through similar situations is not for you?"

He stood up and pulled his keys out of his pocket, making a point of jiggling them near the phone. "I've got to pick up Trudy Frost from DIA, so I'd better get going. It's Sunday afternoon. The traffic's going to be crazy."

He looked at his watch and calculated he had four hours until the plane landed. He stepped to the door, deciding, although he was making the excuse to get off the phone, his argument was valid. Even in the middle of summer, supposedly off-season for the mountains, the traffic was bad, made worse by the road construction, which was everywhere while the weather was good in the Colorado high country.

"I'm out the door."

She hesitated. "This isn't over."

He hung up.

Jet wagged his tail.

"Stay here."

Jet turned around and seemed just as content to curl up on some slices of sunlight on the floor.

CHAPTER 9

FOR THE MAN, staring at the flaming reds and oranges of a sunset, its infinite patterns shifting anew each day, was like staring into the eye of God.

Which was why he'd despised sunsets for years.

No one should be so unfortunate to live through what that all-knowing presence on the horizon had put him through.

For thirty-seven years, the man had been a devout Mormon, learning and living by the word of God in the footsteps of his father, and his father before him—both of who had died from the strange blood affliction, as had two of his brothers, as had six of his cousins, as had his uncle.

God was chastising him now. He could feel it plain as the heat on his eyelids, and he just didn't care. If He had a problem with what the man was doing, then He should have poisoned his blood, too, and taken him.

The man pursed his lips and glared at the setting sun. The orb seared his eyes, but he stared a second longer in defiance before stepping away from the outbuilding doorway and dialing a phone number.

"Hello?" His daughter-in-law had a soft, lilting voice he

loved so much. If he'd been in his son's shoes he would have married the same woman.

"How's he doing?" He blinked and the afterimage of God swam in his vision.

The way her breath came out of the earpiece of his cell phone was a clear enough answer. Her pained sigh was code for *not doing well*. He was suffering. He was watching cartoons to try to forget the throbbing pain in his bones, the hot sweats, the nausea from the crappy drugs provided by the cheap, inadequate doctor from the cheap, inadequate circle approved by the cheap, inadequate healthcare coverage—the kind of stuff a seven-year-old should never have to deal with on a minute-by-minute basis.

"I'll be coming up later this week with the money. I just have to ... go through some more stuff with the lawyers. You know lawyers—they want every 't' crossed, every 'i' dotted."

She sniffed into the phone.

In his mind's eye, he could see her nodding and wiping her pretty button nose.

"Don't you worry. It's going to be a good year for once," he said.

"Okay," she whispered.

"Shoot. I was talking to one of the lawyers about Edinburgh. You know what they wear over there?"

"Kilts?"

"Yeah. Man-skirts."

She laughed.

He smiled and laughed, too, and a tear slid down his cheek. "When we go over there, I'm going to put on a man-skirt before I march my grandson into that doctor's office. I'm going to pull it up, and underneath it's going to be a wad of cash so big, and I'm going to say, 'Give my grandson a new life!'"

"No, no. You're terrible."

He smiled even wider. "You wait and see. That's a promise."

The conversation died to silence and he nodded. "I'll be up there to see you in a couple days, all right?"

"Okay."

"What's that?"

"Okay," she said in a louder voice.

"Bye, baby doll."

"Bye."

He kept the phone to his ear, listening for the call to end, then dropped it in his pocket and pulled out a throwaway phone he'd purchased from Walmart.

"Yeah." The man's voice on the other end was squeaky, his tone impatient.

"Well? How was the rest of your day today?"

"How was the rest of my day? Let's see ... very bad. Truly the worst day of my life. Thanks for asking."

The man turned away from the sun and switched the cell phone to his other ear.

Three mourning doves whistled by on the warm wind. It was almost bearable outside at this hour.

"And what did you find out?"

"To use a big lump of money like this is very difficult."

"But doable. People do it all the time."

The voice scoffed. "The people who do it all the time are called criminals. Most of them are caught by federal agents with sophisticated surveillance techniques. They monitor financial transactions. Certain behavior sends up red flags."

The man clenched his fists. He hated this defeatist talk. He hated the lies.

"And what was your plan in the first place? You were going to split the money with the professor, fifty–fifty. That's four hundred and fifty K."

"I was going to leak it to myself over several years. You're asking the impossible if you want a deposit like this showing up in your account overnight."

"By Thursday."

The man tittered through the earpiece. He was cracking. "I can't believe you shot ..."

The man narrowed his eyelids. "So what's the plan?"

"I don't have a plan!"

The man stared at the oak trees near the river. The boughs swayed in the wind, the leaves sounding like a roaring river.

"I don't know if I can do this." The tinny voice in his ear was barely a breath. "I'm not a killer."

The man stared at the phone and considered a response, but found none worthy for such a coward, so he pressed the call-end button.

He looked at his watch and did some calculations. They were going to have visitors from the south, that much was certain.

It had already been the longest of weekends, and it had just gotten longer with that phone call. But at least his cut had just doubled.

CHAPTER 10

THE LAST TIME Wolf had descended to the plains had been to see the other woman in his life who called him every week—his mother. Mom had given up the mountain life, moving to Denver when his father had died all those years ago, and never looked back. She may have been a flatlander at heart, but Wolf was not. And as he coasted down I-70 with his foot on the brake for the third straight hour in bumper-to-bumper traffic with the rest of the weekend warriors returning to their city life, he vowed it would be another year before he did this again.

The steep, winding final stretch of chaotic highway, past Morrison and the jutting megaliths of Red Rocks Amphitheater, finally flattened and straightened and the traffic opened. He drove onward on I-70 through Denver, past the fragrant dog-food plant, and out into what seemed like halfway to Kansas before he pulled into the arrivals drive-up at Denver International Airport.

Trudy Frost was waiting patiently on the curb, staring into nothing and sitting on her luggage in the dark. Her long blonde hair was pulled in a ponytail lying against her straight back.

He squeaked to a stop and got out; by the time he'd rounded

the back of his SUV, she'd already opened the rear door and dumped her luggage in back. He got there in time to help shut the passenger door.

Climbing back behind the wheel, Wolf said, "Sorry. I misjudged the traffic."

She waved a dismissive hand.

He checked his mirror and then turned to her. In a soft tone, he said, "I'm sorry." This time he was apologizing for Ryan.

She kept her eyes on the windshield. They welled and tears cascaded down her cheeks, but she said nothing.

He shifted into drive and let off the brake. She remained silent for the entire return trip, as did Wolf. Back through Denver, past the hogbacks near Morrison, up Floyd Hill, past Idaho Springs, through Eisenhower Tunnel, past the darkened slopes of Copper Mountain, past Vail, down south through Cave Creek—they said nothing, and Wolf swore he never saw her blink.

Growing up, Trudy had been a beautiful girl, and now she was a beautiful woman. It's where her daughter got her looks. She and Wolf had kissed once in first grade. It was one of those tiny memories imprinted on his mind—a peck underneath a sheet while playing hide and seek. She was a memorable woman, Wolf guessed, and Wolf knew he would remember this drive for the rest of his life. The grief inside his vehicle was like a thick fog and it steamed off Trudy Frost's unblinking eyes.

They pulled into Rocky Points and headed up the hills toward Nate's house, which sent a fresh wave of tears flowing down Trudy's cheeks, probably because the route to Nate's was roughly the same as going to the Frosts' home, reminding her anew of what had just happened to her husband, and the emptiness that waited at home for her.

Pulling into Nate's driveway, Wolf could see the lights

blazing bright inside the log home. Stepping out, he was surprised at the cool stillness of the air.

He opened the door for Trudy and she trudged to the front door, standing motionless before it until Wolf opened it for her

Nate's wife, Brittnie, was standing inside, waiting with sympathetic wet eyes.

The house was quiet and subdued, the opposite of the usual state of Nate's household. Circus music normally played in his head upon entering this residence, but not tonight.

Brittnie opened her arms and Trudy walked into them.

Wolf set down the baggage and stepped back onto the front porch. Nate walked down the hall and joined him outside.

Sliding the door shut, Nate turned to him with a *holy shit* expression and walked down the stairs into the driveway.

"How's it been in there?" Wolf asked.

"Not good. Cassidy and Keegan are in the living room. Jack and Brian are upstairs." Brian was Nate's oldest son and Jack's best friend. "The other kids are asleep. Christ, look at that."

Nate stopped and looked up.

Wolf had already seen the phenomenon on the way into Rocky Points.

"That's ..." Nate let his sentence die and shook his head.

The moon was full, high above the eastern peaks, and blood red, tinted by smoke.

"Smoke from the Durango fire," Wolf said. "They say rain's rolling in tomorrow night. Going to be a monsoonal flow."

"I was gonna say creepy. Frickin' blood red."

Wolf stared up. "Yeah. I guess it is."

"Well, that's good ... about the rain. Now we can put off cutting those trees of yours for another few years."

Wolf smiled, feeling grateful for the tiny jab at humor after the long solemn drive.

"I think I have more respect for you now," Nate said.

"You had respect for me to begin with?"

"I know you always dealt with this type of thing on a first-hand basis, but I didn't know how hard it was. How draining. You know, being so close to the bad stuff. And that's just what you *do*. All day. Know what I mean? Shit, sorry. Don't want to depress you or anything. I'm just saying."

Wolf stared at the moon, opting for a change in subject. "I'm headed up to Windfield tomorrow."

"Big oil up there," Nate said. "I guess you'll be putting off your conversation with Jack then, too."

"What conversation?"

"I could tell you were bent out of shape about it today. Learning Cassidy and Jack were together last night."

Wolf sighed. There was something else that he could put off for another few years.

"Head in?"

Wolf nodded. "Yeah."

They walked inside and down the hallway, and Wolf stopped short at the scene in the family room.

Trudy stood arm in arm with her two children, Keegan and Cassidy, like they were lined up and going to say something in unison, like they were acting out a scene in a depressing version of a Disney movie. Six red-rimmed eyes, all an identical shade of Trudy Frost-blue, stared at Wolf with such ferocity that Wolf straightened.

"Are you going to get the piece of shit that did this to my husband?" Trudy asked.

Wolf swallowed and nodded. "Yes."

CHAPTER 11

WOLF DIALED the number for the head of the University of Utah's paleontology department again and listened to the message.

"You've reached the office of Dr. James Talbot. I'm not in the office at—"

Hanging up, he checked the dash clock, which said 7:55 a.m., and added a mental note to try again in an hour.

He'd been driving on two-lane highways for just under three hours when he passed a sign that said *Windfield 2 miles.*

The hundred and seventy-one miles to that point had been mountains, valleys, and rivers until Grand Junction, where he turned north and the land became harsher–less-inhabited plateaus, flat wastelands, and cliffs shaped by ancient seas.

Now two miles away, Windfield winked in the morning light, its streets a checkerboard on the tilted floor of a wide sage-brush valley. Beyond it, the terrain rose in white and red rock cliffs covered in juniper and pinyon trees.

As he rolled into the town limits, he noted Windfield was a less majestic site than its backdrop. The gray asphalt was cracked with lines that had faded out years ago. The lawns were bleached yellow, the trees more brown than green, and the houses different configurations of single and double-wide trailers standing in varying levels of decay.

A stray dog got Jet's attention as it trotted alongside Wolf's SUV, and a kid on a four-wheeler drove by on the other side of a barbed-wire fence, his sister in the rear. The boy couldn't have been more than twelve, the girl ten, and she was holding a baby. Monday-morning traffic in Windfield.

Wolf considered stopping and yelling at the kid to get back home and leave the baby, but the kid turned around and sped off in the other direction.

"Here we are," he announced to Jet instead.

Jet dropped his jaw and panted in the rear-view mirror. Wolf had had no choice but to take the dog with him that morning. His presence so far had been unobtrusive, save the occasional blast of gas. The medicine was working, albeit slowly.

Two turns later and he arrived at the Windfield County Sheriff's Office without a hitch.

The building was a basic wooden rectangle with a large window in front and a glass door next to it. To Wolf, the structure looked like a nineteen-fifties hardware storefront, but the sign above the door confirmed it to be the Windfield County Sheriff's Department, along with two brown-painted long-bed trucks with gold WCSD logos on the doors parked in front.

Wolf pulled into a midnight-black asphalt lot and parked between two freshly painted white lines opposite the trucks. He got out, stretching his arms overhead, and let Jet out from the back seat.

The heat rising off the pristine parking lot travelled up his pants legs, and he wondered if his leg hair might curl. His feet sank ever so slightly in the asphalt with each step. With an internal groan, he noted his watch read only 8:05 a.m.

He gazed at the higher elevations, hoping the quarry was on the top, and up on top was cooler.

The two Windfield Sheriff's Department trucks were Ford long beds, about five to eight years old by the looks of the body design and wear. As Wolf walked in between them toward the front of the building he looked down at the tires, noting they were Goodyear P265/70R17. Both matches to his crime scene.

A blast of cool air pushed his uniform shirt against his chest as he pulled open the front door. Sleigh bells clanked against the glass, announcing his arrival.

Jet hurried in past his legs inside and Wolf followed.

The room was rectangular, just like the exterior hinted it would be, filled with three desks facing the front window.

A lone man stood up from behind a computer. "Hello. You Deputy Wolf?"

"Yes. Detective Wolf," he said.

"Deputy Etzel," the man said, holding out his hand. He was low and squat. Despite the cool air, sweat marks darkened his uniform underneath his arms.

Etzel's hand was puffy, but clamped onto Wolf's like a bear trap.

"One moment please." Etzel walked to the back of the room to an open doorway and leaned against the doorjamb.

It seemed like Etzel had pressing business to discuss, and then, as an afterthought, jerked a thumb over his shoulder and eyed Wolf.

After waddling back to his desk, Etzel said, "He'll be right out."

"Detective Wolf!" The sheriff came out of his office fast, with hand outstretched. He was just about Wolf's height but a bit thicker and softer, probably ten years older than Wolf—early fifties by the look of his graying, closely cropped full head of hair that was cut into a cube. His skin was tan and his mouth stretched in a smile that failed to reach his eyes. "Sheriff Shumway. Nice to meet you."

"Nice to meet you, too Sheriff."

"And who's this?" Shumway asked, bending down to scratch Jet's head.

"That's Jet."

"I didn't know you were bringing a K-9 unit." Shumway stood straight and shrugged, looking slightly annoyed. "I guess he could come in handy."

"He's a retired dog from the Vail PD. Just a pet now. I'm taking care of him. I hope you don't mind."

The sheriff smiled again and walked back to the doorway. "No, no problem. Come on back. Maybe he could stay out here, though. I'm allergic."

"Stay here," Wolf said to Jet, and he pointed by the front door.

Jet did as he was told.

Shumway waited patiently at the entryway to his office and slapped a hand on Wolf's back as he passed. "Have a seat."

Wolf sat in a squeaking metal chair covered with cracked fake leather.

The wooden desk in front of Wolf was immaculately clean, smelling like polish. A green glass pull-chain lamp perched on one corner and two manila folders—one thick, one thin—sat conspicuously in the center.

"Have a good drive?" Shumway asked as he walked around his desk. His khaki sheriff's uniform was dusty and wrinkled, like it was on its fourth day of use between dry cleanings. With a grunt, he collapsed into a pillowed leather chair and put his hands on the folders.

"Not bad," Wolf said.

"You must have gotten an early start."

"I did."

"I have to say, we've all heard about the Cold Lake incident you had down there last year." He shook his head and whistled. "What a whacky case that was. Can't even make that stuff up."

"It was interesting."

He gave Wolf a smoky-eyed nod. "I was sorry to hear about your loss. We were all sorry."

"Thank you," Wolf nodded.

"I talked to Sheriff MacLean last night for a while. He had nothing but praise for you. How're you liking being chief detective?"

"It suits me."

"Don't miss the politics of the Sheriff's Office, eh?"

Wolf shook his head.

Shumway leaned his head back and laughed, and it shook the room. When he was done, he pulled back one of the folders and glanced inside, then shoved it in the top drawer of his desk.

The room fell silent and Shumway seemed lost in thought.

"You guys have something else going on too?" Wolf asked.

"What's that? Oh, no. No, it's just ... a personal matter." He slapped the thick folder that remained and opened it up. "So, damn shame what we have going on. I heard about your personal connection to the victim. Goddamn shame, and we're here to help you catch these sons of bitches. No matter what it takes."

He gazed hard into Wolf's eyes.

"Good," Wolf said.

"Status is: There's one way in and out of that dino quarry we've got up there, and I sent two deputies to monitor it as soon as I talked to Sheriff MacLean last night." He opened the folder and slapped a piece of paper down. "I got a warrant to search the dig camp for the murder weapon, the pistol used to shoot and kill Mr. Frost, and for the two pairs of shoes that left those tracks at the scene."

"And the dig team is still there?" Wolf asked.

"Yep. My two deputies went into the park and confirmed last night, then they fell back and monitored to make sure they didn't leave." Shumway raised his eyebrows. "I followed MacLean's request to stand down on bringing them in."

"Thanks. I'd like to be there for the pickup and initial questioning."

"I understand." Shumway spread three photographs that were on top of the stack. "Here's what we have on our students at the dig. They had to submit photographs along with a digging permit application with the county. We had them on file here."

"A permit to dig ... in the dinosaur quarry park? On BLM parkland?"

"Neither. They're on private property. Still have to file though. They've set up camp in the park. They straddle the line, with the dig right on the other side of a dry river bed in private property and their access to it through the BLM park."

Wolf nodded. "I see."

Shumway tapped the first photograph. "First guy here? Steven Kennedy. We picked him up for DUI last year in town. Stuck him here in our jail cell for two days until his wife bailed him out. How he's still on the university-sponsored dig team after that, I have no idea."

The man in the mugshot photo was in his mid-twenties, handsome, but looked like he'd seen better days. Brown hair askew, his green eyes were puffy and drunk, his thin face covered with a two-day brown beard. He held up a black sign with his name, date, and booking number on it.

Shumway pointed at the next photo. "Felicia Kennedy, Steven's wife."

The picture was a full-body shot, taken outdoors, of a brown-haired woman also in her mid-twenties. She was dressed in a tank top, cargo shorts, and a big hat that shaded most of her face, but Wolf could still tell she was very beautiful. Thin and athletic, she was tanned deeply from being out in the sun. Her eyes were kind and her smile wide, flashing perfect teeth.

"She's also in the graduate program at the University of Utah. I've never met her. I wasn't here when she bailed out her husband."

Shumway tapped his index finger on the third photo. It was another full-body shot of a woman. On the heavier side, this woman was dressed in a flannel shirt and cargo shorts, flashing bright white legs. Her hair was bleached blonde and spiked, and her face was pale and serious, with smallish eyes glaring into the camera.

"Molly Waters. Another paleontology graduate student at the University of Utah."

Wolf picked a fourth photo out of the stack, which was a full-body photograph of Green. All skin and bones, the man wore khaki pants cinched too high on his waist, a dusty button-up shirt rolled to the elbows, and a satchel on his hip with the strap slung across his torso. He rounded out his outfit with a brown hat that plunged his spectacled face in shadow.

"Then we have Indiana Jones," Shumway said with a chuckle.

Wolf nodded. "You ever met Green?"

Shumway shrugged. "I've seen him around. Never really talked to him. He's kind of ... I don't know ... mousy. Runs around town with his head down, never talks to anyone. Doesn't break any laws as far as I can tell, so we don't butt heads with him. But, of course, now he's involved in some stuff, isn't he?"

"Looks that way."

"The way I see it, looks pretty cut and dried."

Wolf leaned back in his chair. "How do you figure?"

"We've got the mentor-professor Green who corrupts the students into agreeing to sell these Allosaurus bones they find.

Probably under the guise they'd be splitting the money four ways. A quarter-million to each of them. Mentor-professor helps students do the work, all the while knowing he's going to take the money and run on these poor saps. Professor plans to skip town to Argentina with the money. Students find out. Students follow professor and kill fossil dealer in the skirmish, and then kill the professor himself. Students take the money. Come back. Done."

Wolf tilted his head side to side.

"You have another theory?"

"I like your train of thought," Wolf said. "But I have some questions that don't add up."

"And what are those?"

"For one, why are they here waiting for the cops?"

Shumway shrugged.

"And where's Green's body? And where's the rental truck?"

Shumway pointed. "You guys said the witness heard three shots fired, and only two slugs were found in the dealer."

Wolf nodded. "Yeah, I know. But until we have a body, until we have a murder weapon, the shoes, the money ... it's all speculation."

With that, Shumway slapped the desk with both hands and pushed back in his chair. "Then let's get to work."

Wolf stood up. "What about this land? Who owns this land they're digging on?"

"It's a guy from Washington State." Shumway hesitated for a second, then walked past Wolf and out the office door.

"Who exactly?" Wolf asked as he caught up.

"Etzel, get the statement paperwork ready. We'll be coming back with those three students I talked about."

Etzel looked up from his desk. "You got it."

Shumway looked at Wolf. "Guy named Errol. James Errol. Lives in Seattle. Owns a shitpot of land all over the west."

"What does he do with it?"

"With that piece out there? Has six thousand acres and eleven oil wells working around the clock." He looked at his watch. "Makes a ton of money, that's what he does with it. You know where the Windfield Dinosaur Quarry visitors' center is?"

"I've got it entered in my GPS. But I'd like to start with the UrMover truck-rental place."

"Right. It's a few blocks over on the edge of town. I'd say we could ride together, but you've got Jet here. Plus, if we want to bring these students back for questioning, it might be best to have two cars."

It was sound logic to Wolf, and he was a little relieved he was off the hook from a morning of sitting in the car with a stranger, struggling with small-talk.

They walked outside.

"Whew. Hot." Shumway climbed in one of the trucks and slammed the door. He fired up the engine and rolled the window down. "You can follow me."

Wolf and Jet climbed into his own SUV, fired it up, and followed Shumway out of the lot.

CHAPTER 12

"I just don't see why he went by himself," Rachette said.

Patterson felt another lurch in her stomach and saliva gushed into her mouth again. "He's with the dog."

Though she was used to starting work at 6 a.m. five days a week, she felt ridiculously tired today. How many drinks had she had at that stupid shower last night? Two? She leaned back in the passenger seat and closed her eyes.

Rachette scoffed. "The dog with the lazy sphincter?"

"It's an ex-police dog."

"He's going to find two killers, and he has a dog that releases toxins from his ass as its secret weapon for backup?"

Patterson breathed deeply through her nose, willing her stomach to relax. "He'll be—"

"Yeah, yeah, working with the locals." Rachette slapped his hand on the steering wheel. "I'm just saying."

She cracked an eye and looked at him. "Bent out of shape about being left on duty with me?"

Rachette said nothing as they continued through the back-and-forth turns of Cave Creek.

Highway 734 followed the meandering path of the Chautauqua River, which had carved the caves that honeycombed the area's hills over the millennia.

"How much longer?" Patterson asked, feeling another wave of nausea wash over her as she lurched side to side in her seat.

"What's your problem?"

"Nothing."

She kept her eyes closed, but felt Rachette studying her.

"We're almost out of the canyon. I don't know, another mile? What's up? Not like you've never been up here."

"Not with my eyes closed."

"Then open them."

"No."

"Don't feel well?" Rachette asked.

"Nice observation."

"You have two drinks of white wine last night or something? You've always been such a lightweight."

She lifted her hand and raised her middle finger.

They rode in silence for another few minutes. Patterson kept her eyes shut until she felt the car straighten out, reaching the flatland north of Cave Creek.

Rachette whistled. "There's that fire."

Patterson shielded her eyes with her hand against the blazing morning sun.

They were passing by brittle grassland, where five antelopes stood with their backs to the wind. The animals looked as parched and unhealthy as the ground they scoured for food. Beyond them a column of smoke rose at an oblique angle from the sagebrush-filled high plateau.

"That's not that bad," Rachette said. "They were making it out to be another land annihilator like the one down in Durango."

She looked at him. "Land annihilator?"

"I just thought of that."

"Clearly."

Her phone rang in her pocket and she pulled it out. "Hernandez," she told Rachette. "Hello?"

"Hey, sister," Hernandez said.

Normally the pet name would have irked her, but she liked Hernandez and in the short five months they'd been working together on the squad she kind of did feel he was like a brother. One that, unlike her three real-life brothers, she got along with all the time.

"What's up?" she asked.

"We've got nothing from Ashland, and nothing from the Cold Lake Junction gas station. Barker's going through the Mackery gas station recording now, and that's the last of what we got ... just a second ..." Hernandez put his hand over the phone. "Yeah ... Barker says that means the truck must have gone north ... like I was just going to tell you ... the *reason* I called you."

Patterson smiled. "All right. Wish us luck."

"Bueno suerte."

Patterson hung up. "They've got nothing on their footage. So it looks like it's up to us."

They rode in silence a beat.

"What do you think of Barker?"

"Could not hate a person more," Rachette said without a millisecond's hesitation. "He's like hotel soap: he does the job, but not well, and ... always leaves a crappy film on your skin."

She looked at him. "You just thought of that?"

"So, can I ask you a personal question?"

She leaned back and closed her eyes again.

"Are you going to go through with this thing?"

"What thing?"

"Your marriage to Scott?"

She opened her eyes and glared at him. "What?"

Rachette raised his eyebrows, keeping his gaze on the road. "What kind of question is that?"

"It just seems like you aren't that excited about it."

Her face went red. What the hell did Rachette know? Is that the impression she was giving off? The thought made her swallow.

"Sorry, I could be wrong. But I saw some serious hesitation in your eyes last night. You know, when you volunteered to go with me instead of to your bridal shower."

She felt too crappy to respond and closed her eyes again.

"Oh. Wait, I see. Is that it?"

Sometimes it was best to ignore Rachette, so she did.

"You know, Charlotte and I are pretty solid right now. So if you're thinking about me, harboring some sort of deep, secret feelings? Well—"

"Pull over!" Patterson rolled down the window and stuck her face into the rush of chilled morning air. "Now!"

Rachette slammed on the brakes and pulled onto the shoulder.

She opened the door and leaned her head toward the ground. A car honked on the way by and the rush of air rocked the SUV. That was enough to send her over the edge. Heaving, she vomited on the side of the road.

"Whoa, you okay? Make sure it goes outside."

She heaved again, then after one more time she was done. Wiping her mouth and nose, she leaned back and slammed the door. "There. Much better."

Rachette stared at her. "Christ, I was kidding."

"Let's go."

"Yeah." Rachette pulled back onto the highway. "You all right?"

"Must have been the food. They had some shrimp that tasted funny."

Rachette got up to speed and made a show of adjusting the rear-view mirror. "Or it could always be ..."

She looked at him.

He raised his eyebrows and nodded to her, like she was supposed to understand what he was saying.

"What?"

"Come on. Sick? It's the morning? Don't tell me you and Scott aren't having sex yet."

The thought slammed Patterson like they'd just hit the side of a mountain.

For the remainder of the drive they rode in silence.

"Here we are." Rachette pulled into the gas station on the southern skirts of Brushing and parked under the awning next to a pump. "Check it." He pointed up. "They have cameras."

They got out.

Patterson stood and took a deep breath, sucking in gasoline fumes and the aroma of dry weeds. She shielded her eyes and faced the sun, and looked at the new wildfire that was still a way to the north and east.

Upon closer inspection, she could see the glint of firefighters' vehicles near the smoke. Beyond the conflagration, the land rose abruptly, carpeted with a rust-colored forest.

"I hope it doesn't reach that," she said.

"No shit."

Pregnant? The thought was enough to make her hurl again. She took the lead and marched through the automatic doors of the convenience store.

The air inside smelled like hotdogs and window cleaner. Speakers in the ceiling played a B-side classic-rock song she'd never heard.

"Can I help you, Officers?" the clerk asked. He was a young man with a lot of hair on his head and face.

"Deputies," Rachette said, pointing at his Sheriff's Department patch.

The clerk looked more confused than educated.

She slapped the warrant onto the counter. "We need to see your security footage."

The clerk stared at the warrant for a second, then back at Patterson. "Yeah, sure. Back here."

The clerk opened the bulletproof glass door and led them both into the cramped space behind the counter and to a tiny office that smelled like all the others—like overflowing toilet and stale cigarette smoke. Her mouth watered.

"I'm going to hit the head."

Rachette eyed her. "You okay?"

"Yeah. Get started without me."

―――

Seven minutes later Patterson left the bathroom and returned to the office behind the counter. Rachette sat in front of the computer and the clerk hovered over his shoulder, helping him navigate the footage.

"Anything?" she asked.

Rachette shook his head as he stared at the black-and-white video screen. "Nothing."

"How much more do you have?" she asked.

"I don't know." Rachette turned in the chair and looked at her. "You gonna live?"

She nodded, ignoring the blushing look from the clerk. "I'll be fine. Thanks for asking."

"Remind me to never eat shrimp again."

Patterson tapped his shoulder. "I'll take the rest."

"You got it." Rachette stood up and the squeak of his shoes disappeared behind her.

"You need help?" the clerk asked.

"No thanks. I'm familiar with the system."

The guy looked relieved. "All right. I'm going out to have a smoke. Let me know if you need anything."

She sat down at the dial-and-knob system she'd gotten accustomed to over the course of her law enforcement career.

For the next ten minutes, black-and-white images of cars, trucks, and motorcycles flitted in and out of view on the screen. The footage took in the aspect from underneath the one fisheye security camera outside. She was ignoring the interior video for now, just trying to catch a glimpse of the moving truck outside. They could scour the interior recordings more carefully later.

The clock on the film said she was looking at the 3 a.m. hour of Monday morning now—almost seven hours after Frost's neighbor had heard the three shots. She stared at nothing happening on the screen for minutes at a time. This was a twenty-four-hour operation, but she doubted they made any money at that time of night.

"Anything?" Rachette returned with a tinge of whine in his voice.

At that moment she was through to the present moment on the video. "Nope."

"Shit."

She grabbed the footage for the interior and left the office.

The clerk twisted around. "You find what you're looking for?"

Patterson held up the USB stick. "We're going to take this."

The clerk shrugged.

"Hey." Rachette was on the other side of the counter, knocking his knuckles on the glass of the slow-rotating cooker. "Are these from yesterday?"

The clerk blundered through an inaudible response.

Rachette leaned forward and stared into the clerk's eyes.

"The hot dogs. The taquitos. When did you make these? Tell me the truth now."

The clerk hung his head, looking ashamed. "Two days ago."

Rachette nodded, then reached in and grabbed two taquitos from the revolving rack. He bared his teeth and hot-potatoed them back and forth in his hands, then put them in a wad of napkins.

"How much?" He pulled out his wallet.

"Uh ... don't worry about it."

"Nonsense. Are you sure?" Rachette gave him a single second to answer. "Well thanks. You want one, Patterson?"

"No," she said.

Rachette shoved half of one in his mouth. "Ah, hot. Thanks, man." He left through the automatic doors.

Patterson walked through the bulletproof door and around to the front of the counter.

Rachette came back inside and Patterson pretended to be perusing the items for sale on the counter. She placed her hand on a disposable cigarette lighter, and then a box of mints.

"I need another napkin," Rachette said, walking behind her. "You coming or what?"

She twisted and looked at the rear of the store toward the coolers. "I'll be right there. Gonna get a drink."

"Get me a water?" He left.

"Yeah. Sure."

She walked to the cooler, grabbed two waters and went back to the counter. Slapping down a twenty-dollar bill, she pulled out the home-pregnancy-test box from her pocket and put it on the counter. "I need to pay for this."

The clerk picked up the box and studied the ripped open box.

She'd peed on one of them and left it in the women's bathroom trash can. Mercifully, it had been negative. Now she just needed to get back to the station, where she had some Pepto sitting in her desk drawer.

"Come on." She pushed the box forward and the guy swiped it with his scanner gun and pushed it back. "Actually, you keep it and throw it away for me, okay? And keep the change."

She nudged the twenty forward and walked out the door, the euphoria of utter relief making her steps light.

"Don't you want the other one, just in case?" the clerk called.

For an instant she ignored the man, and then she stopped dead and came back inside, the tension already roiling her gut. "What? Why?"

He shrugged. "That's how my kid came. My girlfriend got a false-negative on one of these things. Talk about a psych-out." He laughed. "I think that's why they have two of 'em."

She stared at him.

The clerk scratched his beard.

"Damn it." She grabbed the box, pocketed it, and left.

CHAPTER 13

THE WINDFIELD MOVING Company was a dust-encrusted stand-alone two-car garage with a dirt lot surrounded by chain-link fence. A single moving truck was parked inside the grounds, and near the building a beat-up American sedan stood baking in the sun.

Wolf parked behind Shumway in front of the building and they stepped out. Jet spilled out of the back door, trotted to the fence, and lifted a leg.

Shumway eyed the dog taking care of his business and hooked a thumb toward the building. "This woman's a little kooky if I remember correctly."

"Jet, stay here," Wolf said.

Jet ignored him and put his nose to the dirt.

The door chimed as Wolf and Shumway entered, and a heavyset woman with greasy gray hair, a dirty blouse, and brown bug eyes looked up from a counter.

"Hello, gentlemen. Can I help you?" She leaned back.

Shumway hitched his belt and leaned on the counter. "This here is Detective Wolf from Rocky Points."

"Oh, yes. Hi, I'm Pamela. Pamela Trunzo. I've been talking to … is it Deputy Patterson?"

Wolf nodded.

"Nice woman, she is."

"She called about one of your trucks, rented by Jeffrey Green?"

"Oh yes, I remember. My heck, I've only been thinking about it non-stop for every waking minute since. Have you found the truck yet?"

"I'm sorry, no, we haven't."

She shook her head. "Muh. Ain't got no insurance on it."

Wolf was unsure how to respond to that, so he moved on. "Was Green with anyone when he rented the truck?"

She squinted and looked to the ceiling, putting a stubby finger on her chin. "I assume he was. He drove off in the truck. And he didn't leave another vehicle here. I remember noticing that when I was helping him back out. Nobody was out there with him. Had no vehicle with him either."

"So someone dropped him off?" Shumway asked.

"I suppose."

"Don't you folks have GPS devices on all these trucks to track them?" Shumway asked.

"Not ours. My stupid husband didn't comply with that. That's why they pulled our insurance. Good for nothin' cheap skate, that man. You know what I really hope?"

She waited for an answer.

Wolf and Shumway raised their eyebrows.

"I hope the truck never gets found. Or if it is, it was dumped off a cliff and it's destroyed to kingdom come. I hope we have to shut this place down so I can move out of this heck-hole. That's what I hope." She slapped the counter.

Shumway gave Wolf a told-you-so look.

"You said you watched him drive away," Wolf said. "Which way did he go?"

She waddled around the counter past them, then pushed open the glass door.

Shumway watched with an amused smile.

She poked her arm out the door. "Went that way."

Shumway frowned and walked to the door. "Which way?"

"That way." She pointed to the rising sun.

Shumway pushed past her. "Come out here, would ya?"

She followed, and the door hissed shut.

Wolf grabbed the paperwork off the counter and followed them outside.

"You mean that way, right?" Shumway pointed to the north, toward the plateaus and the dinosaur quarry contained within.

"No. I watched him roll down 11 to the east. Right there. I told you, I helped him back out of the spot here, and he drove away. I remember plain as day. Heck, I've had one customer all month, and it was him. And that's why I've gotta get the heck out of here." She turned to Wolf. "I'm bored. Oh yeah. And broke."

Wolf raised the paperwork. "Is this the time Green rented the truck? Right here?"

The woman walked over, wheezing heavily. She mashed her breasts into his forearm and looked at the forms. "Yeah. 12:42 p.m. Customers get twenty-four hours with the truck. Anything over that, and I gotta charge 'em another day, so gotta be precise with the time."

"Of course," he said, handing the papers back to her. "Thanks for your help. And you're sure you didn't see anyone else with him?"

She widened her already bulging eyes and stared at him.

They stood in silence for a beat.

"Okay," Wolf said. "Thanks."

"You're welcome." She waved a hand and disappeared back inside through the jingling door.

Shumway gave a half-smile. "Told ya."

"What was all that directional pointing about?"

"She was saying Green drove off east. There's nothin' east. No access to the quarry up there."

Wolf frowned. "Then where was he going?"

"If she's telling the truth."

"She seemed pretty sure."

"Pretty crazy," Shumway said. "That's what she seemed like. Let's get up to the quarry."

Wolf followed Shumway back to their vehicles.

CHAPTER 14

WOLF FOLLOWED the local sheriff out of town to the north and into the red and white cliff plateaus that overlooked Windfield. He'd entered the dinosaur quarry into the GPS, and a red line appeared over the green digital map display on his dash computer, indicating his route.

It seemed unnecessary, because he passed the third brown-painted sign that said Windfield Dinosaur Quarry with an arrow pointing ahead.

It was past 9 a.m. now so he pressed the number for Talbot at the University of Utah and put the phone to his ear.

"Dr. Talbot's office," a female voice answered.

"Could I speak to Dr. Talbot please?"

"He's not in. May I take a message?"

"This is Detective Wolf from the Sluice–Byron County Sheriff's Department in Colorado. I'd like to speak to him as soon as possible."

"Oh, yes. I just heard your messages. What's going on that's so important?"

"Just a few questions I have for him. Do you know when he'll be in the office?"

"Well he ... ready ..."

He eyed his cell phone screen and saw a single dot filled for reception, along with a combination of letters he'd never seen.

He took his foot off the gas. "Can you hear me?"

"Yes."

He pulled to the side of the road and slowed to a stop. "Sorry, I didn't catch the last thing you said."

Shumway continued ahead of him and disappeared around a bend.

"I said he's usually here. I come in at 8:30 and he's always here before me. I'm not sure what's going on this morning."

He nodded. "Okay."

"So what's Professor Green done this time?" she asked in a conspiratorial tone.

Wolf hesitated. "What do you mean by 'this time'?"

She laughed. "Professor Green? Oh, never mind."

"No, really," Wolf said. "What do you mean?"

"Well ... he just likes to think of himself as some kind of paleontology swashbuckler. Has all these stories about things."

"Like what?"

"Oh ... like getting bones out of Mongolia before the *corrupt president* catches him, or paying off the *corrupt customs officials* to get a skeleton out of Argentina, or some other bull-puck story."

"Argentina?"

"Uh, yeah. I guess he's spent a lot of time there."

Maybe there was some truth to the stories she'd heard, at least about bribing customs officials.

"Well, I'll tell Dr. Talbot to give you a ring as soon as he gets in. Should be any minute now."

"Thanks."

He pushed the button and dropped the phone in his center console.

Re-checking the GPS, he hit the gas to catch up.

The paved road wound and climbed. Without a human escort, the GPS readout did fine enough, telling him to take a right at a fork in the road where the pavement ended and a graded dirt road began. He continued for fifteen minutes, all the while tilting back in his seat as the road climbed higher, past two-track offshoots that disappeared up dry washes into the juniper hills.

As he ascended, the road turned rockier, and he passed over a stripe of mustard dirt that changed to bright purple for a few yards, then red, and he mused it was easy to imagine they were pulling dinosaur bones out of the ground here, because he felt like he was stepping into the past with so much geology on display.

He turned a final sharp corner around a hill and a building abruptly came into sight, along with a majestic view.

The Windfield Dinosaur Quarry tourist center was set on a high plateau and tucked against the base of a rounded mountain that towered behind it. It was built from concrete and steel, jutting from the ground to look like a wind sail. Or a dinosaur spine, Wolf realized.

He rolled into a circular drive looping in front of the building, passing four American-made full-sized pickup trucks parked next to one another. Three had upside-down triangle logos of the Department of the Interior on their door, and the fourth was Sheriff Shumway's.

He pulled in next to Shumway's, edging his bumper up to a jagged black boulder that had been laid out to mark the boundary of the parking lot. Beyond the rocks stood twisted junipers, which covered the landscape on the high plateau.

Climbing out of his SUV, he stood in the parking lot, once again stretching his arms overhead, ignoring the ache in his leg and back.

It was still, completely silent, and still oven-hot, noticeably devoid of buzzing insects, which had apparently burrowed themselves into the cool depths of the earth to escape spontaneous combustion. The only signs of life were two children climbing on rocks near a picnic table, and some people standing inside the windows of the building looking out. They were looking at him.

Wolf nodded and waved, recognizing Shumway standing next to a man and woman on the other side of the glass.

When he opened the rear door, Jet lifted his head and squinted as hot air hit his eyeballs.

"Yeah. I know. I think they have air conditioning inside."

The dog stood with a groan and spilled out.

They followed a dirt walkway indicated with more black rocks to a concrete pad and the building's steel-and-glass entrance. A sign said *Windfield Dinosaur Quarry*, and there was a cartoonish dinosaur-skull impression stamped in the concrete wall next to it.

In the distance stood three army-green yurts, constructed of heavy fabric and lashed to the rocky soil with thick straps. Beyond them, wide-open landscape filled the horizon. Mounds of white rock jutted and lunged, striped with red and white sedimentary layers tilting every which way, all of it dotted with pinyon pines and juniper trees. Underneath the high vantage, the land waves darkened to a deep blue before melting into the horizon God knew how many miles away.

Somewhere below, Wolf knew the Yampa River was cutting its way through the rock. How far down, he couldn't tell. He made a mental note to study the GPS later.

Pulling himself back to the space around him, he ignored the staring faces in the window and opened the door next to it.

A man in a khaki button-up shirt with a BLM patch pushed the door open for Wolf and Jet, letting out a wintry blast of air.

He had a bushy, round silver goatee that was groomed to display his friendly smile. His gray hair was curled upward at the edges of his yellow ball cap. Judging by the wrinkles on his face, Wolf pegged him in his early sixties.

Looking down at Jet the man said, "Hey, who are you?"

Jet ignored him and beelined it to the cool interior.

The man splayed his hand in an oh-well gesture.

"That's Jet," Wolf said, holding out his hand. "I'm Detective Wolf. Sluice–Byron County Sheriff's Department. Colorado."

"I'm Bradley. Bradley Boydell."

Boydell took his hand in a tight grip. "Nice to meet you. Please, come in. It's already hotter than heck out there."

The door yawned wide for Wolf to enter. Just when he was about to close, the two children Wolf had seen earlier shot through with delighted squeals.

"Whoa! Watch it!" Boydell called after them as they disappeared into the visitors' center.

The children bobbed into the distance, passing under a huge skeleton that looked like a Tyrannosaurs rex but smaller, with, just as one would expect, a mouth wide open in a silent roar. An Allosaurus fragilis, Wolf recognized from his internet searches the night before. The twenty-foot-high fossil specimen fit comfortably in the light interior of the building, as if the center had been built around it.

"Allosaurus," Boydell said, watching Wolf.

Wolf nodded and looked to Shumway and the woman, who turned out to be younger than Wolf had thought at first glance through the window. She had bright-blue eyes and a wide smile. Her skin was tanned from head to toe and her blonde hair was naturally bleached from the sun and pulled back in a tight ponytail. She wore a tight tank top, short shorts, and flip-flops. Her scent was a mixture of coconut-oil and perfume.

"Hi, I'm Megan." She thrust out a skinny arm.

Wolf nodded and shook her dainty hand.

She held his grip a second too long and eyed him up and down.

He pulled his hand away, feeling heat rise in his face at the forwardness of the greeting.

She walked to Jet and bent over with straight legs, as if she were trying to display her firm backside. Gripping the dog's face, she cooed while she scratched. "Look at you. You're so cute."

Jet licked his lips and wagged his tail.

Wolf noticed Shumway's eyes ping-ponged between her butt and the men's eyes in the room, as if he were keeping mental tabs of who was looking.

Wolf turned to Boydell, whose eyes had already wandered to the ceiling.

"You're going to escort us out to the dig site?" Wolf asked Boydell.

"Yes, sir. Like I told the deputies last night, it's best that I do. There're some tricky parts."

A late-teens, early twenties, man stood behind a round reception desk as if waiting introduction.

"That's Phil," Boydell said. "He and Megan are both interns from the University of Utah."

Phil had a flop of brown hair that covered most of a pimple-plastered forehead. "Hi," he said, smiling awkwardly.

Wolf shook his hand, too.

"You guys rent out those yurts outside to tourists?" Wolf asked.

Boydell chuckled. "No, that's where we live. I'm in the far one, year-round, and Megan and Phil live in the other two for the summer."

"I see. And what's that in the distance?" Wolf pointed out

the window at a line of blue and red dots tucked among the bushes and trees.

"Good eyes," Boydell said. "That's Dig 1."

"That's where Professor Green and his students are digging?"

"No, they're further on, down the valley beyond. We call Professor Green's site Dig 2. I know, we're creative."

"How many digs are there?" Wolf asked.

"Two," Boydell said.

Wolf nodded and gestured out the rear windows toward a steel building that looked like an oversized shed. "I looked at your website last night. That's where they're digging the predator trap?"

Shumway looked at his watch.

Megan had turned away from Jet now and was staring at him with a half-smile on her lips.

Boydell nodded. "You're right, that's the predator trap—a big bunch of disarticulated bones from a range of species from the Cretaceous period. Mostly predators. No one knows exactly why there's such a collection of bones, and broken into so many pieces." Boydell smiled sheepishly. "At least, that's what they tell me. I'm just a BLM employee, not a dino expert like these two kids."

"You're right, Mr. Boydell," Megan chimed.

Wolf nodded at the big skeleton. "And where was this specimen found?"

"That's a replica of one found back in 1982, down in the same valley Dig 2's at right now. But on the park side of the gulch."

"Park side of the gulch?" Wolf asked. "Rather than the private-land side, you mean?"

Megan and Shumway exchanged a glance, but Wolf failed to read anything into it.

"I'm not comfortable with bringing you to the Dig 2 site," Wolf said to Boydell.

"Why not?" Boydell pulled his eyebrows together. "I escorted those deputies last night."

Megan put her hands on her hips. "Are you two going to tell us what's going on, or what?"

"No, we're not," Shumway said. "It's official business and we need you two to stay up here. In fact, Bradley, if you can just give us directions, you don't even need to come out with us."

Boydell looked skeptical. "I wouldn't know where to begin giving you directions. There's a maze of two-track roads out there, and you have to avoid some problem spots. I'll get you to Dig 1 and then let you guys go on by yourselves. It's easy from there."

Shumway and Wolf exchanged glances and nodded.

"All right. You'll lead us, I'll follow, and Detective Wolf can take the rear."

"Sounds good," Boydell said.

Wolf nodded and clapped a hand on his leg. "Let's go, Jet."

Shumway was out the door first, not bothering to wait for them.

Boydell shuffled forward and held the door for Wolf and Jet.

"Bye." Megan sang the word looking straight at Wolf. "Bye cutie."

Jet left reluctantly and Wolf followed him out into the blazing heat.

Boydell stepped alongside him. "Try and keep close. It'll make things easier on your vehicles."

Shumway gave a thumbs-up as he climbed in his truck. He put his seatbelt on and fired up the engine.

Boydell jogged to his truck and climbed in, then started backing out.

"Let's go, Jet." Wolf opened his rear door and slapped his leg.

Jet paced back and forth with a look that Wolf had come to recognize as his bathroom face.

"Not a good time. Come on."

Jet dropped his head and walked to him.

That seemed to be the go-ahead for Boydell and Shumway, because they shot off in a cloud of dust around the corner.

Jet whined and turned around, then made his way toward the junipers and crouched in a pooping position.

Wolf sighed. "Make it quick."

"Uh-oh, they ditched you." Megan was outside and flip-flopping her way to his SUV. "You're going to need my help."

"No thanks. They're right there." Though the two vehicles were out of sight and around the bend, Wolf had heard the squeak of brakes and running engines. "They're waiting. Thanks, though."

She walked to the passenger side, got in, and shut the door.

Jet came over with a bounce in his step and Wolf let him in the back. Tail wagging, he stood on the rear bench seat and stuck his head in front over Megan's shoulder.

"Sit down," Wolf said.

Jet complied.

Before Wolf could climb inside, Megan had her butt in the air again, bending over the seat to pet Jet.

"Sit down," he said again.

Megan took her time, but eventually sat down and faced forward.

"And now get out," he said, firing up the engine.

She frowned and looked at him. "That's not very nice."

"Get out, please."

She shook her head. "You're not going to be able to find the turn-off."

"They're right around the corner waiting for me."

"And if you lose them on the way there?"

"I don't think your father would appreciate it if I brought you in my car. This isn't a joyride."

She turned to face him. Her eyes were cold and her mouth downturned. "My father can suck eggs. I work here. He doesn't."

Wolf leaned back in his seat. "So that *is* your father."

"Huh?"

"Your father is the sheriff."

She looked at him then smiled. "You didn't know before?"

"No. Please, hop out."

"You just figured that out?" With lips parted, she looked him up and down again. "You're a good cop. I can tell."

"Get out." He backed up, turned and then scraped to a stop at the walkway. "Now."

"Nope." She took off a flip-flop and put a foot out the window. Her toes bounced in front of the side-view mirror. She leaned back and closed her eyes, like she was enjoying a nice country drive.

Wolf took a deep, cleansing breath and pushed the accelerator.

CHAPTER 15

PATTERSON STOOD in the county-building bathroom in front of the mirror. She was panting, her chest heaving. Her fingers cramped from pinching the freshly peed-on device in her fingers.

With a deep breath, she steeled herself and looked at it.

Negative.

What were the chances of a double false-negative? Probably small. And the chances of her birth control failing? Very slim according to the doctor who'd placed the device inside her.

She stared at herself in the mirror. Her normally tanned, vibrant face—if she did say so herself—looked pale and sunken.

Geez, was it that big of a deal to be impregnated by the man she loved? And she did love Scott. She had already addressed that issue after she'd failed to answer Scott's third proposal, which led to a fourth and final one, to which she'd said yes.

That she had made Scott do all that just to win her hand was already borderline psycho. Okay, it was over the psycho line. And now? She was a fifth-degree black belt in karate. The mental and physical fortitude to get to that level was beyond the capability of a normal person—again, if she did say so herself.

So what was her problem?

She'd had bad shrimp and she was ill. That's why she looked like this, and why she felt sick, and why her hand shook, and why she couldn't keep away from the toilet.

A vision of her pregnant fat ass waddling into the squad room flashed in her mind. Check that—it was her pregnant fat ass waddling *out* of the squad room. Out of the entire building. For good.

"Hey, you all right?" Deputy Charlotte Munford had snuck inside the bathroom. Damn the perfectly silent new doors in this building.

Patterson slam dunked the box and pregnancy test into the trash hole in the counter and got busy washing her hands. "I just feel like crap after the food last night."

"Oh, yeah. The bridal shower. How was it? Get some good gifts?" Munford smiled with that perfect lots-of-gum-like-a-young-Meg-Ryan smile of hers, her blue eyes alight with mischief, like they were girlfriends or something. "Those in-laws can be tough. My sister got married, and her husband's mother was a nightmare."

Patterson nodded, then dried her hands with a larger-than-needed wad of paper towels and threw them into the trash to bury the evidence.

"Rachette and I are so excited to go to the wedding," Munford said. "It's going to be so beautiful. On the top of the mountain like that? Oh. My. God."

Patterson knew she looked disgusted by the conversation, because she was looking at herself in the mirror. A fake smile was all she could muster in response.

Munford dug inside her bag and frowned. "Shit. You have any more of those?"

Patterson froze. "What?"

"Tampons."

"Oh. No. Sorry, last one."

"Damn. All right." Munford looked at a loss for a second, then turned to leave. "See you." Before she got to the door she stopped and turned around. "I hope we can be friends some-day." Then she left out the door.

The words sailed through the flowery air of the bathroom and jabbed Patterson in the heart. She looked at herself in the mirror. Her mouth was wide open, her eyes staring in shock.

A minute later she was back in the squad room at her desk, watching a fisheye-view black-and-white video of the customer counter at the Brushing gas station from earlier that morning.

Hand on her chin, she watched yet another patron, a man, walk into the convenience store. This man wore a wide-brimmed cowboy hat that hid his face. He wandered to the candy-bar aisle, picked one, then grabbed a plastic gas can from the floor and went to the counter. Nothing too out of the ordinary—there had been other men who'd worn ball caps or other hats that obscured their faces—but the time stamp said 9:21 p.m., which was right in the timeline that the perps could have been passing through the gas station after shooting Ryan Frost.

Twisting to the laptop she'd set up next to the desktop, she checked the exterior footage for the same time.

She fast-forwarded, then let the recording roll, and saw a Honda Civic parked in front of one of the gas terminals.

No moving truck.

She clicked the mouse and let the interior footage play again. The man paid with cash, grabbed something from a counter display, then walked out with the gas can in hand.

"You got anything?" Barker asked from his desk, not both-ering to look away from his computer screen.

"Still nothing," she said, hitting the fast-forward button again.

"Just let me know about anything out of the ordinary," he said.

She glared at Barker's round head of shaved red hair. Let *me* know?

Everything that came out of this guy's mouth was a brand-new WTF moment. Who did he think he was? Wolf? Even Wolf wouldn't have said "me." Because Wolf included his deputies, didn't treat them like employees that fed his all-knowing mind, so that he, alone, could work out the answer.

"Let *me* know?" Rachette looked over his shoulder with a raised eyebrow. He was standing with Hernandez at the printout map they'd pinned onto a roll-stand corkboard.

The map had a red radius circle drawn on it, indicating how far the rental truck could have gone on its journey before fueling up. Rachette and Hernandez were marking off the gas stations with red push-pins indicating which footage had already been studied thoroughly.

"Yeah, I'm the ranking deputy," Barker said. "Let me know."

Rachette shook his head and pushed a pin into the map.

"You got a problem with that?" Barker said, his chair creaking as he leaned back and twisted toward Rachette. "When you do the time, like I have, you can take a little more responsibility yourself."

Rachette ignored him and pushed in another pin, this time north of Cave Creek. "Patty, you done with that footage?"

She looked down. "No."

He took out the pin. "Let me know when you're done."

Barker stood up. "You making fun of me now, asshole?"

"You're an idiot."

Barker walked over and squared off with Rachette.

Patterson rolled her eyes and leaned into her computer screen. She'd seen so much friction between these two that it now bored her.

"Hey, boys." Deputy Charlotte Munford's voice appeared out of nowhere. "Greg, please calm down, okay?" she said in a soft tone.

Barker puffed up even larger. At six foot one, he towered over Rachette's five-foot-seven frame, but Patterson had to hand it to Rachette—the guy never backed down an inch.

"Hey." Munford pulled Barker away gently by the arm and Barker backed up without resistance.

The way Barker slobbered over Munford was so glaringly obvious it was comical. And Rachette had Munford sleeping in his bed. Real daytime television stuff. Patterson hated daytime TV.

"What the hell's going on?" MacLean's voice echoed in the squad room.

Patterson sat up straight and turned around.

MacLean stood outside his office with his hands on his hips. "Where's the moving truck?"

Nobody answered.

"I asked a question!"

"Sir, Patterson hasn't found anything on the gas-station videos yet," Barker said.

"And that's all you got?" MacLean wore the same face that he'd had after smelling Jet's gas. "Where's the truck?"

They stood in silence.

"And what are you doing here?" MacLean pointed at Munford. "I want every deputy out on CP, except for these four, who are supposed to be finding a goddamned moving truck."

Munford's shoes squeaked as she hurried out of the squad room.

Patterson cleared her throat. "Sir, it's true. We've scoured just about every bit of footage and there's no sign—"

"Just about? It's nearly ten and you haven't gotten through all the video?"

She wondered why 10 a.m. was the cut-off between diligent and lazy work.

"There was no sign of the truck at any of the gas stations," she said, "and now I'm looking at the stores' interior recordings."

"Why?" MacLean shook his head. "If it didn't show up on the exterior footage, then it didn't refuel. So what are you going to look for on interior footage?"

Patterson opted to remain silent.

"Since it didn't refuel," MacLean said, "not in town, not anywhere within our agreed-upon radius, then they must have ditched it somewhere. So I'll tell you how to find this truck, okay? Listen close. Ready?"

They stood frozen.

MacLean's face turned red. "Get in your goddamn cars and start driving!"

Barker marched out of the room at full speed. "Hernandez, let's do it."

Hernandez shuffled after him.

Patterson powered down her computer tower and looked at Rachette.

Rachette pushed his pin into the map and went to his desk.

"I'm not feeling impressed by your enthusiasm right now," MacLean said.

Patterson shut the laptop and shoved her chair in, banging it loudly into her desk. It was much, much more of a ruckus than she'd meant to cause, but something had snapped inside her, releasing anger through her limbs.

"Is there a problem, Deputy Patterson?" MacLean walked over.

Patterson shook her head. "No."

"No. Tell me, what is it? You have a problem with following orders?"

MacLean leaned in close. His breath reeked of coffee.

"No, sir."

"Good. Now get your asses out there and find me a UrMover truck. Preferably with a pile of bones inside."

Patterson followed Rachette out of the squad room.

"And, Deputies?"

They slowed and turned around. MacLean had a finger pointing at the ceiling. "Do not come back until you've found it."

The sheriff's eyes meant every word.

"Yes, sir."

"Yes, sir."

CHAPTER 16

"How did you know?"

Wolf leaned toward the windshield and squinted. Shumway's and Boydell's trucks had kicked up a cloud of dust. There was no way to tell how far ahead they were, but it looked like they were going fast.

The dirt road twisted with the occasional straightaway, all the while descending back off the plateau's top.

"How did I know what?"

"That I'm the sheriff's daughter." She was preoccupied with rubbing something on the inside of her propped leg.

Wolf kept his eyes out the windshield. "You two have the same blue eyes. Identical. And you have the same inflection in your voices, the same pronunciation of certain words."

"Really?" She leaned back and laughed. "You are so cute."

"I'm forty years old. What are you, twenty?"

"Bingo. Right again. I bet you think I'm a lot better looking than my dad, though. Right?"

He saw her staring at him in his peripheral.

"I was going to say I'm old enough to be your dad."

"My dad's fifty."

Trying to comprehend her logic, Wolf leaned forward and slowed the SUV. The cloud of dust seemed to get denser, more immediate, but he saw no brake lights.

Then the cloud dissipated, and he broke into clearer air, so he pressed the accelerator again.

She laughed. "You might want to slow down."

"Why?"

"Because you just passed them."

Wolf saw the two trucks in the side-view mirror. They had pulled off and Boydell was out of his truck, staring after him. Behind his truck stood Shumway's, close on his bumper.

Wolf skidded to a stop and turned around.

As he drove back to them, Boydell was swinging open a wooden gate set in barbed wire, before Wolf had reached Shumway's bumper they were already on the move again.

"See?" Megan said. "I told you you'd need me."

Like a hole in the head.

The SUV drove spongily as they followed in the caravan, sliding in a sandy wash meandering through boulder-strewn terrain. The rocks were cinnamon-colored and streaked with black watermarks, some of them dwarfing the SUV. Canyon walls towered on both sides, with layers of white on top and maroon underneath.

With the dust now settled, the scent of juniper flowed through the window, mixing with the dog fur and coconut oil inside.

The curves were tight and Shumway's truck rarely came into view, so Wolf concentrated on the well-worn tracks in the sand.

"Just go along this wash. I'll tell you when you need to turn. It'll be a right in about a half-mile."

"Okay ... thanks."

She smiled, and Wolf regretted encouraging her.

"So ... what's this all about?" She bounced her eyebrows.

He ignored her.

"Oh, come on."

"Is that why you're here?" Wolf asked. "To get the inside scoop?"

She shrugged. "I want to go visit Dig 1. I have a friend there."

They rode in silence for another beat.

"And I want to help. Feel free to ask me any question you want to."

Wolf twisted the wheel and they turned a tight corner.

"So, what about you?" she asked. "How's Sluice ... what county are you from?"

"Sluice–Byron."

"And how's that?"

Wolf raised an eyebrow and sighed. "It's nice."

"Where do you live?"

"Town called Rocky Points."

"Oh, I've heard of that. Skiing. I've never been, but I bet I'd love it."

Wolf plucked his cell phone out of the center console and checked it. It said *No Service* in the corner of the screen.

"No service except for in town. Doesn't matter which carrier you have," she said. "Okay, turn up here."

They climbed out of the wash. It was steep, and they were pressed back in their seats, looking at blue sky. He pressed the gas and the tires spun in the sand, but they ascended without stopping, and then the landscape swung back up into view as they dropped down the other side of a hill.

The other two trucks were in the distance, meandering through trees and rocks, approaching a rise on the left. Above the vehicles stood the flat plateau, and the route started making sense to Wolf. They were going to the dig they'd seen from the visitors' center, but along a circuitous route off the plateau and back onto it.

To their right, rolling hills and plateaus dotted with more juniper stood like frozen waves.

"Pretty beautiful," Wolf said.

She looked at him with a bashful smile.

He resisted rolling his eyes and concentrated on tire marks ahead of him.

"The other dig is down there." She pointed down the valley.

He craned his neck, and for an instant he saw a blue spot—a tent or a tarp—and then it was gone behind a hill.

"Dig 2?"

"Well, you missed it," she said. "But we'll be able to see it again from the top of the plateau."

They bounced in their seats as he cranked the wheel and feathered the gas, avoiding the twisted overhanging wood of the pinyons and junipers, and any rocks that looked too jagged to roll over.

"Used to be our land, you know," she said.

He eyed her. "What used to be your land?"

She put her hand out the window. "That whole thing, thousands of acres. Until my dad lost it."

He blinked. "What do you mean? Where?"

"The private land that Dig 2 is on used to be our family's land."

Wolf kept his face neutral, but his mind was racing.

"And when my grandfather died, somehow my dad screwed up the whole transfer of land ... or my grandfather did ... or whatever—nobody will tell me what happened. But, anyway, we lost it. Some other guy got it."

She clamped her lips shut and looked out the window. She was blinking a lot. Fighting back tears?

"Watch out!" She pointed out the windshield.

He jammed the brakes, stopping just short of a boulder.

Jet let out a squeal from the back seat as he fell on the floor.

"Oh, are you okay?" Megan pursed her lips and reached back to scratch Jet's head.

Jet shuffled back into his comfortable position with Megan's help.

"Megan."

She turned around. "What?"

"Can you please finish your story about the land your family lost?"

"I thought I did."

"Not really."

"Yeah, I did. Dad lost land. Done."

They sat silent in the idling car. Sun rays cooked his arm through the open window.

"Are we going to go?" She looked over with a devilish grin. "Or just stay here?"

He backed away from the boulder and drove on.

CHAPTER 17

JUST SHORT OF the crest of the plateau, they passed a red tent and a full-sized Dodge pickup off to the left side of the two-track.

"Who camps here?" Wolf asked.

"That's Levi's camp. One of the grad students at Dig 1. Levi Joseph. See? Aren't you glad I'm here to answer all these questions for you?" Megan smiled.

Wolf slowed to a stop next to the truck and peered at the tires. They were the wrong brand.

"Hello?" Wolf called out.

No one answered.

"Probably up—"

Jet barked, and the sound filled the interior of the cab with the volume of a jackhammer.

Megan screeched and plugged her ears.

"Jet!"

Jet was standing on the rear seat, staring out the passenger-side rear window and barking with snapping jaws. Saliva stuck to the glass. After every second or third bark he shut his mouth, looked at Wolf, and whined.

He shoved the truck in park and got out. When he opened the rear door, Jet leapt down, almost barreling him over.

With ears raised, Jet trotted around the rear of the SUV and turned, barking and staring at Wolf again.

He looked at his watch and shrugged. "Go!"

Jet took off down the steep slope, weaving his way through the brush rocks.

"What the hell?" He stepped to the road's edge and watched the dog trot halfway down the mountain before he stopped and started barking again.

Megan got out and stood next to Wolf. "What's he doing?"

"I don't know. Hey! Let's go!"

Jet ignored him, preoccupied with something. Whines floated up on the breeze.

"Probably chasing an animal," Megan said. "Growing up, we had a dog that would chase jackrabbits. He would go crazy, just like this."

Wolf nodded. Jet looked like he had an animal cornered.

"Jet! Come! Now!"

Jet hesitated for another few moments and then trotted back up the slope, weaving in and out of the trees, stopping every few yards and looking back.

"Now!"

Finally, Jet reached them with a lowered head and followed Wolf's prompting back into the truck.

Slamming the door, Wolf turned and surveyed the valley below. It must have been five hundred feet to the valley floor. A lone blue tent stood amid the foliage and rock.

"Oh, yeah. There's Dig 2."

She stared intently below.

"You know them?" he asked.

"What was that?"

"The students at Dig 2. Do you know them?"

"Yeah, I guess." She shrugged, looking nonchalant, but Wolf sensed she was putting on an act. "I know everyone. Everyone knows everyone."

"Is there anyone here that wears Converse All Star shoes?"

She swallowed and looked at him, perplexed. "Converse All Stars?"

He nodded.

She shrugged and looked away. "I haven't noticed. Why?"

He stared at the back of her head until she turned around.

"Are you telling me the truth?"

"Am I telling you the truth? Geez. I mean, I have a pair. Why? Why are you asking?"

Resigned, he walked back to the driver's-side door.

They got in and Wolf eyed Jet in the rear-view mirror. "You got that out of your system now?"

Jet barked and looked out his window again.

"All right, that's enough." He put the truck in drive and the tires spat dirt.

A few seconds later they were at the top of the plateau, and looking at the flat expanse he'd seen earlier from the visitor center, but from a different angle. Off to his left he could see the gleaming windows of the structure far away, and the shining red mountain of rock that butted up to its rear. Further down the two-track in front of them, Boydell and Shumway had parked their trucks next to a red one, and they were milling around a complex of tents and tarps with a man and a woman.

"So, Levi camps all the way down here and walks to the dig? Do you know why that is?" Wolf asked.

She laughed, like Wolf had asked the funniest question in history. "He probably can't sleep with all the sex noises coming from the other tent."

He raised his eyebrows.

She stopped laughing and looked at him. "A guy named Dr.

Mathis heads up this dig, and the other student besides Levi is a girl named Karen. Dr. Mathis and Karen think they're keeping it secret, but they're clearly screwing. So Levi gives them their space. Although now that I think about it, even if they weren't screwing, Levi would probably be camping back there. He's kind of a loner."

"And you're friends with Levi, too?"

She looked out the window. "Yeah, I guess. We've gotten to know each other."

A few minutes later of relatively smooth driving over the flat terrain, Wolf and Megan approached the camp. Outside, Shumway stopped in mid-sentence with Boydell and shielded his eyes. His facial expression showed he'd just realized his daughter was in the car with Wolf, and he was none too happy about it.

"Stop here. Wait," Megan said. "Wait, wait, wait ..."

Wolf stopped the car.

Before he could ask why, he pressed himself back into his seat as Megan leaned over him and out his window.

"What the hell are you doing?" he asked.

"Hey, sister!" Megan shouted out the window. "Long time no see!"

The woman Wolf assumed was Karen paused in mid-sentence and waved.

"When did you get back?" Megan asked.

Sheriff Shumway stood next to Karen, his head tilted, his eyes wide and locked on Wolf's.

Megan and Karen chatted for another few moments, and then Megan drew a hand down into the cab and planted it squarely in Wolf's crotch as she launched back into her seat. Without a word, she opened the door, jumped out, and slammed it. With a happy jog, she ran around the front of the SUV and went to embrace her friend.

Wolf sat still for a second, then let his foot off the gas and pulled alongside the other trucks.

A few seconds later, Wolf had Jet out from the back seat and they were walking toward the camp—Wolf pointedly ignoring Shumway's red-faced glare.

With the commotion, he almost forgot his duty. He stopped and turned around, and went back to study the trucks.

Bradley Boydell's BLM truck had the Goodyear P265/70R17s, and so did the red truck with civilian Utah plates, which, since they'd passed Levi's truck, by process of elimination would have to be either Mathis's or Karen's.

Add Sheriff Shumway's tires, which also matched, and the whole tread piece of evidence seemed less useful by the second. But, as Wolf knew, that's how the truth lulled you to sleep—by hiding in a sea of anonymity.

CHAPTER 18

"Hello, I'm Detective Wolf." Wolf held out his hand to the man standing next to Shumway.

"I'm Dr. Mathis."

The short man stepped forward and pumped Wolf's hand with a firm, rough grip. He wore Birkenstock sandals with dusty white socks, cargo shorts and a T-shirt that had a picture of a dinosaur with glasses and *The Saurus Knows All The Words* written underneath.

"Welcome to Dig 1, as they call us."

"I'm Karen." A bright-eyed woman stepped away from Megan with an outstretched arm.

Wolf took in her slender hand, which was callused and dusty. She was a couple of inches taller than Mathis, a comparison Wolf made only because of Megan letting him in on the "secret." Karen wore jeans shorts that displayed thick tanned legs. A mesh, wide-brimmed hat sat on her head of short black hair, shading a smile that was bright and pleasant.

"And where's your other grad student?" Wolf asked. "Levi Joseph?"

Mathis and Karen looked at one another. "Beats us. Been gone all morning. Heck, he was gone all day yesterday too."

"Without taking his truck?" Shumway asked.

"Sometimes he takes long hikes," Karen said with a shrug.

Mathis looked skeptical. "Yes, but he usually tells us when he goes on his little treks. He brags about them first, talks about the route for days, then shows us the map in case he doesn't come back." He waved a hand. "Sorry, we've just been discussing it. He kind of up and disappeared on us this weekend."

Shumway glared at Boydell. "You haven't seen him?"

Boydell shook his head.

Shumway put his hands on his hips and shook his head. Then he gave his daughter a sidelong glance.

There was real urgency in Shumway's tone.

"Should we be putting out a search party?" Wolf asked.

"Oh my," Karen gasped.

Shumway peered down the two-track toward Levi's camp, which was out of sight over the edge of the plateau. "No, but keep us posted if he doesn't show himself."

They stood mute for a few seconds, and then Wolf cleared his throat.

"I'm not sure what Sheriff Shumway has told you two yet, but he and I are conducting an investigation and we have some questions."

"Yes, he told us. What's it about?" Mathis asked. "What kind?"

"I can't discuss the particulars."

Mathis gave a skeptical frown. "Well then we can't answer any questions you might have. I'm sure you understand, Detective. I don't want to implicate myself in anything. So I'm going to respectfully decline speaking to either of you. And I advise Karen to do the same."

Karen looked dumbfounded.

Mathis folded his arms and pretended that everyone around him had vanished.

"We've had a homicide," Wolf said. "A fossil dealer in Rocky Points was shot twice and killed."

Megan gasped, then put her hand over her mouth.

Karen blinked rapidly.

"Wow. A murder in Colorado?" Mathis unfolded his arms and pulled his eyebrows together. "So why are you here?"

Wolf nodded toward the centerpiece of the camp, which was a wide, shallow hole in the ground. "Could I see your dig?"

"Yes, sure." Mathis looked at him suspiciously for a moment, then led the way and waved them to follow.

They stopped at the edge of the hole. Inside the opening, a grid of string bounced on the breeze. Underneath it, digging tools were strewn near exposed fossils.

"What are we looking at here?" Wolf asked.

Mathis's face lit up. "It's really quite a find. An ornithopod from the late Cretaceous. A hadrosaur."

Wolf made a show of not knowing what the heck he was talking about.

"An iguanodon?"

"Yeah, okay. I remember those," Wolf said, referring to memories from his own childhood dinosaur phase.

"The hadrosaurs were prolific in the late Jurassic through the Cretaceous. In the Jurassic they were small, and then," he paused for effect as he stopped at the edge of the hole and spread his arms, "they grew into giants, like these."

Shumway leaned over and squinted, looking unimpressed.

The pieces of bone were a jumbled mass that was hard to put into context in the mind's eye.

Boydell kicked at a rock.

Mathis eyed them all in turn. "Well, you'd have to see the GPR readouts to really get a sense of it."

"GPR?" Wolf asked.

"Ground-penetrating radar."

"Ah."

Mathis looked dejected, like he was surrounded by three-year-olds.

They were standing in fine dirt, and Wolf took the opportunity to study shoes. None of the prints they were leaving matched the crime scene at Rocky Points. Mathis's sandals didn't match. Megan's and Karen's feet were way too small. Boydell's feet were average size, about a ten, but the imprints of his well-worn boots didn't fit either of the patterns at the scene.

And Shumway's? They were about the same size as Boydell's, but the tread was deep and jagged, not the same pattern either. Wolf had the circles, squares, and rectangles of the killer's shoe sole memorized, and none of these matched.

He realized they were stuck in silence once again. "Do any of you own a pair of Converse All Star shoes?"

Megan raised her hand.

"That's quite a change of subject," Mathis said.

Wolf shrugged. "It's what I do."

"Not me." Mathis looked at his own feet, "I just stick to my good ol' Birks. These students, though, they wear that kind of stuff. Used to be popular in the eighties, and now they're all the rave again."

"Steven has a pair," Karen said.

Wolf looked at her.

"Purple ones. Can't miss him when he's got those things on."

Wolf and Shumway exchanged a glance.

"We're talking about Steven Kennedy?" Wolf asked. "Down at Dig 2?"

Karen nodded. "Yep."

Megan avoided eye contact with Wolf. He noticed her face turning red.

"Did Steven kill a fossil dealer?" Mathis asked. There was a hint of amusement in his eyes.

Wolf gestured to the bones in the ground. "Were these predators? Or plant eaters?"

"Ha!" Mathis leaned his head back. "The subject changes once again. Yes, it's an herbivore. Did Steven Kennedy kill someone? I think we have a right to know, him being so close."

"We're not sure who killed the fossil dealer at this point."

They stood in silence.

"How often do you two visit Professor Green's dig?" Wolf asked.

Mathis and Karen looked at each other.

"Last time we saw it was last year."

"Early last year," Karen said.

"When Green and his students used to be more social," Mathis said.

"Yeah," Karen said. "Now we all call them the hermits."

"And why's that?" Wolf asked.

"Professor Green's made it clear he doesn't want anyone near his dig." Mathis stepped around the pit. "It's like he's protecting some art masterpiece he isn't ready to unveil to the world yet."

Wolf frowned. "Can't you just go down there?"

Mathis shrugged. "Done that a couple of times. Trying to sneak a peek. But the last time I went, they had it all covered up. Told me point blank to get back to my own dig. He did pretty much the same thing the first time I went down. And when I asked him about it he just flat told me to leave. I said fine. No sense dealing with crazy people."

"So you haven't seen the dig at all?" Wolf asked.

"Yeah, at the beginning, but not recently, though, no."

"So you have no idea how far along they are with their specimen?" Wolf asked.

"No."

"You and Professor Green both work at the University of Utah, correct?" Wolf asked.

"Yes."

"We've gathered that Dr. Talbot is Professor Green's boss … is he your boss, too?"

"Yes, he's the head of the paleontology department."

Wolf nodded. "That is odd, you being part of the same university and all. I would think the two teams would be on the same side."

"You're telling me." Mathis leaned forward and stepped into the pit by accident.

"Why do you think they're acting the way they are?" Wolf asked.

"Internal politics that we don't know about," Karen said. "Gotta be. Green's vying for a job, doesn't want to share any credit. That, and he's straight crazy."

"Pssh." Mathis waved a hand. "We both have tenure and the guy is most definitely not looking for more responsibility, believe me. The guy doesn't even read half the papers he makes his students write. If anything, he wants less responsibility."

Karen made a sour face and glared at Mathis.

Mathis shook his head. "Anyway, politics wouldn't make sense. That's not how things work."

"When Dr. Talbot came a month ago for his 'surprise' visit, they drove away together," Karen said. "Went to lunch or something. Remember that? I'm telling you, Green's looking for some sort of promotion or something. Maybe it has to do with—"

Shumway cleared his throat. "If we could maybe get back on track here?"

"Dr. Talbot came in a month ago to check the dig?" Wolf asked.

"He does that from time to time," Mathis said with another wave of his hand. "Comes down and checks our progress, updates for his report to the board of regents. Peels his butt off his desk chair and makes the obligatory rounds."

Twisting on his heels, Wolf gazed back toward the two-track road that ran on a straight line across the plateau. "Have you seen Professor Green or any of his dig members drive a moving truck through here recently?"

Mathis looked confused.

"A UrMover truck," Shumway said. "Like a rental truck you use to move from one house to the next."

"You just drove up that road. You think one of those could get up here?" Mathis chuckled.

Shumway looked nonplussed. "So is that a no?"

"Yes, that's a no."

Karen shook her head. "I haven't seen anything like that."

"So, Professor Green is secretive. What about the other three students of his dig team? What do they act like?" Wolf asked.

Karen and Megan glanced at one another.

"They're all right," Karen said. "They're definitely friendlier than Professor Green. At least Mo will come up and have a beer or two. We're kind of friends."

"Mo. Meaning, Molly Waters?" Wolf asked.

"Yeah. She goes by Mo."

"She's a lesbian," Mathis said.

Karen looked horrified. "So what, Ted?"

"What? I'm just saying. She is."

"And what does she say about the dig when she comes up from her camp?" Wolf asked.

Karen peeled her death stare away from Mathis. "Not much."

"She keeps her lips as tight as Professor Green," Mathis said. He ticked off three fingers. "Steve, Felicia, Mo, they're all just like Green. The whole team's the same. They're all hiding something down there."

Like an empty hole, Wolf thought.

"Did you see Professor Green leave past here on Saturday afternoon at all?" Wolf asked.

"Yeah," said Karen. "I do remember him leaving. It was like noonish. I think Felicia was with him, and Steven followed them in his truck."

"And not Mo?" Wolf asked.

"No. They always keep someone there to keep guard," Mathis said. "Someone at the camp to make sure we don't snoop."

"And this was at noon?" Wolf asked.

"Yep. Right around noon."

"Did you see them return?"

They both pondered.

"Steven's truck came back," Mathis said. "Not Professor Green's."

"Oh, yeah," Karen said to Mathis. "You're right."

"Do you remember who was in Steven's truck when he came back?"

"Felicia," Mathis said. "It was Steven and Felicia."

Karen agreed and glanced at Megan once again.

"So, no Professor Green," Shumway said, his eyes narrowing.

"Yeah. That's right. No Professor Green." Mathis eyed Shumway, and then Wolf. "Why?"

"And what time was this they returned?" Shumway asked.

"A few hours later, I guess. We were sitting here grilling, so must have been like four?"

"So at noon they left," Wolf said, "and they came back at four. Four hours."

Karen nodded.

Shumway had his head leaned back, eyeing Wolf.

Mathis looked between them. "What? Why?"

"Like I said, Dr. Mathis, I really can't discuss the particulars," Wolf said.

Mathis rolled his eyes and folded his arms.

"Is this road the only way in and out of here for Dig 2?" Wolf asked, this time addressing the whole group.

"Yep," Karen said.

Mathis silently agreed.

"Technically, no." Boydell raised a finger. "It's a little rough but you can keep following the wash along the bottom of the plateau. You don't have to climb up here."

Wolf nodded. "Was there any other vehicle traffic past here Saturday?"

They shook their heads.

"And how about the rest of the weekend? Sunday?"

Karen shrugged. "Just the two deputies last night, and Mr. Boydell with them."

Boydell nodded. "I escorted them in."

Wolf looked at Mathis and Karen. "And what were you two doing Saturday night?"

Mathis raised a finger and shook it. "Now, wait a minute. Do we need a lawyer now? What is this? Are you saying we're involved?"

Shumway held up both hands. "Dr. Mathis, Detective Wolf is just covering every base. It's within your rights to not answer, but—"

"We were here all night. I thought that much was clear," Mathis said.

Karen nodded so hard her hat threatened to fall off.

They looked like they were telling the truth.

"And so it's clear now," Wolf said. "Thank you. You two have been a real help."

"The second Levi comes back, tell him I want to speak to him," Shumway said. "Tell him to come down to the station. It's very urgent."

"Sure, yeah. We'll tell him," Mathis said.

"I may be around for a while," Wolf said. "I'd appreciate it if you'd stay available if I have more questions."

Mathis shrugged. "Where else are we going to go?"

"Of course we will," Karen said.

"Thank you." Wolf exchanged glances with Boydell and Shumway, and they stepped away.

"Uh ... Detective?"

Wolf paused and turned around.

They smiled and pointed at Wolf's feet.

Jet stared up with a quizzical brow, a hand shovel in his mouth. He dropped the utensil in front of Wolf, backed up, and sat.

Wolf took the slimy shovel, wiped it dry on his shirt, and handed it to Karen. "Sorry."

"No problem." She laughed and turned to Mathis. "We should get a dog."

Wolf left them to debate the point. "Jet, come."

"I'd like a word, Detective," Shumway said, stepping next to Wolf. "What was my daughter doing with you?"

He chose his words. "I had little choice, Sheriff."

Shumway nodded and scratched his chin. "Yeah. She's a real ... goddamned handful. I'm sorry for the embarrassment you had to endure because of her."

Wolf eyed him. "It's no problem. She's a ... seems like a good kid."

Shumway snorted and stopped suddenly. "Boydell, you'll take Megan back?"

Boydell poked up the bill of his cap and nodded.

Megan stretched her arms overhead, ignoring the conversation about her.

"And how do we get down to Dig 2?" Shumway asked.

Boydell stepped to them. "Can't miss it. Just keep going, and then down the hill. It's steep, and at the very end there's a doozy of a bump, so go slow. It curves right. Follow it and you'll hit the camp a quarter-mile up the wash."

"Thanks."

Boydell nodded. "I'll keep you posted if I see Levi."

"Maybe you could swing by his camp tonight," Shumway said.

Boydell walked to his truck. "Will do."

"I'll lead the way," Shumway said, walking to his own truck and climbing in.

"Up," Wolf told Jet as he opened his rear door.

Wolf watched Megan as she walked silently to Boydell's passenger door like an inmate being escorted to a prison bus. A pair of purple Converse like the one's Karen said Steven Kennedy wore was hard to miss, and Wolf had specifically asked her whether anyone had worn them. She'd inserted herself into the situation, and now she'd made herself out as a liar.

With eyes laser focused on the ground in front of her, she opened the door and got in.

CHAPTER 19

PATTERSON CRANKED up the air conditioner in the SUV and leaned toward the windshield.

"Okay, sounds good, honey. I love you," Rachette said in a cuddly voice that threatened to make Patterson's stomach turn again.

He hung up the phone and slowed, creeping around a tight turn. They were five minutes off Rocky Points' main strip and already socked into pine trees and steep hills.

"This is dumb."

Rachette looked at her. "This is necessary work. That's something you'd say to me."

"Wandering around on hundreds of miles of road, only able to see a few hundred feet in front of us until the next bend, with no clue as to where we're going? This is dumb." She shook her head. "We need to think this through, not waste our time because MacLean wants to look like he's doing something for Senator Levenworthless and his precious bones. And while you're at it, speed it up."

Rachette let out a rhythmic hiss between his teeth. "Whoa,

woman. You are not in the best of moods today. You need to find a toilet again or something?"

She ignored him, relaxing her jaw as she realized it had been locked shut.

"Hernandez says Senator Levenworth is buddy-buddy with everyone," Rachette said, "which includes the district judge."

"Whatever. Doesn't mean the guy can get evidence crucial to a double murder released," she said, hoping her skepticism was founded on reality. Could this senator really corrupt the system so flagrantly?

They rode in silence for a while.

"Hey."

With a roll of her eyes she looked over, taking the Rachette bait.

"It's going to be all right, okay? I know you're probably going through some ... stuff with the wedding coming up and all. Maybe some second thoughts?" He held up his hands. "Hell, I don't know. And I saw the way you looked when I mentioned the pregnancy thing."

She turned back to her window. "This is dumb."

After another few moments Rachette asked, "So?"

"So what?"

"What did it say?"

"What are you talking about?"

"Oh, come on. You think Charlotte's blind? She saw the pregnancy test in your hand. What did it say?"

Patterson's heart raced. "When the hell did you guys even discuss that? Just now?"

"That was her on the phone."

"Well, duh. That was like a two-minute phone call."

"Not gonna tell me?" He eyed her. "I don't see why you're so cranked up about kids. Charlotte's ready to churn them out when she gets married. Shit ... I guess I need to pop the question soon. You think it's too early?"

Patterson stared out the window.

"Fine. Thanks for the pep talk." Rachette pulled his phone out again and dialed a number. "Damn. It goes straight to voicemail."

"He's out of range."

Rachette shook his head and clanked the phone in the center console.

"What's the problem?"

"Nothing."

Was he mad that Wolf had not taken him? Was he worried? Patterson would have paid a few bucks to know her partner's thoughts. She'd always marveled at Rachette's loyalty to Wolf. She felt it too, but clearly not at his level.

"So ... seriously?" Rachette turned to her with a sly smile. "You're not going to tell me? Preggers? Heather Patterson, a mom?"

Maybe she would pay a few cents.

She leaned back and closed her eyes, focusing on her *hara*, the spot just below her naval. She pushed as she drew breath in, filling her lungs from bottom to top. Then she exhaled, pulling in her abdomen, blowing the air out of her nose in a steady, powerful stream.

The abdominal breathing was a technique she'd learned from her sensei in Aspen long ago to calm her mind and promote peace within her body. It was a technique that came in handy being Deputy Thomas Rachette's partner.

With each exhale, the built-up tension in her body released, the fire within extinguished. In the real world, fire grew hotter, blew embers and spread with wind, but in her body the air dissipated the heat away from her, setting Rachette alight.

She opened her eyes and sat upright. "Wait. Stop."

"What?"

"Stop the car!"

"Shit." Rachette cranked the wheel and jammed the brakes. The SUV scraped to a stop. "Get the door open! Don't puke in here!"

She looked at him. "I'm not going to vomit."

"Then what the hell?"

"I figured out where the moving truck is."

"What? How? Where?"

Patterson glared in thought, nodding her head. "Yeah, I'm sure of it. Turn around and head north."

"Why? I'm not going back to the station. I don't care if you're pregnant or not, you can get out and walk your ass back there."

"Shut up for a second and listen. Tell me this. When did that fire start?"

Rachette blinked. "Which one? The Durango or the new one?"

"The new one."

"Sunday morning? That's when I heard about it."

"Could have been Saturday night, though."

Rachette narrowed his eyes. "Yeah ... I guess. I don't know."

"And what was the cause?"

Rachette sat silent.

"Before we left the station, I watched a video of a guy purchasing a gas can. The Brushing gas station. The gas station near that fire."

"With taquito-boy?"

"There was a guy who went inside with a big hat on. He bought a gas can, a candy bar or something, and then he picked something up off the counter after he was done paying."

Rachette shrugged.

"When you were mooching your taquitos, do you remember what was on the counter, just to the right of the clerk window?"

"Napkins?"

She rolled her eyes. "Matches. The guy purchased the gas can, then grabbed some matches and walked out."

Picking up his can of chewing tobacco from the cup holder, Rachette opened it, took a pinch and slid it between his lip and gum.

Patterson ignored the smell as it permeated the cab and climbed up her nostrils. Normally it was a well-established rule that Rachette put his "dips" in outside, in the bathroom, anywhere but in front of her, but he'd had a little sister he liked to beat up on when he was a kid, and enjoyed treating Patterson the same way from time to time.

"It fits," Rachette said, finally looking over. "Embers blow off the truck, set the brush on fire."

"No shit."

"But Barker called up there and they said they hadn't seen the truck."

She shrugged. "We know how communication can get muddled sometimes."

Rachette cranked the wheel, hit the lights, and pushed the gas. "It fits," he said again, tapping the wheel. "Nice work."

"It all came from the thought of setting you on fire."

"I'm glad I could help."

CHAPTER 20

THE SUV KICKED sideways off another rock and Wolf lurched in his seat.

Shumway reached the bottom of the decline well ahead of Wolf. Hitting the forewarned spot way too fast, his truck bucked and bounced high with an explosion of dust.

Wolf edged his way over the same depression and reached a flat dirt two-track road below.

They were at the bottom of a canyon now. Juniper, pinyon, and boulders covered the hills on both sides. A dry wash lay to Wolf's left.

After hanging a hairpin right, the road continued over a low hill ahead.

Mathis had been right—there was no way a UrMover truck could have made it down that slope. Much less back up it.

So how had they got the bones out? There was no way they'd packed a seventy-five-percent-complete, twenty-five-foot-high set of dinosaur bones into the bed of one truck and gone up that hill on Saturday afternoon. They'd probably split the bones between the two trucks.

Or maybe there was a storage unit, Wolf thought with a

nod. That would make more sense—shuttle a few bones out, store them in a unit, repeat the process over time until the whole skeleton was out, then load them all up in a rented UrMover truck and drive down to Rocky Points.

Wolf eyed Jet in the rear-view mirror. "You all right?"

Jet opened his mouth and panted.

Winding side to side, up and down, the drive was easy, following a dry wash at the bottom of the valley.

A quarter-mile later, Wolf pulled up behind Shumway's parked truck.

Shumway was already out and leaning on his door.

Wolf shut off the engine and stepped outside.

The whine of a commercial jet lingered overhead. A blast-furnace wind rustled the sage and juniper, blowing sand across the ground with a soft hiss.

A tarp flapped near the bottom of the wash. Wolf peeked through the swaying foliage and saw three people near a camp looking back at him.

He opened the rear door and after a brief protest Jet lumbered out, loped to the shade of a tree and lay down in the powdery dirt.

Wolf grabbed a couple pairs of rubber gloves from the box on the floor and shut the door.

Shumway stood patiently with a hand on his holstered Glock.

"You have the warrant?" Wolf asked, holding out a pair of rubber gloves to the sheriff.

Shumway took the gloves, nodded, and extended a hand. *After you.*

Wolf passed him and led the way off the road and down a gradual slope.

They approached a complex of tents—red to the right, then blue beyond that, and a darker blue one to the left. A tarp, set up at an angle to shade a large pit, fluttered in the distance.

The camp had all the fixings of a paleontology dig, with shovels of all sizes and types strewn about, dusty brushes near the hole in the ground, leather gloves, and the paleontologists themselves.

"Good afternoon," Wolf announced.

They were all there—Steven Kennedy, his wife Felicia, and Molly "Mo" Waters—and they were all staring with unreadable looks. A trio of camp chairs sat underneath a white shade tent that was staked at the corners. Three paper plates with half-eaten sandwiches lay on a fold-out table. Underneath the table a box lay filled haphazardly with dry goods, and in the dirt stood a half-empty bottle of Scotch.

"I'm Detective Wolf from Sluice–Byron County, Colorado, and this is Sheriff Shumway from here in Windfield County."

They nodded, their faces frozen masks.

Steven stepped forward first and held out a hand.

Standing just about Wolf's height, six two or three, he was slim and fit, looking better in the face than he had in the DUI photo Wolf had seen earlier. His eyes were clear and bright, intelligent, and his skin was deeply tanned.

"Steven Kennedy. Nice to meet you. This is my wife, Felicia."

Steven's smile was confident and easy, framed by dark-brown stubble. He tipped up a worn New York Yankees ball cap with one hand and shook with the other.

Felicia squinted underneath a wide-brimmed hat and offered an outstretched hand. "Hi. I'm Felicia."

Felicia was thin, small and athletic, and looked like she feared no ultraviolet radiation anywhere but on her face, because she wore a tank top and short cargo shorts that displayed her sunbaked cocoa skin.

Molly Waters was next. She wore a baggy T-shirt, jeans, and hiking shoes. A few strands of white hair jutted out from underneath her floppy hat, which shadowed her freckled face. She glared at Wolf with small eyes and swallowed, offering no greeting.

"Mo?" Wolf asked.

Her grip was rock solid. "Molly. My friends call me Mo."

Wolf nodded. "Then I'll call you Molly. And Professor Green? Where's he?"

Molly's hard gaze dropped and she took a step back.

"He's up at the university," Steven said. "Had some business. What's this about?"

"What kind of business?" Wolf asked.

Steven shrugged and the two women looked like they'd gone deaf.

"Eighteen-year, huh?" Wolf asked.

They all three frowned with confusion.

"The Scotch." Wolf pointed behind them. "Glenlivet 18. That's an eighty-dollar bottle there. You guys must be connoisseurs. Or are you celebrating something?"

They all kept their attention on the bottle, lips closed, waiting for someone to say something.

"Yeah," Steven said with another winning smile. "We don't drink much, but when we do we want it to be the good stuff. What can we do for you two?"

Shumway stepped up next to Wolf.

Steven raised his chin and eyed the sheriff.

"We're looking for Professor Green," Wolf said.

"And like I said, he's not here. Is there anything else we can help you with?"

"Yes," Wolf said. "We need to take a look around your camp. You can help by standing still right here while we do."

Wolf made a production out of pulling on his rubber gloves, unnecessarily snapping the material a few times.

"You can't do that without a warrant," Steven said.

Shumway produced the warrant and handed it to Steven. "Well then, luckily we have one right here."

Wolf stood still and studied their boots while Steven read the warrant with Felicia.

"Hey, what the hell? It says here you're looking for a gun. W-what?" Steven's confidence had disappeared. "Why are you looking for a gun?"

Wolf watched as each of their faces dropped, but Molly seemed the most openly perturbed by the news.

"Something wrong, Molly?" Wolf asked.

"Yeah, you're looking for a gun. What the hell does that mean? Someone's been shot and you think we did it?"

"I never said anyone's been shot," Wolf said. "Do any of you have any weapons on you now? A gun?"

"No, we don't," Steven said.

Wolf pointed to Molly. "Can you please lift your shirt? Show me your waistline."

She did as she was asked, displaying a leather belt cinched around a ghost-white belly and nothing more.

Wolf walked to the red tent and unzipped it. He pulled open one flap and saw the interior was strewn with women's clothing, though he couldn't tell which woman's it was. Outside the tent's opening hung two pairs of panties clipped to clothes hangers.

"Like what you see?" Felicia asked.

Wolf caught the tail end of a sneer on Felicia's face as he ducked inside the opening. It smelled like perfume and campfire. He shuffled in on his hands and knees and moved the sleeping bag aside, then looked under each piece of clothing.

"Just tell them," Molly said outside.

"I will, just—"

"Tell us what?" Shumway asked.

Wolf started to duck out of the tent and then paused as a revelation unfolded. Clearly Felicia lived out of the tent, but there was no sign of her husband ever being there—no sleeping bag, no musky body-odor scent of a man who showered little. No men's clothing. He thought it odd, but then again, maybe they just liked their personal space.

Wolf backed out and stood up. "Tell us what, Molly?"

"We have a gun," Felicia said.

Shumway raised his eyebrows and gripped his pistol.

"Where?" Wolf asked.

"It's for emergencies, you know?" Steven said, twisting and pleading to Shumway too. "There's frickin' animals out here. Rattlesnakes galore. It's dangerous. Not that we ever use it. We've actually never used it. It's Green's gun."

Wolf nodded. "I understand. Can you show me where the gun is, please?"

Steven stepped to the backside of the second tent.

"Slowly now," Shumway said, drawing his pistol all the way out.

Steven gave him a double take and raised his arms. "Jesus, I'm not ... it's there. Hanging from Professor Green's tent." He pointed and his jaw dropped.

"Come back over here." Shumway crooked a finger and held his pistol loosely at his side.

Steven stood frozen, still looking down.

"Right now," Shumway said.

Steven raised his arms higher and walked fast, back next to the two women.

Wolf rounded to the other side of the second tent. An empty leather holster hung from a hook off the tent fabric. The retention strap was unbuttoned and bouncing in the breeze.

"I swear it's usually there," Steven said.

"What?" Molly's eyes widened. "What do you mean? It's not there?"

"I don't know, he must have taken it," Steven said with clenched teeth.

"Oh my God." Felicia put both hands over her eyes.

Wolf went to the front of the second tent and peeled open the half-circle zipper. It was hot inside, the air stagnant, and a single fly buzzed against the domed nylon interior.

A light cloth sleeping bag was neatly laid out with a pillow at its head opening. Two pairs of white socks were lined up next to each other, and next to that lay a stack of neatly folded clothing. The shirts were all button-up, the shorts cargo. A worn copy of a book called *Systematics and The Fossil Record* lay next to it all.

Wolf lifted the lid of a wooden box. It was full of rocks and crystals, and a carton of .38 special rounds. He pulled a pen from his chest pocket and lifted open the box lid. Half the rounds were missing.

Backing out of the tent he said, "Got a box of .38 specials. Half of them are gone."

"Well, this is definitely not looking good for you three," Shumway said.

"Why?" Steven turned around. "What did we do? That's Professor Green's tent."

Wolf walked to the third tent and poked his head inside. There was a dirty pair of men's jeans wadded up in the corner, and a man's T-shirt lying near it. But the size of the clothing told him it was Mo's tent.

He dug through the clothing and personal effects and found no pistol or pair of Converse, not that she would have worn a size-sixteen shoe.

He ducked back out and stood, making a show of looking around. "I'm confused. Where do you sleep, Steven?"

Steven glanced at his wife, who didn't return the gesture. "Down the wash a ways."

Wolf pointed to his right and then left.

"That way." Steven pointed to the west.

"Why do you sleep away from the rest of the camp?"

"That's not really any of your business."

Felicia stared into the distance. She'd thoroughly checked out of the conversation.

Shumway was squinting in thought, flicking his gaze between them. He'd seen Felicia's reaction, or non-reaction, too.

"You have a pair of Converse All Stars, Steven?" Wolf asked.

"Nope," he answered without hesitation.

Felicia's steely gaze cracked, and she scratched an eyebrow.

Molly seemed to flinch at the question too.

"We had a homicide down in Rocky Points, Saturday night," Wolf said. "A fossil dealer was shot once in the head and once in the back. The two slugs found in his corpse were .38 specials, which I'm sure we're going to find match those bullets in that box."

They said nothing.

"We just had a conversation with the people at Dig 1, Steven, and they say you have a pair of purple Converse All Stars."

Steven made a *so what* gesture and said, "Not anymore. Haven't had them for over a month."

"So you do have them," Shumway said.

"I said I did. I don't anymore."

"And why's that?" Wolf asked.

Steven licked his lips. "I lost them over a month ago. They just disappeared. I think an animal took them."

Shumway snorted. "An animal took them?"

"Did I stutter? I keep my shoes outside the tent. One morning they were gone. So, like I told you, I don't have a pair of Converse All Stars. Why are you asking me, anyway?"

Wolf looked at Mo and Felicia. They met his gaze now, as if Steven's explanation had relieved their earlier stress.

"How far?" Wolf asked.

"How far what?"

"How far to your tent?"

"Up a couple of bends."

"And your truck?"

"Up next to my tent."

"Okay. Let's go take a look. You lead the way. Felicia and Molly can follow. The sheriff and I will take up the rear. But first, I want you to take us by the dinosaur bones and show us those."

The three students stood in frozen silence.

"Why?" Steven asked.

Wolf waved his hand. "Let's go."

Steven exhaled and crunched past Wolf. Felicia came next, smelling like a fresh spray of the perfume that permeated her tent. Mo Waters followed, giving Wolf an unreadable look on the way by.

Shumway gave him the *after you* hand again.

They passed underneath the shade tent and squished their way through the dry wash, then climbed up a few yards onto the other side.

"Is this a private-land dig?" Wolf asked. "Or part of the BLM park?"

Mo turned around. "The dig is on private land. That side of the wash is BLM."

Wolf nodded, sneaking a glance at Shumway. The sheriff

might have blinked, but that was it. "And where will these bones go once they're dug up?"

"To the university," Steven said, stopping at the edge of a deep, wide pit. "The landowner donated them."

Wolf was confused by Steven's actions. He was looking down like the bones were still there, like he was willing to play this out until the last bitter second.

Wolf and Shumway reached the edge of the pit too, and Wolf stiffened. *What the hell?*

Inside the enormous pit were stone-colored fossils. Judging by the skull and the rest of the bones, it was an Allosaurus, and to Wolf's untrained eye it looked to be about eighty percent complete.

CHAPTER 21

PATTERSON STEPPED on a burnt stick and it crumbled under her boot.

A gust of wind kicked up a blast of soot and ash from the surrounding landscape and whipped it into their faces.

"Shit, ah," Rachette said behind her.

Patterson's eyes stung as she clamped them shut. Holding her breath, she put her face into her sleeve and tried to wait it out.

She dared a peek and saw Rachette stumbling away. Thinking better of remaining among the charred sagebrush, she followed her partner's lead back outside the fire line.

"Damn. Nice idea going out there." Rachette brushed his face and scalp.

Tasting charcoal, Patterson spat and saw flecks of black in her saliva.

A Brushing fireman named Danny Chase, a quick-talking individual with a bushy goatee, stepped away from Patterson. "Careful." He smiled and winked, and then his eyes raked her up and down for the third time in as many minutes.

They stood at the apex of a V-shaped burn pattern, the line of scorched earth extending away from them in two directions.

"Nothing at all?" Patterson asked.

"Couldn't find anything," Chase said. "Not that uncommon. It was a fire. The source of it could've burned up in the flames. But this is definitely the ignition point. Like I said, our lead investigator is due in later today and he'll check it out. Sorry." He lifted his hands and turned a circle. "No charred moving truck."

She turned to face the county road where their vehicles were parked a dozen or so yards away up a slope.

"Classic cigarette-butt fire," Chase said. "If you ask me."

"But you didn't find the butt."

"Right. But those were some high winds Saturday night. It could have landed in the top of these bushes here, ignited them, and then kept blowing along with the flames until"—he snapped his fingers—"poof. Gone."

Rachette expelled a wad of chew from his mouth and began his ritual of swirling his tongue around and spitting profusely.

"Ugh." She turned away and walked back toward the SUV.

Rachette kicked pebbles against her heels as he followed. "You like it up here in Brushing?"

"Not bad. Wish I was in Rocky Points like you guys. A lot more action down there. Got my application in with your department, actually. I guess they're hiring a driver down there. We'll see."

Rachette made an uninterested noise.

They ducked through the barbed wire, Chase making too much effort to help Patterson in the process, and reached their SUVs.

"Thanks, Chase," Rachette said. "We'll let you get back to work."

"It's no problem. We've got it contained so the work's pretty much over. Anyway, glad I could assist, but sorry I couldn't help with what you're looking for."

Patterson scratched her chin with her engagement-ring finger, just in case Chase got any bold ideas, and glared at the line of cars moving like ants in the distance. She spotted the gas station, and then another car cutting left across the valley on a road that looked to be parallel to the one they stood on. "What's that road?"

Chase furrowed his brow. "I don't know, uh ... 83? No ... wait ..."

"How far could a burning ember travel on the wind?"

"Upwards of a mile, given the right conditions. That's why we have so many of us still here, to make sure there aren't any embers blowing out."

Patterson shook her head. "No, an ember from a moving truck."

Chase followed her gaze. "You think your truck was burned on that far road, and a burning ember blew all that way here?"

"If you check the direction of that burn, and follow it backwards, it points to that grove of oak trees up there, right next to that road. If I was going to burn a truck, I'd probably do it near those trees. It would hide the flames from people passing by the highway. Otherwise it would draw a lot of attention, right? What is it to that farther road, four hundred yards?" Patterson asked.

"No." Rachette said. "Like five hundred. A short par five."

Patterson and Chase looked at him.

"What? I play golf, and it's about five hundred yards to that road. I can tell."

"What's that, like a driver and two three woods for you?" Chase asked with a straight face.

Rachette appraised him and smiled. "And another chip and three putts, if I'm lucky. You play golf too?"

"Yeah."

"What's your handicap?"

"Psh, I don't know. Used to be a—"

"Excuse me," Patterson said. "But we're going to leave now."

CHAPTER 22

PATTERSON'S ARM SIZZLED, looking like a burnt hot dog as it rested on the edge of the open window.

Rachette's window was up and he had the air conditioning blasting on him.

"Why don't you roll down your window? What if we can smell something?"

Rachette looked at her.

"We checked your clump of trees and it was empty. There's nothing here."

She shook her head. She knew what she'd seen on that video. It fit.

Danny Chase was no longer behind them. He'd been just as dejected as Patterson when the oak trees lining the creek had held no burned secrets and had returned to his prior task of burying embers on the burn line.

Now Patterson and Rachette crept along another quarter mile past the point Rachette had given up, reaping nothing but more anger from him with each roll of the tires.

A short distance later there was a ninety-degree turn to the right.

Rachette stopped. "All right. End of the line, the road curves even further away from the fire."

She leaned into the windshield. "Keep going. A little more. Look at that."

Rachette took the turn and hit the gas, seeing what she was looking at.

There was a mound in the road up ahead with a sign that said *Hedge Creek*.

When they passed the sign, he rolled down his window and stuck his head out. Letting off the gas he said, "Look for tracks going off the road."

A second later Patterson saw them. "Stop!"

Rachette scraped to a halt and jammed the SUV in park.

They'd found their quarry. She stepped outside and punched a fist into the wind. "I knew it."

She pointed down. "Dual rear tires."

"Stay off 'em," he said.

They stepped over them and followed the barbed-wire fence down to the creek, which was a trickle of water in a twenty-foot-wide swath of dirt that passed directly under the road ahead.

The tracks left bent weeds and stalks of grass where it had driven. Rachette kicked up grasshoppers, leading the way down a gentle slope to the water's edge.

"Thar she blows," he said, coming to a stop.

A box-culvert ran underneath the road, and inside were the tangled, black remains of a truck.

"Whoa." Rachette's voice echoed in the culvert. "I'm no fire expert, but it looks like it burned hot."

Patterson nodded, entranced by the twisted skeleton of the vehicle.

The wind whipped at their back and sucked past them into the hole.

"It's like a wind tunnel," she said. "So you're right. It probably burned hot with a constant fan hitting it. Strange. Look how there's barely anything burnt beyond it."

Through the space between the truck and the blackened concrete walls there was brush land and another grove of oaks hugging the creek's banks—all of it unscathed by flame.

From here, the trees obstructed a view of the fire trucks so the culvert had been invisible from their earlier vantage point.

The vehicle was twisted and mangled, so much reduced to ash that it was barely recognizable.

"Check out the footprints in the dirt next to the tire."

Patterson nodded. The tread was the same diamond pattern.

Patterson tilted her head and stepped nearer the charred remains. "These are bones."

"What kind of bones?"

She touched a gray piece of material and it disintegrated to dust, revealing a human skull underneath it.

Rachette stepped back. "Shit. You think it's Green?"

She snapped on rubber gloves and poked her finger at some wire next to the blackened skull. "Looks like eyeglasses. I think it's him. I recognize the front teeth. One of them is set in front of the other. Remember his smile? I remember thinking he looked like a chipmunk with those teeth. Lorber can make the call, but I'd bet your salary it's him."

"Confidence. I like that in a woman." Rachette walked past her to the side of the truck. Leaning his head past a twisted piece of metal, he pointed at a lump. "What's this? There's a ton of it."

She stepped over and pressed it with her finger in various places. It was firm. She picked up a rock and tapped it against the lump, then smacked it down hard.

"What are you doing?"

She hit it again, and a piece of material flaked off, revealing a lighter shade beneath. She hit it again, revealing an area stark white against the blackened exterior.

"Casting material," she said.

"Casting material." Rachette made an "O" with his lips. "More bones."

"Yep. But these are a lot older."

CHAPTER 23

"WHAT KIND OF DINOSAUR IS THIS?" Wolf knew the answer but could think of no other questions as he gaped down at the hole.

"Allosaurus fragilis," Steven said. "It's a good specimen. Female, more than seventy-five percent complete by our estimates. One of the best finds in history."

Wolf had never seen anything like the full skeleton sitting in the ground, precisely in the spot where it had died millions of years ago. He stared at it, trying to imagine the beast alive. The head was fully cleared of dirt, and looked to be ready to remove. The skull was huge, jaws agape—Wolf could've wedged half his body inside.

Steven watched him. "Classic death pose."

"What?" Wolf asked.

"That's what they call that position the skeleton is in. Head thrown back, jaws wide open. Thought to be strong ligaments in the animals' necks tightening after death, or just how water deposits them—it's all up for debate."

Shumway stood looking down, thumbs hitched on his duty

belt. "Why have you guys been keeping this a secret from everyone up at Dig 1?"

Steven shrugged. "It's a rare find. We wanted to keep it a secret until the bones were all uncovered. Superstition, I guess. We didn't want to jinx it. You know ... say we're finding a great specimen, one of the most complete ever, and then we suddenly can't find any more bones."

The two women stared at the bones with frozen expressions.

"What were you three doing on Saturday?" Wolf asked.

Steven made a show of thinking about it, and then shrugged. "I don't remember. Not much. We don't usually work much on the weekends. Try to keep a normal schedule to avoid burnout. What did—"

"We went into town," Felicia said.

Steven froze.

Wolf nodded. "Yeah, the team up there said three of you left and went into town in the afternoon, and Molly stayed here. What were you doing?"

"We dropped Professor Green in Windfield," Felicia said. "He was renting a moving truck."

Steven turned his head slightly toward his wife but held his poker face.

"You dropped him off?" Wolf asked.

Felicia nodded.

"And where did you go?"

"Back here," she said.

"Where did Professor Green go?" Shumway asked.

Felicia shrugged. "Said he was going up to the university. Wouldn't tell us why."

"Mo," Wolf said.

Mo jerked to attention.

"Is that true? They dropped off Professor Green and then came back here?"

Mo took her time and then nodded.

"And where's Professor Green's truck?" Wolf asked. "His pickup?"

"He left it in town," Felicia said. "Near the moving place. Steven and I came back together in Steven's truck because Professor Green needed his truck when he came back."

"But he didn't tell you when he was coming back." Wolf nodded.

"Nope."

"And what did you do after you dropped him off?"

"Just came back here."

"Four hours later."

Felicia's eyes darted. "Four hours later?"

"That's what the Dig 1 team says. They saw you leave at noon, and saw you return at around four."

"Oh, yeah ... we got a bite to eat. Did some shopping."

"Got some scotch," Wolf said.

Felicia blinked. "Yeah."

Steven slid his gaze back and forth between Wolf and Shumway.

"Okay," Wolf said. "Let's take that walk to your camp, Steven."

Steven began walking, and Felicia and Mo followed silently.

Wolf looked at Shumway and held back a few steps.

"What the hell is going on?" Shumway whispered to Wolf. "I saw those photos of the dinosaur bones Green was selling. They were out of the ground. There was date proof from one of the pictures in our local newspaper. That gives time and location of those bones being dug up somewhere around here."

Wolf nodded but said nothing.

"So, where did those bones come from?" Shumway's voice was barely audible over the squish of their footsteps on the sand and pebbles.

"I don't know," Wolf said.

They walked in silence for another beat and Shumway leaned close again. "I'm thinking, we really have nothing. I mean, nothing. Not unless we find that revolver and that pair of shoes up here."

"We have something. They're lying about the four hours they killed on Saturday afternoon. I don't know about you, but I didn't see any vehicles parked near Windfield Moving Company. We have mountains of probable cause for arrest. Steven and Felicia look like they might lawyer up and not talk, but Molly's conflicted. We just have to separate them."

Shumway nodded. "Yeah. Okay, then let's bring them in. We can separate them by putting Molly in your car, and I'll take the other two. We have two interrogation rooms and two holding cells back at the station." The sheriff eyed the wash ahead. "This is strange. Why's he camping all the way up here?"

Wolf wondered the same thing.

Molly, Felicia, and Steven marched in silence. Their heads were down, their shoulders slumped, like they were approaching execution.

Steven looked over his shoulder. "Just up here. Next bend."

As they followed the swerve of the wash, a pickup truck gleamed on the hill to the right. A blue tent was erected near it —the same blue Wolf had seen from the top of the plateau at Levi Joseph's camp.

He did a double take to the top of the mountain. Megan Shumway was standing against the sky, staring down at them.

Steven stopped. "Here it is."

Felicia and Molly stopped next to Steven and folded their arms.

"You three stay here," Wolf said.

They failed to respond because they were all now looking up too.

Megan and Boydell must have stopped at Levi's camp, Wolf thought. Boydell's truck was parked near Megan. When everyone looked up at her, she walked to the vehicle and climbed inside.

Shumway's daughter seemed like she was on a single-minded mission to shake up her father, and Wolf was an integral prop in her act. He felt his face warm.

"You," Shumway said. "It was you."

He turned, hearing thumping footfalls come up behind him.

The sheriff launched past him and barreled head first into Steven's chest.

Steven was too slow to react and took the collision standing still. Shumway thumped into him, sending him through the air and onto his back.

Shumway fell square on top of him, got to his knees, and started punching.

Wolf got there in time to catch the third right-hander in its backswing. "Sheriff!"

Shumway ignored him and wrenched his arm free, then started another flurry of punches, this time with alternating rights and lefts.

Wolf pointed at the two women. "Stay back!"

They were wide-eyed and already shuffling away.

Wolf straddled Shumway's back and pulled him off and into the air. He dropped him on his feet and then grabbed his arm, securing it in a wrap wrist lock.

"Dah! What are you doing?" Shumway sucked in air through his teeth. "Stop, stop."

Wolf held firm as he walked them up the wash.

"Calm down," Wolf said.

"You're gonna break my wrist!"

Wolf let go and Shumway spun on him.

The sheriff's chest was heaving, eyes wide. He pushed his torso into Wolf's and then backed away, pointing at Steven. "You son of a bitch. It was you. Don't think I don't know. It was you."

Steven was slow getting to his feet, checking the blood seeping from his lip with the back of his hand.

"It was you," Shumway said. He bent over and put both hands on his knees to catch his breath.

Wolf noted the conspicuous distance Felicia Kennedy stood from Steven lying on the ground, like she had no concern for her husband at all.

They all turned toward a sound traveling up the draw. It was strange at first, impossible to discern, but coming closer and getting louder, nonetheless. Then the noise sharpened to rhythmic breathing and footsteps coming at fearsome speed. Jet came skidding around the corner and barked with snapping jaws.

The murderous expression on Jet's face surprised Wolf. "Jet! Heel!"

Jet immediately slid to a stop.

"Sit!"

He sat.

"Keep that thing away," Steven said, scooting back on his butt.

Wolf stood catching his breath, taking it all in. Felicia and Mo kept their distance from both Steven and Jet. Steven rubbed his chin, dejected and humiliated. Shumway clenched his fists and glared at him.

"You three stay right here. You move and Jet runs you down." Wolf had no intention of using the attack command. In fact, Jet's Vail handler had made Wolf swear to never use it, but the threat had the desired effect.

He jerked his head at Shumway and walked up the wash.

Shumway stepped over with more than a little reluctance.

"What the hell was that?" Wolf asked, leading them behind a juniper tree.

"I don't want to talk about it. But that guy deserves a hell of a lot more than what he got."

"We need to keep the situation at hand under control."

Shumway put his hands on his hips and nodded.

Wolf backed up a few steps and peeked around the tree.

Jet watched the three graduate students; they stared back, frozen in place.

"I'm going to search that tent," Wolf said. "And I want you to come with me."

Shumway rolled his eyes. "Yeah, all right."

Wolf gave him the *after you* hand.

Steven's tent was a three-man design, much like his other dig team members. Nearby he had a firepit dug out of the dirt and ringed with rocks—blackened and well used. A lone camping chair sat next to it, and a gas stove and fold-out table stood under an overhanging juniper tree.

There was a black plastic trash can next to a bush. Wolf opened it and looked inside, finding dozens of empty cans and food packets.

Shumway went to the tent and studied some hiking and running shoes lined up on the exterior wall.

"Got your gloves?" Wolf asked.

Shumway pulled them out of his pocket and put them on.

Wolf kept an eye on the other three as the sheriff peeled back the zipper and knelt inside the tent, rummaged around, then came out with his hands splayed.

"No gun. These are size fifteen and a half," Shumway said,

picking up one of the running shoes. "And these are sixteen. Phew, I can see why he keeps these things outside."

Wolf caught the scent of untreated athlete's foot coming off the shoes as he ducked in for a look himself inside the tent.

Keeping his ears open in case Shumway made any sudden movements outside, Wolf sifted through an explosion of dirty clothing. The tent held a superheated pocket of air saturated with body and foot odor, so he held his breath and made haste.

He rifled through everything and found no other shoes, and just like Shumway had said, no gun.

After thoroughly searching every nook and cranny, he backed out of the tent and sucked in a breath.

Shumway was staring toward the wash, his fists clenching and releasing. "They're talking."

Wolf nodded. "I'm sure they are."

"They're going to lawyer up."

Wolf searched the rest of the camp. He opened a cooler and looked inside. Lifted a conspicuous-looking rock with his toe.

Walking to the Ford pickup truck, he bent down and checked the tires: Goodyear P265/70R17.

"A match?" Shumway asked.

"Yep."

"You know, I have those tires too," Shumway said.

"So I saw."

"I'm pretty sure any government vehicle up here's going to have them. You've got the same ones but sixteens."

Wolf nodded.

Shumway said nothing.

Wolf lifted the passenger handle and the door squeaked open. It smelled faintly of cologne and coconut oil. *Faintly like Megan Shumway*, Wolf thought. He thoroughly checked the interior, found no gun or shoes, and shut the door. The rear of the truck had tiny chunks of white crumbly material—like plaster used for encasing fossils.

"Check out these tracks." Shumway was in the trees, pointing down at tire marks.

"Looks like they've been taking another way out of camp."

Wolf took off his rubber gloves and wiped the sweat from his hands on his jeans. He bent down and felt the dirt. It was hot and soft, and held no shape or tire-tread pattern, but the depressions clearly came from the opposite way they'd come in and ran all the way to Steven's truck.

"This looks like an old road," Wolf said.

Shumway nodded. "Sure does."

Wolf eyed him. "You've never been out here on this road?"

"No. What? Why you lookin' at me like that?"

"Megan told me this was your land, growing up."

Shumway shrugged. "It was our family's land. Just had some cattle. I never spent much time here. We'd go visit my granddad at his ranch house, which is south over that hill a long way. My mom and dad moved in there when he died. I'd already moved out by that point. My dad might have come out here but I never did. It was a big piece of property. I haven't been on a lot of it."

"And you got rid of the land when your father passed away?" Wolf asked.

"When my dad died, my brother and I sold everything—the cattle, equipment, the land. We weren't going to ranch and it wasn't making us any money the way it was."

Wolf nodded. "You didn't know about the oil?"

"Psh. That bastard knew something we didn't when he bought it from us, that's for sure. We should have charged him twenty times the price and he would have taken it."

Megan had told Wolf her father had lost the land to the new owner, implying her father was at fault for getting rid of it against his will. Wolf detected no animosity with Shumway about the deal, only seller's remorse for not getting more money.

"What?" Shumway asked.

"Nothing."

Wolf looked down the road. "Let's photograph these tracks leading to Steven's truck and follow this route too."

CHAPTER 24

WOLF KEPT his eyes on the sandy desert bottom and followed the tire depressions as they weaved around trees and boulders.

He met Steven's eyes in the rear-view mirror again, and Steven turned away and looked out the window.

"That wasn't me. It was your dog."

"You were displaying a lot of control over those two women back there," Wolf said, rolling down the windows.

Steven blew air between his lips.

"What was Shumway's outburst all about back there, anyway? Megan?"

The question hit home. Steven closed his eyes and shook his head.

"That Megan is something else," Wolf said.

Steven glared at him in the rear-view.

"Apparently you know that. And, apparently, so does your wife and Sheriff Shumway."

Steven looked out his window.

"I've heard of being in the dog house, but what you have going on is ... well, that's another level living in exile up the wash like that."

"I'm not going to talk to you," Steven said for the fourth time. "None of us will."

"What I don't get is if you got caught messing around with Megan Shumway, why are you sticking around? You just moved up the wash? Why not just leave altogether and save your wife the heartache?"

"I'm not talking."

Wolf nodded. He wondered how much Shumway was learning in the truck behind him.

"It doesn't matter if you talk to me or not," he said. "The evidence will speak for itself."

Steven smiled. "What evidence?"

Wolf slowed as the tracks disappeared over an edge and out of sight.

"This a navigable hill?" Wolf asked.

Steven said nothing.

Wolf got out and checked. The slope was a good thirty degrees and there were deep gouges where vehicles had gone up and down. At the bottom there were more bushes and boulders, and then the dry wash they'd driven up earlier behind Boydell.

Wolf climbed back behind the wheel and drove over the edge. "Speaking of evidence, here's the way you and the girls could've left your camp without the other dig team knowing. According to Dig 1, you three came back in your truck at around 4 p.m. on Saturday. With that ten-minute jaunt we just took, and the rest of the drive down to Windfield ... I'd say it takes just about three and a half hours to drive down to Rocky Points from your camp. If you left at 4 p.m., that could have put you guys in Rocky Points right in time to commit the murder."

Steven shook his head. "I have no idea what you're talking about, man."

"That was smart of you guys to do a drive-by past Dig 1. Make it look like you were returning for the night."

Steven shook his head.

They drove in silence the rest of the way down the wash.

The barbed-wire gate near the main road had been left open, so he drove through and pulled over. He waved Shumway past him to lead the way back to the station.

Wolf rolled up the windows and turned on the air conditioning. His stomach was empty, churning air, making him well beyond irritable and only a lot of food was going to remedy that. Jet had to be starving too.

Steven scrunched up his nose. "Oh, man, roll down the windows again."

Wolf followed the good advice and then pulled over and let Jet out.

While Jet found the shade of a juniper and did his business, Wolf's phone beeped and vibrated as multiple messages streamed in.

There were two text messages from Rachette and two voice-mails, one from Rachette and one from MacLean.

Rachette's message said:

Patterson and I found the truck! It was burned out. Green's body inside, and the bones.

Where are you? Call us when you get this. We're getting worried.

Wolf read the message again, then lowered the phone and eyed Steven in the rear of his truck.

Steven sat with closed eyes.

Wolf walked down the road out of earshot and pressed Rachette's number.

"Hey, where the hell are you?" Rachette said.

"Hey."

"We've been trying to get ahold of you."

"You found the truck?"

"Yeah, we did." Wind ruffled the microphone on Rachette's

side. "We're all at the scene now. Patterson got a hunch from looking at the video footage from the Brushing gas station. They doused the truck with gas and left it to burn in a culvert under County Road 39. Turns out the truck started that fire outside Brushing. We're here with Summit SD now, and Lorber's up here. He confirmed it's Green's body. MacLean's up here with Senator Levenworth. They've got a hard-on for me and Patterson right now for finding the bones."

"What bones?" Wolf asked, looking over his shoulder at his SUV. Steven still sat motionless in the back.

"The fossils. The Allosaurus bones Levenworth was buying. Hello?"

Wolf stared at the ground, trying to process the information.

"You there?"

"Yeah ... I just saw the bones up here. Sitting in the ground. Are you sure they were the bones we're looking for?"

"Yeah. Levenworth just cracked one out of its shell and looked. Identified it as an Allosaurus shin bone or some shit."

"Out of its shell?"

"Yeah. They're all encased in casting material. Levenworth said they call it a field jacket. Protects the bones ... or the *fossils*, sorry ... Patterson's correcting me here. You say they had a full skeleton sitting in the ground?"

"Yes."

"Well, there's definitely a full skeleton in the back of this truck, too. So ... there must have been two sets of bones?"

Wolf eyed Steven again, thinking of the white plaster in the back of his truck.

"You there?"

"Yeah, sorry. Just trying to understand what's going on."

"Sounds to me like they have a second dig site," Rachette said. "Anyway, I'll let you give that news to MacLean. He's been calling you too. Have you talked to him?"

"Yeah, I saw. What about that security video from the gas station? Can we get a good look at the guy on it?"

"Not really. We still need to go back and take a closer look at the footage. I haven't even seen it yet."

"Let me talk to Patterson."

There was a rustling and then Patterson came on. "Yes, sir?"

"What did you see in this footage?"

"I saw a man wearing a big cowboy hat, which covered his face. He purchased a candy bar, a gas can, and then took a book of matches off the counter. But I didn't realize about the matches until later. Then we had a hunch and checked near the Brushing fire, and found the truck. There're the same shoeprints here as at Ryan Frost's."

"Definitely a man in the footage?" Wolf asked.

"Yes ... I'm almost positive."

"What about height? Weight?"

"I can't say for sure. I'd need to look at the recording again."

"Get back to the station ASAP and do that, please. And call me back."

"Okay," she said, "but what's going on up there in Windfield? What did you just tell Rachette?"

"I'll let Rachette relay it to you. Check the video footage and call me."

"Yes, sir."

He hung up and pocketed his phone. Climbing in behind the wheel, he glanced in the rear-view, knowing now they were being lied to by all three of them.

Steven was looking at him.

Wolf ignored him and shifted into drive. Then they were rumbling down the road back to Windfield.

CHAPTER 25

"You think she's gonna crack?" Shumway asked.

Wolf swallowed the half-cheeseburger in his mouth and sucked down a third of the grown-adult-head-sized Coke and exhaled. "I don't know."

Shumway dug into the greasy bag and produced a box of French fries and pushed them in front of Wolf.

"Thanks."

Shumway shook his head. "These Kennedys are tough. I don't see any budging in them. But Mo Waters? I was watching her in the truck on the way down here. Felicia was trying to give her steely looks, like 'we can do this,' and Mo was ignoring her."

Wolf finished chewing a handful of salty fries. "That's good, I guess."

Shumway eyed the clock on the wall. "Lawyers are coming from Ogden. Three o'clock now ... that'll put them here at six or seven. So, we have some time, but not much. Maybe one of the women will talk."

Wolf shoved the second half of the first cheeseburger in his mouth.

The sound of Jet chomping on a bowl of kibble echoed from the front of the station all the way into Shumway's office.

"I think the location of the UrMover truck points to Steven and these other two," Shumway said. "Ditched on the side of the road heading north from Rocky Points on the route to Wind-field? What a bunch of dumbasses. I would've left it south, or east, or west, or just left it sitting there at the crime scene. Anything would have been a smarter move."

"It was burned out under a bridge on a remote road," Wolf said.

"Yeah, whatever. To the *north*. On the way here. And burning it? What if someone saw the flames? They would've been caught."

Wolf chewed some fries. "I think it means they had to burn it. They had no choice."

"Why?"

"To hide something."

"Like what?"

Wolf took another sip. "Like forensic evidence that would prove who'd been in the truck. Which begs the question, why take so much precaution with the forensic evidence and be so flagrant with the shoeprints?"

"Yeah. And now we can't find his shoes. He's ditched them. So we have nothing."

"Or he's telling the truth about his shoe-stealing coyote," Wolf said.

"You're saying someone stole his shoes and committed the two murders with them on?"

Wolf chewed another handful of fries.

"Could have been the two women." Shumway glared at his desk and went silent.

"You gonna tell me what the hell happened up at that camp with you and Steven Kennedy?"

Shumway concentrated on eating his fries. "You have a kid."

"Yep."

"Teenager, right?"

Wolf nodded.

"Yeah, but you have a boy. Girls are ... they just ..." Shumway shook his head. "They're so damned hard sometimes. I don't know what to do. She's promiscuous. Do you know what a nightmare that is?"

Wolf said nothing.

"It's tough raising a kid alone, right?"

Wolf unwrapped his second cheeseburger. "Yeah, but you're still not answering my question."

Shumway slapped his cup onto the desk. "I sure as hell am. Don't you get it? She was screwing that guy we have in the holding cell. A married man. There. You happy?" He grabbed a handful of fries and shoved them into his mouth.

Wolf ate the second burger in silence, then said, "You yelled, 'It was you,' and then you tackled him."

"So what?"

"It was an interesting choice of words. So you knew someone was sleeping with her, and you'd been searching?"

Shumway leaned back. "Bingo. Now can we be done with this topic?"

"I'm just trying to understand the full situation I've walked into here."

"You think my daughter and Steven Kennedy being with one another has anything to do with this?"

"Why is Steven Kennedy still at that camp? After that? Most men getting caught doing that would have tucked their tails and run. And he'd obviously been caught. That's why he's sleeping up the wash. Then there's the DUI he got last year."

"So what?"

"So that's two very big strikes against him, and yet he's still part of this university-sponsored dig. It's like he's ... I don't know."

"Untouchable," Shumway said, gritting his teeth.

"Yeah. Or something."

Shumway dropped his cheeseburger in the wrapper and lifted the trashcan off the floor, and then raked the rest of his meal into it. "I'm not hungry anymore."

Wiping his hands on his already dirty pants, he stood and walked past Wolf and out of the office.

Wolf finished his third cheeseburger and fries, and then dug Shumway's unsullied fries out of the trash and finished those.

He'd once known a field surgeon in the army who would slap him on the back and repeat the surgeon's maxim, *Eat when you can, sleep when you can, and don't fuck with the pancreas.*

CHAPTER 26

MOLLY "Mo" Waters sat like a rock in the interrogation chair, arms resting in her lap and rarely blinking.

Wolf pulled the wobbly plastic-and-metal chair back and took a seat. "We found size-sixteen shoe prints at our murder scene. We have our crime-scene techs looking to match those bullets we found in your camp to those that murdered two people."

Molly frowned but said nothing.

"We just found Green's body in the moving truck he rented on Saturday. The truck your two dig-team members took him to rent."

Her chest rose and fell faster now. Her eyes darted.

"The truck was burned to a crisp with his body inside. It looks like he was shot, point blank with a .38 revolver, much like the one missing from your camp. We also found size-sixteen shoe prints. Converse All Stars. Steven's size. He has these shoes, doesn't he?"

She said nothing.

"And if we find him guilty, and you keep acting the way you

are, you're going to be charged as an accessory. What other choice do we have?"

She closed her eyes and her mouth dropped open.

"He ..."

"He what?" Shumway asked loud.

Wolf gave him a sharp glance.

"I'm pretty sure Steven left that night," Molly said, looking like she'd betrayed her own mother.

Wolf looked at Shumway again. "Okay. Just so we're clear, which night are we talking about?"

"Saturday night."

"Thank you. Can you please elaborate? He left?"

"When he and Felicia got back, he went to his camp. Later that night I was outside and saw his headlights. He was driving into his camp."

"Coming in the way we drove *out* of camp today?" Wolf asked. "The shortcut that leads to the wash, rather than going up and over the plateau."

She nodded. "I could see his lights as he drove in. Couldn't see his truck, just the lights. I was outside, going to the bathroom. But it sounded like his truck."

Wolf nodded. "And what time did Steven and Felicia get back from giving Professor Green a ride to the truck-rental place?"

"I guess four or five?"

Wolf tapped a finger on the wooden table separating them. "And what time did you see Steven returning that night?"

She shrugged. "Must have been midnight, I guess."

Wolf nodded. "Are you sure about that time?"

"Pretty sure."

"Was Felicia with you all night Saturday?"

Molly frowned and looked up at him. "Yes."

"Did you know where Professor Green was going with that rental truck?"

Molly said nothing and lowered her eyes.

"Was he going to pick up the second skeleton?"

She narrowed her eyes for a moment but said nothing.

"He was found dead with a full Allosaurus skeleton in the back of the truck, Molly. And Felicia said that she and Steven came back right after dropping Professor Green off at the rental-truck business. But we know from your testimony right now that they came back four or five hours later. What were they doing?"

She said nothing.

"Were they helping load up this second skeleton into that truck?"

She closed her eyes and swallowed.

"Where? Where did this second skeleton come from? Are there more people we need to be worried about? There could be more dead people, do you get that? Or they could be out there, the ones getting away with murder."

She shook her head a little, then a lot. "No."

"No, what? Tell me. We're confused here. You don't have to go along with Felicia and Steven's lies anymore, Molly. They're not here. Tell us. It's the only way out of this."

She screwed her eyes shut and shook her head.

Wolf softened his voice. "Do you think Steven did this, Molly?"

She opened her eyes. "No. It doesn't make any sense. He'd never even fired that gun before. He's a wimp with it. Felicia and I have fired it, but he never has. And he's telling the truth about those shoes. I haven't seen him wear those things for over a month."

Wolf nodded. "Okay. So where do you think he was that night?"

She looked at Shumway, then back at Wolf. "I don't know."

Wolf stared hard into her eyes until she looked down.

"We're going to figure all this out," Wolf said, "and it's not going to go well for you if you're hiding knowledge of who did this."

"I told you what I know. I'm done talking. I have to talk with my lawyer first."

Wolf checked his watch: 6:14 p.m. They'd gotten nowhere, and the lawyers were going to be there any minute to consult with their clients. Apparently, the legal team had made it clear to all three of them to not speak, because Molly was the only one who'd said a word all afternoon. Felicia and Steven had said nothing.

Legally, they had another sixty-nine hours to hold these three, but they had nothing beyond circumstantial at the moment.

Wolf tapped a finger.

Molly Waters bounced her leg and her shoe squeaked.

He thought of Cassidy's tiny shoe prints next to her dead father and the heat rose in his face. He wanted to reach across the table and grab Molly by the neck, but instead he stood and walked out of the room.

Shumway followed on his heels.

As they reached the hallway they almost ran into Deputy Etzel, who held a wireless phone toward Shumway. "Sir, you have a call."

Shumway took it. "Shumway ... yes. Hi Bradley." Shumway looked at Wolf with narrowed eyes. "We'll meet you at the gate in a few minutes." He hung up and handed the phone back to Etzel. "That was Boydell. Levi Joseph still hasn't come back to his camp."

CHAPTER 27

PATTERSON REACHED her desk and pulled open the laptop. It whirred and clicked, laboring through a full minute of startup. As she typed in her access password she felt a presence at her back and recognized Munford's perfume.

"You told Rachette about the pregnancy test, huh?" Patterson said.

Munford said nothing, so Patterson swiveled in her chair and looked up at her.

"He ... told you about that?" Munford's mouth dropped open.

"That's your boyfriend for ya." Patterson poked the power button on her desktop, beginning the warm-up process for her second computer. "In case you haven't learned by now, Tom Rachette has the secret-holding ability of a five-year-old."

"I'm sorry." Munford stepped into her peripheral vision. "I wasn't being vindictive or anything. I was concerned for you. You looked very upset, and that's what I was talking to Tom about."

"Whatever." Patterson concentrated on pulling up the footage of the man in the huge cowboy hat.

"What's going on?" Munford asked.

"Just doing some work." She paused for effect. "What are you doing?"

Munford narrowed her eyes for a second. "What's your problem with me, Heather? What have I done to you?"

Patterson's face flushed and she tapped on her keyboard. A few seconds later she opened the recording. As she drew the video-player slider to the right, the interior footage flickered in ultra-fast motion, until she found the spot and pressed play.

Cowboy Hat walked in and did his thing again—grabbed a candy bar, a gas can, paid cash, grabbed some matches, and went out. It was impossible to gauge a height because the man stooped as he left past the height strip, which stood inside every convenience store doorway for such an occasion.

Smart bastard.

Munford stepped behind Patterson and mouth-breathed over her shoulder. "Where's Tom?" she asked.

Patterson rolled her eyes and opened the exterior footage on her desktop. "With Barker and Hernandez up at the gas station. Trying to get some prints. It's gonna be futile."

"Ah."

She pulled the video-player slider to the appropriate spot on the exterior footage and pressed play.

Cowboy Hat walked out and went to a far gas terminal and ducked down behind it.

"What's he doing?" Munford asked.

"Filling up ten bucks worth of prepaid gas."

She rewound to a point where the man was shown walking and leaned into the screen. His shoes were barely visible underneath the wide leg of his jeans, but they were unmistakable—Converse All-Stars. She took a screen shot of the man in mid-stride and saved it to her desktop.

"He's wearing the shoes."

Patterson flinched. Munford's breath was on her neck.

"Jesus, can you back up a bit?"

"Sorry. I just heard about the case from Barker."

Patterson took a deep breath and continued with the video, taking note how carefully the man shielded his face with his hat.

After filling his gas can, the man stood and walked away, out of the video footage forever.

"Did you see that?" Munford asked.

"What?"

Munford came up next to her and sat on the edge of the desk. "If I tell you, you have to tell me what your problem is with me."

Patterson stared at Munford for a second and shook her head. "I don't have any problem with you."

"Bullshit."

"What did you see on that footage?"

Munford reached onto the side of Patterson's monitor and fiddled with the dials. The screen went almost completely dark.

"I saw shit footage. The contrast is way too high. Rewind it and look again."

Patterson was intrigued because, now, the video recording was much darker and held more detail. Whited-out areas popped with shadow while gray areas darkened to black. The scene was sharper.

Patterson rewound, and was astonished to see an off-white rectangle appear in the upper-right-hand corner. She picked up a picture of the truck they'd gotten from Windfield Moving Company and held it to the monitor. "The truck. The white side of it was washed out in the footage."

Munford showed serious gum as she smiled wide.

"Okay." Patterson felt like an idiot. She'd have probably gotten to messing with the contrast a few minutes later, but there was no ignoring the sheer joy radiating from Munford's face. "Nice work," she said.

Munford leaned into the screen. "I saw the truck already. I want to look at the guy's shoes. Rewind a little bit more."

Patterson pulled the slider back until it showed the man in mid-stride.

"Check those shoes out," Munford said.

Patterson frowned. "I already said I saw the shoes. They're Converse."

Munford looked at Patterson, as if waiting for her.

Patterson shook her head and looked closer. The white fronts of the shoes had been almost completely invisible in the initial overexposed footage. Now they were light gray against an almost black background. And their true size became clearer.

"This guy's feet are huge," Patterson said.

Munford nodded, her eyes alight. "Too huge."

Patterson pulled her cell phone from her pocket and dialed Wolf's number. It went straight to voicemail. "Sir, call me as soon as possible."

She relayed their discovery, taking care to mention Munford's help, much to her delight.

She hung up, then stood and paced. "Damn it. There's shit cell service up there."

Munford sat quietly, then looked away and stood. "Okay. Well, have a good one."

"Wait."

Munford stopped and turned. "Yeah?"

"I really don't have a problem with you. I just ... have a problem with what you ... I really have a problem with myself."

"Okay. And being rude to me makes you feel better?"

Patterson rolled her eyes. "I'm about to get married."

"Yeah?"

"And I'm going to get some pressure to start a family now."

"So? Do you not want kids?"

"I do."

"So what's the problem?"

"There. That's the problem."

Munford frowned. "I'm not following."

"I mean, I've seen how you talk about family—about having a family—and I can't even imagine doing that and keeping this job. It's impossible, isn't it?"

Munford shrugged. "Says who?"

Patterson felt a surge of annoyance. "This is what I'm talking about here. You don't see the roadblocks standing in front of you. I watched my mother resent us for years because she had to quit her job as a public prosecutor to raise four kids. You think you can keep a career with the department and have a family?"

Munford shrugged again. "I think I can do whatever the fuck I want."

Patterson smiled momentarily and shook her head.

"I think y—"

"Period." Munford glared at her. "My mom kept her job and raised three kids. She had no choice because my dad got coked up and ditched us, and if she'd stopped working we would've starved. If she can do it, I can."

Patterson blinked.

"I think that if you have concerns, you should talk to Wolf, not me. But if you want my opinion, life is what you make it."

Patterson suddenly felt dumb. She knew what it meant to make a goal and commit until it was accomplished. Her martial arts, her career so far? That had been how she'd lived her entire life.

"Thanks."

Charlotte smiled. "You got it."

CHAPTER 28

JET HAD BEEN TRAINED by the Vail PD as a detection dog. He would ride around with an officer in the pre-legalized-marijuana era and assist on routine traffic stops, often sniffing out weed, magic mushrooms, and other illicit substances that Coloradans tended to carry around in their cars more often than jumper cables.

It was lights, pull to the shoulder, "Do you know how fast you were going?", and then Jet had his paws on the trunk, sniffing a hit inside.

Other specialty dogs included cadaver and search and rescue, both of which spent their days sniffing out human scents. Cadaver dogs were often bloodhounds. SAR K-9 units were German shepherds in Vail. Vail had enough money to fill its back bowls with twenty-dollar bills. If they needed another SAR dog, they'd get one and train it. Same with a cadaver dog. Multi-tasking a dog would be out of the question. Or so Wolf had thought.

Because now, for the second time that day, Wolf followed Shumway and Boydell up the dry wash and onto the plateau. And for the second time that day, Jet went berserk when they reached Levi's camp. And now Wolf had the sinking feeling that this dog had some other specialty experience under its collar.

Wolf endured the air-shaking barks as he pulled up behind Shumway's truck and parked. He shut off the engine and let Jet out. Once again Jet went to the back of his SUV and stood expectantly.

"What's going on?" Shumway asked.

"I don't know. Go on, Jet."

Jet sprang off the edge of the road and scurried down the side of the hill, weaving his way past bushes and trees, heading in the same general direction as before.

Wolf followed.

"Where you going?" Shumway asked.

"I'll let you know when I get there."

Wolf slid on his heels down the steep dirt road shoulder.

Jet disappeared among the trees and shrubs, so he stopped and listened. Panting, and paws pattering the dry earth, came from below and to the right.

Assisted by gravity, Wolf paced at a fast jog, slaloming to avoid sage and cactus, ducking to miss juniper and pinyon boughs, jumping up and over red and white rocks and downed logs.

As he rounded a large sage, Jet came into view. The dog's rear was low, his ears standing straight up, head bouncing and jaw snapping as he barked.

Wolf walked up and put a hand on Jet's back. He stopped barking and whined.

"Good boy," Wolf said.

Jet sat.

Wolf stared at a low mound of sandy dirt. The shape unmistakable. He tilted his head. A sand-encrusted patch of grass at his feet had been uncovered by Jet, and Wolf stepped back as he realized it was a tuft of hair.

"What d'ya got?" Shumway yelled down.

Shovel marks were gouged into the earth all around—next to the mound, behind Wolf's feet—and amid those, a flurry of shoe prints with the diamond pattern.

"Wolf!"

"You need to come down here. Mr. Boydell needs to stay up there."

CHAPTER 29

WOLF STOOD BACK as Shumway snapped on a pair of gloves and pushed the piled earth away, revealing ghost white skin crusted with maroon dirt.

There was more hair, this part caked with red mud, and brown eyebrows and then dirt-packed slit eyes. As Shumway continued to remove the fine earth with his rubber-gloved hands, a crooked-looking face emerged.

"Levi Joseph?" Wolf asked.

Shumway looked at him and nodded. "Yeah, that's him."

"What's happening down there?" Boydell, who'd been pacing the road on top, now stopped. He was a silhouette against the reddening sky. "What did you find?"

"Don't say anything," Shumway said in a low voice. "Boydell was close to this kid."

Wolf was standing and out in the open from Boydell's vantage. He held up a finger and said, "We'll let you know when we know, Bradley."

Boydell scoffed and resumed pacing.

"Holy mother of ..." Shumway said as he brushed away dirt

from the neck area, revealing a slash of dark red across the throat. "Just about cut off his head."

Wolf watched as Shumway worked.

"Chest is slashed to hell," Shumway said unnecessarily, because the shredded, red-stained clothing and dirt-packed crevices explained it all.

Wolf grabbed a rock and bent down next to the body. He scraped off some of the caked-on dirt and revealed a wound underneath seven or eight inches from end to end, canoed up on both sides.

"A shovel," Wolf said.

Shumway shook his head. "My God."

They stood in silence for a moment, neither needing to point out how many stabs with a shovel it would take to make a body look like it did.

"Shit," Shumway said, standing up.

"What is it?" Boydell called down from up above.

"Uh, just ... hold your horses, Bradley! We're trying to make sense of this now."

"Make sense of this?" Boydell shook his head and started pacing again.

Shumway turned downhill and lowered his voice. "There's more to this, Wolf."

Wolf stared at him.

"What the hell is this?" Boydell was yelling at the top of the hill now, pointing down on the ground. "What is this?"

"What is what?" Shumway yelled back.

Boydell was further down the road than he'd been before, a good twenty yards behind Wolf's rear bumper. Boydell bent down, then stood up abruptly and staggered back. "Is this blood? Oh my God, is this blood? What did you find down there, Sheriff?"

"Shit," Shumway turned around and hesitated, assessing the climb back up to the road.

"I'll go up," Wolf said.

"Hell, I'll come up too. Gonna have to radio everyone. It's gonna be a long one tonight."

CHAPTER 30

WOLF CLIMBED BACK UP to the road as fast as he could with legs that ached from so much driving and activity in one day.

Bradley Boydell was leaning on his elbows against the front of his truck. Head down, tears streamed onto the hood, making a tiny puddle that reflected the orange clouds. "It's Levi, isn't it?"

Wolf stood breathing hard next to his SUV.

Shumway was grunting his way up the slope behind him and Jet was sniffing over where Boydell had been earlier.

"Jet, come."

Jet came over and sat down.

Wolf studied a bloody scrape mark that went across the road. He'd driven over it twice without seeing it, and so had Shumway and Boydell, leaving numerous tire tracks running through it. But it was visible now, plain as day.

It was no wonder they'd missed it. The road was rusty orange, made from the pulverized rock from the area. The blood was a darker shade of the same color. Without the prior discovery of a mutilated corpse, the marks looked like nothing.

Wolf spotted his elusive set of Converse footprints, sitting right there on the road in plain sight after all. He followed from the camp across the road. There was a gouge in the soft shoulder where the killer had dragged the body off the edge, and then below, drag marks disappeared into the bushes.

Shumway crunched up next to him, his lungs wheezing. "My deputies are on their way up. They'll call in the crime-scene techs. They're on-callers, spread out all over the county, so it'll take a while."

Wolf pointed and lowered his voice. "The Converse tracks go down with the body there, and come back up a few feet over."

Shumway nodded, still breathing hard.

"We need to get Boydell out of here," Wolf said.

Shumway coughed. "Yeah, I know. But we don't want to have him drive over this. Shit."

Boydell was standing next to his truck now, staring at them. His eyes were red, his cheeks wet.

"Mr. Boydell," Wolf said, walking toward him, "I'm afraid it's exactly what it looks like here."

Boydell sagged and closed his eyes. "My God."

Wolf stopped in front of him and hooked his thumbs in his jeans pockets. "I'm sorry, Bradley. We need to get you back to your quarters. This is a crime scene now and we need to restrict access to law enforcement only. I know you understand."

Boydell opened his eyes. "Is this why you asked about the Converse shoes? Because I saw those shoe prints just now. Those are the same as you found in Rocky Points, aren't' they?"

Wolf drew his mouth in a line, but said nothing.

Boydell looked at Shumway. "Was this Steven?"

Wolf turned and eyed Shumway.

"Uh ... listen, Bradley." He put his hands on his hips and studied the camp. "I tell you what, let's walk it back to your quarters. We'll need to keep this road right here as pristine as possible for evidence gathering." He raised his hands and dropped them. "I'll walk you back."

Boydell waved the offer away and turned. "I can walk myself."

"No, Bradley, I can—"

Boydell turned around with raised eyebrows. "Sheriff, I said I can walk myself. You stay here and do your job, figure out who did this."

"Mr. Boydell," Wolf said.

"What?"

"What were you doing Saturday night?"

Boydell's face dropped. "What?"

Wolf nodded.

"I was in my quarters. You can ask Megan and Phil." He looked at Shumway with a pleading look.

"Okay, thanks Bradley," Shumway said. "You know we have to cover every base, right?"

"I was up at my quarters."

Wolf nodded. "Okay."

Boydell gave Wolf a final resentful look and turned around. He opened his truck door and dropped his car key inside on the seat. "In case you need it." Then he slammed it, walked up the road, and disappeared over the top.

Shumway shook his head. "What the hell was that?"

"And what were *you* doing Saturday night?" Wolf asked.

Shumway stared long at Wolf. "Are you serious?"

"I am. What were you doing?"

Shumway shook his head.

Wolf held his gaze. "Just covering every base."

"You're runnin' the wrong direction around the bases, Detective."

"Am I? You have motive, just like the rest of the people I'm meeting."

"Motive? What motive do I have?"

"That land used to be yours. I don't know, maybe you've been resentful of their find all along, wishing you still had the land, so you could make all that money with a fossil sale. Maybe you know a lot more about fossil trade than you're letting on. Maybe you know exactly where that second skeleton came from —somewhere on your family's land.

"Megan told me you lost the land. She didn't say you sold it. Maybe she was telling the truth. Is she?"

They stared at one another for a few seconds, and then Shumway stormed away toward his truck.

The sheriff opened his door and bent inside, searching the floor for something. He looked in the side pocket on his door, then picked a slip of paper out and brandished it at Wolf.

"Here." Shumway walked over and handed it to him.

Wolf took it, and saw it was a credit-card receipt for a place called Chuck's Grill and Tavern.

"Look at the address."

Wolf did. It said *1823 Garland Street, Windfield, Colorado.*

"And look at the time. The date."

10:29 p.m. Saturday, August 11th.

Wolf shrugged. "So your credit card was at Chuck's Grill Saturday night. Doesn't mean you were."

Shumway put his hands on his hips. "Okay, fine." He walked back to his truck and leaned inside. "What does that total say on there?"

"What?"

"The total price after tip?"

Wolf was already convinced now. The man was telling the truth and all it would have taken to verify it was a trip to Chuck's Grill and Tavern, but he went along with Shumway anyway. "Forty-eight dollars."

Shumway scribbled something on a piece of paper, ripped it

out of a notebook and walked back to Wolf.

"Let's do a little handwriting check, shall we?" Shumway said.

He held the piece of paper next to the receipt, both showing the number forty-eight with two zeros scrawled on them. The handwriting was identical, written in such terrible chicken scratch that there was little doubt they were both Shumway's hand.

"So that puts *me* at the bar, right? If you want, we can go in there and ask around."

Wolf gave him back the receipt. "Okay. I believe you."

Wolf rubbed his temples and walked toward the ring of scorched earth Levi had used as a firepit. Nearby, a patch of dry grass was smattered with blood.

The spatter was barely visible in the oblique light, but it was there, telling a gruesome story. Wolf pictured the killer hauling up and driving the shovel down, then repeating.

He turned to the final rays of the sun and closed his eyes, trying to erase the movie playing in his mind.

With a deep breath, he cracked his eyelids and gazed out at the hills and jutting rocks casting long shadows that streaked the dusty air.

"This is where he was killed."

Shumway walked up next to him.

"We're missing something."

"Yeah, no shit. Who's killing these people."

Wolf shook his head and walked to the edge of the road. "Look at this. The footprints go off the edge of the road here, then come back up the hill ..."

"Yeah, you said that earlier. So what?" Shumway said.

"If it was Steven, wouldn't there be a set of tracks from his camp up to this camp and back? Not from this camp, and then back up?"

"Not if he drove up here, got out and murdered him, then put Levi down there and hiked back up to his truck."

Wolf nodded. "In the process leaving a shitpot of evidence, once again. He leaves footprints that everyone knows are his. And, literally, he drags the body in the direction of his own camp?" Wolf pointed down at Steven's tent and truck in the darkened valley.

"Yeah. Okay. You're saying it wasn't a coyote who stole his shoes. You think someone's setting Steven up."

Wolf said nothing.

"Maybe he just let the shoe prints slip," Shumway said. "Maybe he realized later that he left the prints, so he made his shoes disappear, and he made up the story."

"Molly said she corroborates that story," Wolf said. "She said he hadn't had the shoes for over a month."

"Maybe she's in on it," Shumway said. "That's why she's the one looking so freaked out all the time."

Wolf folded his arms and stared down at Steven's tent and truck. "And then there's that pit this morning down at Dig 2 ... and my deputies said they found the bones in that burned truck encased in plaster. And there's chunks of plaster sitting in the back of Steven's truck down there."

"Yeah," Shumway said. "I saw that stuff in there. So what are you saying? I'm not sure I'm following all your tangents here. Where's this stream of consciousness coming out of your mouth flowing to?"

Wolf walked away toward his truck.

"Hey. Where are you going?"

"Down to Dig 2."

"What just happened? What about this crime scene?"

"We're going to find he was killed with a shovel. The shovel's going to be missing, and the only evidence worth anything will be those shoe prints. I'm done with this crime scene."

CHAPTER 31

WOLF DROVE up the road onto the crest of the plateau, leaving Shumway shaking his head in the side-view mirror.

As he twisted on his headlights, the straight two-track lit up. Then he clicked on his brights and the tents and tarps of Dig 1 reflected back at him.

Karen Orpia and Mathis stood up from their camp chairs next to a flickering fire and moved steadily toward the road to intercept Wolf as he passed.

Slowing to a halt, Wolf leaned an elbow out his window.

"Hello, Detective," Mathis said. The doctor wore a head-lamp, and pointed it downward, averting the beam from Wolf's eyes. "We were just about to head that way and see what all the commotion was. What's happening?"

Wolf sat for a moment in silence, then asked, "When exactly was the last time you two saw Levi?"

They looked at one another.

"Shit, is that why you're there?" Mathis asked. "He still hasn't shown up?"

Karen leaned her head on Mathis's shoulder.

"Is that true?" Mathis asked.

Wolf nodded. "When was it?"

"Uh, I guess it must have been ... I hardly know what day it is when we're out here."

"It's Monday," Karen said. "We saw him Saturday. Saturday morning he came in and had coffee with us, then went back to his camp. We haven't seen him since."

Mathis nodded, his beam of light bouncing up and down. "Yes. And he never mentioned where he was going that day. Not once. Never even said he was going hiking."

Wolf nodded. "Can I ask you two for a favor?"

They nodded.

"Can you come down with me to Dig 2? I have some questions I need answered and the Dig 2 team is no longer there."

Mathis's light beam twisted to Karen. Her eyebrows were raised high.

In unison they said, "Yeah."

CHAPTER 32

WOLF PARKED at Dig 2 and kept the headlights pointed toward the camp. They got out and walked through the dust swirling in the beams of light, down the hill toward the cluster of tents.

"Where are they?" Karen asked quietly.

Wolf flipped on his flashlight beam. "They're in jail at the moment."

"Jail?" Mathis stopped and swiveled his headlamp beam in Wolf's face. "You're kidding, right? They're your murder suspects?"

"This way." Wolf led them between the tents, past the uneaten sandwiches the team had been eating when Wolf and Shumway had first visited, which were now swarmed with insects.

"Shit," Karen said, focusing her beam on a hairy spider walking on a piece of bread.

Jet sniffed close and the spider raised its front legs.

"Jet, no."

Jet whined and followed.

"Where are you taking us?" Mathis asked. "To the pit, I hope."

Wolf stepped to the open pit and stopped.

Mathis had beaten him there and had all but skidded to a stop, kicking some dirt into the hole.

"My heck." Mathis swept his headlamp beam up and down the length of the spine of the fossilized skeleton. "My ... heck ..."

The doctor methodically probed the bones with his headlamp beam, inhaling sharply while staring at a leg bone, then turning and studying the claws, then gasping as he stared at the skull.

"This is the most complete Allosaurus specimen I've ever seen. And the condition ... it's spectacular. Female ... you can tell by the pelvic structure and the lacrimal crest."

Karen gripped Mathis's arm, following the beam of light with wide eyes.

"What a bunch of assholes, keeping this a secret," she said. "Why? It's so spectacular."

"Look at the skull," Mathis said. "It's larger than Omega by at least ten centimeters. Look at the quality of fossilization."

"What's Omega?" Wolf asked.

"Oh, the replica in the visitors' center," Karen said.

Wolf put his hands on his hips. "How do you go about finding a skeleton like this? Do you use that GPR you were talking about earlier today and search a grid pattern or something?"

Mathis laughed. "A lot of people think exactly what you just said—that in this day and age we can head out into the wilds of Colorado, or Utah, or Siberia, or Australia with our ground-penetrating radar and just start scanning until we find the mother lode, like the one we're looking at right now. Sure, that's the hope one day. In fact, there are some people working on scanning by aircraft ... but that technology is farther in the future than we'd like. In reality, finding a fossil is akin to the old-time prospectors looking for a vein of gold.

"Firstly, we seek out a place where known dinosaur fossils have been found. Like, say, Dinosaur National Monument and surrounding areas. Check. Secondly, we seek out places where erosion is taking place year-round, doing the unearthing of the bones for us." Mathis twisted with his arms out. "This dry riverbed in this ancient valley for instance. Check. Thirdly, we walk up and down the bottom of the valley with our foreheads inches from the ground, searching for tiny fragments of fossilized bone. When we find them, we move upstream, looking for larger chunks. When the fossils peter out to nothing, we know we've passed the potential mother lode and move our way up the sides of the hills and look for the larger bones.

"More often than not we find absolutely nothing. Sometimes we find a large fossil specimen, say, a leg bone or an arm bone, or a rib, and the rest of the skeleton sat in the wrong material for millions of years and simply decayed away into nothing.

"But in the rarest of cases, we find something as magnificent as this. The animal died, and before scavengers could devour it, it was buried rapidly, say, by a mud or landslide event. Perhaps the catastrophic event that killed the animal in the first place. Then, over thousands of years, the organic material decomposed, the minerals seeped in to replace the decomposing bone, and now here we are. We're left with rock in the shape of the original bones. And in this case, rock curved and hardened into a magnificent three-dimensional picture of exactly how the animal *existed* underneath its skin at that very moment of death almost a hundred million years ago."

Mathis's chest heaved.

"And that's what they did here?" Wolf asked. "They found a piece of bone, followed the other pieces upstream, came a few yards up this hill, and excavated this?"

Mathis nodded, knelt in the pit, and wrapped both hands around a huge bone. "Green liked to tell the story to anyone who'd listen. They found a claw, then some smaller fragments, then came upon a femur sticking out of the ground. And voila."

"Isn't that a femur you're grasping in your hands right now?" Wolf asked.

Mathis froze for a few seconds then let go, like he'd just realized he was holding a hunk of plutonium.

"And how about that other bone right next to it," Wolf asked.

Mathis stood up. "What in the heck? What's going on?" He twisted in a circle. His light swiveled wildly in the hole.

"Which leads me to my next question," Wolf said. "What are the odds of pulling out two complete fossil specimens like this from the same hole?"

CHAPTER 33

"Two skeletons?" Karen asked with a chuckle. "Not likely at all."

Mathis shined his light on Wolf and held up a finger. "Karen," Mathis nodded at her, "remember the first time we saw the progress of this dig? It was two years ago. We'd been here for two months, flipping dust off partial caudal vertebrae, and here comes Green and his students finding an Allosaurus femur poking out of the ground. And less than a mile away from us."

Karen said nothing.

"Are you listening to me? It was that *femur* he wouldn't shut up about it."

Karen shook her head, then nodded. "Yeah, okay. It was. So what?"

"Yes, it was. Do you remember the disgust we had with them for being so stupidly lucky?" Mathis asked with a chuckle. "The anguish?"

Karen rolled her eyes and wiped her nose. "Whatever."

"And do you remember the location of it?" Mathis tilted his head.

Karen nodded, and then her eyes widened in comprehension as she took in the huge hole in front of her. "It was right on the surface."

Mathis looked at Wolf. "So you're right—they must have found bones from two dinosaurs. There's no other explanation. These bones are almost three meters below the surface. I'm looking at two femurs right now, and we saw a femur sticking out of the ground. Heck, look at the amount of earth they've removed. But you asked if they pulled a second, complete skeleton out of this same hole. No. No way. The odds would be astronomical."

"We found a second skeleton," Wolf said. "Allosaurus. Female. Thought to be almost eighty percent complete."

Mathis stepped toward Wolf. "What do you mean, 'We found a second skeleton'?"

Wolf nodded. "At one of our crime scenes."

Mathis looked down. "That's impossible, isn't it?" He went to the edge of the pit and dug a chunk off the side. "Sandy, but very dense. I guess it could be."

"And now it makes sense why they were hiding the pit for a year and a half," Karen said. "All this time, they were keeping their two-skeleton find secret."

"They excavated the top bones, encased them in field casting, and transported them out to store somewhere, off-site," Wolf said. "But how would they hide this kind of thing from your boss? You talked about using ground-penetrating radar on your dig up there. Wouldn't they be able to see a second skeleton underneath it from the beginning readouts?"

Mathis bent down and picked some more soil off the edge of the hole. "Not necessarily. We do GPR readings for initial funding. This soil is pretty dense, and we use a 1,000 MHz antenna for fossil detection. With the second skeleton this low? Could have gone undetected until they found the second one with their bare hands. Or maybe it was ... yeah ..." He walked to the end of the hole and on into the dark. "This specimen ends here, and there's another pit to the side of it. This over here must be where the first skeleton was found. So they weren't exactly on top of one another. They were side by side, this one being a little deeper.

"You can check it all for certain. They'll have the funding package on file at the university—you can bet on that. And, really, you couldn't hide a second skeleton if it came up on the readout. Smart people write those funding checks."

Mathis shook his head. "Okay, all this is making sense now. Green was going to sell one of the skeletons. His whole team was in on it. That's why they kept it all so secretive all this time. The conniving bastards." He chuckled and then stopped and looked at Wolf. "What happened down in Colorado? Did he kill a fossil dealer or something? Was he selling the bones and decided to ... or wait a minute ... did Professor Green die?"

Karen's and Mathis's faces dropped.

When they turned their eyes on Wolf, he pulled his lips into a line.

"He did." Karen covered her mouth. "That's why he's suddenly gone."

"Or he killed someone," Mathis said. "Is that it?"

Wolf waved a hand. "I'm sorry. I really can't discuss the details. But I can say thanks. You've really helped."

"Psh. He changes the subject again." Mathis chuckled. "It is a good question, though: How did he hide this from Dr. Talbot? That's what I want to know. Must have crapped himself the last time Talbot came into town. What if they'd been caught? 'Oh, yeah, by the way, we found a second skeleton and have been excavating it for months. We were going to tell you, I swear.'"

Wolf turned to leave.

"Mr. Wolf?" Karen called after him. "Are you leaving?"

Wolf kept walking. "I'm headed into town. You guys don't mind walking back up to your camp, do you?"

Wolf heard an answer but didn't listen. He and Jet climbed into the SUV and drove away from the main camp toward Steven's truck. He passed the pickup and Steven's tent, and then underneath a swarm of lights on the side of the mountain, some of which pointed his way. As he followed the tracks through the Colorado desert, he thought he heard a shout through the open windows say, "Wolf! Where are you going?"

He switched on his radio and it auto-tuned to the Sheriff's Department's active frequency.

Thumbing the button, he said, "Sheriff Shumway, this is Detective Wolf. Come in."

"Wolf!" Shumway's voice was crisp and clear. "Where are you going?"

"Back to the station. I need to speak to you."

There was a long hesitation. "Negative, I'm too busy here."

"It's urgent."

"Then stop and come back up here and tell me about it."

Wolf kept his foot on the gas. "I need to speak to the students again."

Another hesitation. "What the hell's going on?"

Wolf pressed the button. "I'll tell you at the station. Over and out."

"Shhhhhhhhit. I'll see you there."

He switched off the radio and spun the wheel to avoid a clump of cacti.

CHAPTER 34

Fatigue had taken hold, and Wolf rubbed an eye as he descended the high country toward Windfield. Jet snored in back.

The dash clock said 9:04 and he was looking forward to joining Jet in dreamland, but he knew it might still be a long time coming.

He picked up his phone again and checked for cell service. Still nothing.

He felt the pressure mounting to get the job done—for Cassidy, and Keegan, and Trudy Frost. He wondered what they were doing right now. Probably wondering how Wolf was getting along in the investigation.

He knew how it felt when someone took away a person you loved with all your heart. After the initial shock and longing for ridiculous things like time reversal, or a miraculous resurrection, next came an insatiable desire for justice. There was no way of moving forward until that justice had been served.

The Frosts were stuck in a kind of mourning purgatory, and it was up to Wolf to help them out. And for once he felt like he was close.

His phone buzzed and he picked it up. He'd missed calls from Jack, MacLean, and Patterson.

He pushed Jack's number and listened to it ring.

"Hello?" Jack's voice was barely audible over the rumbling of Wolf's SUV.

"Hey, it's me. How's it going?"

"What's going on? Are you all right?" Jack asked. "I've been calling you."

"Yeah, I'm all right. Bad cell service up here. How about you?"

"I'm good."

"How are Cassidy and her family doing?"

A long pause. "Not too well. They keep crying and they don't talk. They're sleeping now, though. I guess that's good."

They sat silently with one another for a few seconds.

"Everyone still at Nate's?"

"Yeah."

"And what are you doing?"

"Sitting out on his deck, worrying about you."

Wolf half-smiled.

"Are you finding anything out?"

Two pinprick headlights shone in Wolf's rear-view mirror—Shumway finally catching up. "Yeah. I think so."

"Good."

"Yeah. Listen, get some sleep. You need it. It's been a long day."

"I will," Jack said. "How's Jet?"

"He's fine. Get your ass to bed."

"I will. I love you."

Jack rarely expressed such sentiment, and the words hit him hard. "I love you, too."

He hung up and opted to dial Patterson next.

"Hello?" Patterson answered in a weak voice.

"Hey, I saw you called. Crap, I guess it was a few hours ago. Sorry, you asleep?"

She cleared her throat. "Don't worry. I was just resting. Yeah, I called. Did you listen to my message?"

"No."

"I went through the footage ... actually Deputy Munford helped ... anyway, the guy at the gas station was careful. He stooped as he left, so the height strip's pretty useless. But we noticed he was wearing Converse All Stars. And his feet were enormous. If you've met a guy with clown feet up there, then he's your man. But, otherwise, I think he was wearing shoes that were too big for him. In fact, I went back to the crime scene for confirmation—the pressure exerted onto the front of the shoe was conspicuously low. Like, either someone never put their full weight on their toes, or they were wearing huge shoes. I'm going with huge shoes by the looks of the video."

The headlights grew in his mirrors.

"Sir?"

"Yeah, okay. You got a color on those shoes?"

"Black-and-white footage, so no. But they're a dark color. Like a blue or black."

"Or purple."

"Yeah, or purple."

"What was he wearing?"

"A cowboy hat, Carhartt jacket, jeans ... I can make a video snippet and send it to your phone."

"Good idea."

She paused. "I'm ... um ..."

"What?"

"Well, I'm at home now. I don't have the footage on my laptop. I left it on a flash drive in the station."

"Don't worry about it. Tomorrow morning's fine. Get some rest and I'll talk to you then. Anything else?"

"Not really. We went back to the gas station and couldn't get any prints off the gas terminal. Let's see ... they found a .38 slug lodged in Green's skull. Matched the other two in Frost."

"Okay."

"And that's about all we've got here. MacLean's on pins and needles, waiting to hear from you. I hope that shoe thing helps."

"It does."

"What's going on up there?"

Wolf had slowed to a crawl and now Shumway was on his bumper, his headlights lighting up the cab through his rear window.

"I gotta go. Talk to you later." He ended the call and dropped the phone in the center console.

He pulled over and Shumway pulled up next to him with a rolled-down window. "What the hell's going on with you?"

"You find anything else up at the scene?" Wolf asked.

"No."

"I went down to Dig 2 with Dr. Mathis and Karen Orpia."

"Yeah?"

Wolf told him about the second skeleton.

"Two skeletons ... that's not possible, is it? What, two dinos were doin' the nasty and got hit by a comet?"

Wolf told him about the location of the bones the team had initially found, the way it was supposedly sticking out of the ground, and the second skeleton being much deeper, and how the university would have pictures of the first skeleton find on file in something Mathis referred to as a "fund package."

"All right. So we go to Utah tomorrow."

Wolf nodded.

Shumway rubbed his chin. "The case against these kids is more solid than the rocks up at that dig. The two-skeleton thing means all three of them are lying. Which means we go back to the original motive we talked about on day one: They were in on the deal to sell one of the skeletons, split four ways. They figured out Green was going to take all the proceeds of the sale and run off to Argentina, so they killed him. They felt betrayed and pissed off, and wanted their cut of the money."

"But why kill Levi?" Wolf asked.

Shumway shrugged.

"And if they did go down to Rocky Points to kill Ryan Frost and Green, why come straight back and wait for the cops to come ask them about everything? They would've known we'd come to them, right? The evidence leads right to them. And the plaster ... they left plaster in Steven's truck. They left buckets down there with plaster all over the place inside of them. If they wanted to pretend the first skeleton didn't exist, why didn't they wipe away all the evidence if they knew the cops were coming?"

"I don't follow."

"I'm just saying, these three students are acting like the last thing they expected was for cops to show up. Their actions are not consistent with having just killed three people. And why Levi?"

Shumway shook his head. Lifted a hand.

"I just talked to my deputy. She has the gas-station video footage showing one of our perps wearing Converse shoes."

Shumway raised his eyebrows. "There we go. So?"

"She says the man's face is covered and he ducks down as he's leaving the convenience store so she can't get a height. But she also says she's positive the man's shoes are several sizes too big for him. Either that or he has clown feet."

Shumway gazed through his windshield. "The coyote?"

"If this deputy thinks something, it's usually right. She'll send us the footage tomorrow morning so we can see for ourselves."

Shumway took a huge breath and let it out. "So what now?"

"Now we know they had a second set of bones. I want to

know where they kept them," Wolf said. "There might be a clue there."

"What are you going to do? Ask those students? That's why you wanna talk to them? Psh. Why do you think they'll talk now?"

Wolf conceded the sheriff had a point.

"I'm stopping for food on the way back," Shumway declared.

"Had to have been a storage unit," Wolf said. "There aren't any in Windfield, so how about east? East of the UrMover truck-rental place. Remember she said Green drove off going east?"

Shumway shifted into park and his truck rocked back and forth. "I told you, Pamela's crazy. She didn't know where she was pointing. I'm hungry."

"And if she isn't crazy?"

"Then she'd be pointing to the nearest town, which is Logan's Ferry, an hour east toward Steamboat Springs on 40."

Wolf did some mental math. "That would fit our timeline. They rent the truck at 12:30 p.m., drive into Logan's Ferry, start loading up the bones at 1:30. Let's say it takes an hour to load them, so they finish at 2:30, come back to Windfield by 3:30, and then the students and Green split—Green goes south to Rocky Points, and Felicia and Steven go back to the dig."

"Okay. Maybe you're onto something. Then, on the way back to the dig, Steven and Felicia make their drive-by of Dig 1 to make it known they're returning. But they take the other route out, past Steven's camp up the wash, and follow Green's route down to Rocky Points."

Wolf pinched one eye shut. "But my deputy says it's someone else in the video footage wearing Steven's shoes. She says the shoes were big looking. So, you're saying Steven and

Felicia went down there and killed them. But Felicia was wearing Steven's shoes? Makes no sense to me."

Shumway rolled his eyes. "I'll believe that footage when I see it."

Wolf tapped his phone screen and searched for storage units in Logan's Ferry. "There aren't any storage rentals in Logan's Ferry."

"Ah, Christ."

They sat for a few moments with their motors idling.

"Where else?" Wolf asked.

Shumway started to say something, then his face dropped. "Wait."

"What?"

"I know where they kept them."

"Where? Let's go."

Shumway pointed to his dash clock. "It's nine frickin' thirty. You said you wanna go talk to these students, and we got a murder scene up there. My stomach thinks my throat's been cut. If anything, let's go eat, and we can get a fresh start on this in the morning."

"You're right. The students aren't going to talk anyway. Tell me where this place is. I'll let you know what I find."

Shumway rolled his eyes and put his truck in gear. "Yeah, right. Follow me."

CHAPTER 35

WOLF FOLLOWED Shumway along a cracked asphalt county road, five miles past the Windfield Moving Company. They were traveling east—the direction Pamela from the UrMover Moving Company had pointed earlier—along flat country lit by the moon, surrounded by dark hills that blotted out a blanket of stars.

Shumway's brake lights blossomed as he slowed and took a left at a grove of deciduous trees that looked to be hugging the banks of a river.

Wolf slowed and followed. Hundreds of insects swam through his headlights as he bumped onto a rutted dirt road.

Continuing on for a quarter-mile, Shumway slowed as their bobbing headlight beams lit a ranch house squatting in a clearing.

The windows of the broken-down house shone, revealing cracks and holes in the glass. A wall of weeds higher than a grown man stood against the warped wood-panel siding. Next to the house sat an aluminum building that looked much newer.

Shumway parked in front of this outbuilding, swiveling his

truck so his headlights illuminated two white oversized garage roll doors.

Slowing to a stop next to him, Wolf shut off the engine, grabbed his Maglite and got out.

Jet moved an ear, but otherwise remained dead asleep, so Wolf left him inside and shut the door.

"This is it." Shumway swiveled and looked around.

Cricket chirps came at them in stereo out of the sweet-smelling grasses and weeds.

"This is what?"

"Where my great grandparents homesteaded a hundred years ago." He pointed to the side of the house. "Where my grandfather taught me how to shoot a .22."

Wolf nodded and waited patiently for Shumway to finish a flashback.

Then Shumway turned around and took hold of a roll-door handle and twisted it. The clack of the locked handle echoed through the huge metal building. The other one was locked too.

"There's a side door."

Wolf followed him and clicked on his Maglite.

The side of the shed was overrun with huge weeds coming out of the gravel. Behind the foliage, a window reflected his flashlight beam, next to which stood a tan door with a cracked concrete landing.

Shumway twisted the knob. "Locked. Damn it."

The sheriff clicked on his own flashlight and parted the weeds, pushing his way to the window.

Wolf stepped next to him and shone his light through the glass.

The interior space was big—metal crossbeams and corrugated aluminum roof and siding, with a crumbling concrete floor. A pickup truck was parked inside, covered in dust.

"Green's truck?" Shumway asked. "Dodge Ram. Black. Can't see the plates but that's gotta be it."

Shumway flipped his Maglite around and smashed the butt-end into the window. It smacked and the glass broke into large pieces and dropped. "Watch out!"

They jumped back as pieces shattered inside and out. A large razor-sharp shard inclined toward Wolf and toppled to the ground in a thousand tinkling splinters.

Wolf glared at him.

"Sorry." Shumway straightened his pants. "You can probably reach inside and unlock it now."

The window frame was now a yawning mouth of glass fangs.

Shumway patted his belly. "I can't reach. Too fat."

Wolf stepped up and knocked the rest of the glass out with his flashlight, then reached inside and twisted a lock on the knob. "Try it now."

Shumway twisted the knob. "I think there's a deadbolt."

There was, so Wolf leaned back in and pulled at it. The bolt was sluggish, like pulling a nail out of wood. He suddenly felt exposed, so he pointed the light in Shumway's eyes.

Shumway held up his hand. "Hey, watch it."

"There," Wolf said as he opened the deadbolt and lowered his flashlight.

"What the hell?" Shumway said.

Wolf ignored him and opened the door. He snapped on a light switch and two fluorescent tube bulbs buzzed overhead. He squinted at the sudden assault on his retinas and walked inside.

The interior was vast, dwarfing even the full-sized pickup truck inside. The once-smooth concrete floor was chipped and cracked, darkened with old oil stains where farm machinery once sat, and on top of that were chunks of white plaster.

"I don't remember that being there." Shumway pointed at a steel-cabled winch attached to a boom arm. The base of the six-foot-high contraption was bolted to the concrete floor.

Wolf pulled on some rubber gloves and went to the passenger-side door of the truck. The handle clicked and the door swung open on silent hinges. He passed the light beam around the interior and opened the glove compartment.

"Registered to Jeffrey Green," he said, reading the Utah registration card.

"You'd better take a look at this," Shumway said from the other side of the truck.

Wolf closed the door and walked over.

Shumway had his beam pointed at a duffel bag tucked against the aluminum wall. On the floor next to it was a shovel with a yellow handle.

"And now we have a murder weapon," Shumway said. "Looks like the same size as those cuts on Levi."

As if there was any doubt. Blood painted the blade and had spattered up the handle, smudging where the cold-blooded killer had gripped it.

Wolf unzipped the bag and parted the opening, revealing stacks of cellophane-covered bundles of hundred-dollar bills. Each stack had a blue $10,000 band on it.

"Jesus. There it all is," Shumway said.

Shumway was referring to the other items in the bag: two purple Converse All Star high-top shoes with huge dollops of blood on them, a Smith and Wesson four-inch barrel revolver, and a pair of leather gloves that were stiff with blood stains.

Shumway sniffed. "Reeks like the rest of Steven's shoes."

Wolf nodded.

"Well ..." Shumway gingerly picked up the shovel and studied the smudge marks. "No prints by the looks of it. Killer wore these gloves—they're going to be the nail in the coffin. We can scrape DNA out of these, check it for a match against Steven, Felicia, and Molly."

Wolf crouched down and pushed aside the stacks of money. "You listening?"

"There's only twenty stacks here. Two hundred thousand. Where's the rest?"

Shumway said nothing.

"What's the point of all this sitting here?" Wolf asked.

Shumway scoffed. "They're in jail now. They haven't had the chance to deal with all this."

Wolf stood up.

Shumway gingerly put down the shovel. "I gotta tell you, I'm liking Mo and Felicia doing this. Let's say Steven is telling the truth, and his shoes were stolen. They come back from loading the bones, and Steven leaves for some reason ... to do something else in his truck. Felicia, or Molly, straps on Steven's shoes. Then the two of them take the gun off the tent and drive down into Rocky Points in this truck... but wait a minute ..." Shumway scrunched his forehead. "The Dig 1 team said Mo didn't leave with the rest of them that afternoon, and Steven and Felicia came back in Steven's truck. So how did Mo get this truck?"

Wolf raised his eyebrows.

"Well?" Shumway sagged and his face turned red. "You have any thoughts? Or are you just going to sit there and stare at me some more?"

Wolf looked at the duffle bag. "I think I agree—if it was Mo and Felicia, then how did they get down to Rocky Points? And there was a second set of shoeprints at our crime scene in Rocky Points that were size ten or eleven. Both men's sizes. Both too big for these women. Huge for them."

"One of the two women and Levi?" Shumway paced. "Is

that it? Maybe this here is Levi's cut of the money. Brought here after the perp killed him. It was a double-cross."

Shumway stopped and held up a finger. "Maybe *all three* of these students were in on this, but Steven didn't know that Mo and Felicia had decided to kill Professor Green. Maybe Steven stayed back Saturday night at the camp, and Felicia and Mo drove down to Rocky Points, telling Steven, 'Hey, we'll be back in a few hours with our cuts of the money.' But they had other plans—they killed Green, putting it all on Steven ... making it look like someone else had been with Steven. They had Steven's shoes, they had the revolver ..."

Wolf stared at him and pulled down the corners of his mouth, because despite the wild look on Shumway's face, the theory fit. "I think we desperately need sleep. I think there's a lot of evidence to process and we need to get your crime techs here, so you'd better get on the radio."

Wolf yawned.

Shumway eyed him and broke into his own yawn. "Where are you sleeping?"

Wolf shrugged. Like always when he left town, he had the essential camping gear in the SUV.

"Let's get CSU down here and we'll go crash. We need to sleep, and we need to eat. Either that or I'm gonna start murdering people."

Wolf conceded with a nod.

"You can sleep at my place." Shumway walked to the door as if it was settled and pulled his radio off his belt. "Deputy Etzel, come in ..."

CHAPTER 36

WOLF WOKE from a dead sleep to the sound of a phone ringing somewhere in the distance. He sat up and momentarily had no clue where he was.

A spring cushion couch squeaked underneath his butt, sounding like an effect on a Looney Tunes cartoon.

Jet stood and stared at him from two feet away.

"Huh?" a gruff voice said.

Only then did Wolf fully snap to and realize he was in Shumway's Windfield home.

"All right ... fantastic ... we'll be in."

Wolf opened his sleeping bag and pushed his bare feet into the soft yarn of a mid-length shag carpet. His watch said 6:20 a.m.

Standing up and stretching his arms high, he bent over and pressed on his lower back, feeling like he'd slept folded in half.

Jet whined, walked to the front door, and stood expectantly.

Wolf opened it and a cool breeze smelling like cut grass and sagebrush fluttered inside. Jet squeezed his way out and squatted on the lawn.

Shumway walked out of his bedroom and put his hands on

his hips. He wore boxer shorts and a white T-shirt that were both twisted on his body. His box of gray hair was now crushed on one side, and his face had a red line where the pillow had pressed into his cheek all night.

"Just talked to Deputy Etzel. The techs worked all morning. Matched the blood on the shovel to Levi, got the ballistics going on the revolver. Found all four of their prints on the shovel—Felicia, Steven, Molly, and Green's."

Wolf nodded. "But not in the blood."

"Nope."

"So it proves the shovel came from their camp, and nothing else."

Shumway smiled with one side of his mouth. "They'll have the DNA-match test done early this morning. They took the gloves and the three students' cheek swabs down to Grand Junction overnight. That'll get us the perp. Coffee?"

Shumway walked down the hall and disappeared into his kitchen.

"Sure," Wolf said, smelling the coffee already brewing.

"Sleep all right?"

"Yep."

Wolf followed him into the room.

Shumway sat down at a table in front of a window and sipped. "Cups to the left of the sink."

He went to the cupboard and dug out a *World's Greatest Dad* cup that had years of swirling scratches inside it.

He filled it with steaming, jet-black coffee, and sat down. His body rejoiced as he swallowed the first sip. The brew was a hazelnut blend, sweeter than Wolf would've liked, but the caffeine started doing its job.

"Hell of a view," he said, gesturing out the window.

"Yeah. Not bad."

A neatly trimmed lawn glistened with dew outside the

panes of glass, ending at a barbed-wire fence. Beyond, sage country gleamed in the morning sun, folded with shadows.

Jet walked in front of the window outside with his nose to the grass, walked to a fence post, and lifted his leg.

"Sorry," Wolf said. "I'll pick up whatever he leaves."

Shumway reached out, touching the side of Wolf's coffee cup.

Wolf saw the sadness in the man's eyes and wished he had chosen a different mug.

"I did lie to you," Shumway said.

Wolf raised the cup and sipped the coffee.

"About the sale of my grandfather's land."

"Okay."

"My brother and I didn't sell it." Shumway stared out the window. "I sold it without my brother's permission. I mean, I didn't really need my brother's permission. My dad left it all to me in his will ... but ... I did need his permission. At least that's what the other people around me thought. Especially my wife. She hated me for it. I sold it to this guy from Washington, and I took the money and ran for the Sheriff's Office with it."

Shumway took a long slurp of his coffee. He hung his head and then chuckled to himself.

"I spent that money wisely. Bought a television-and-radio-ad campaign. It was for the future of my family, for God's sake. Got myself into the minds of the people in Windfield County. And then ... my opponent died of a heart attack before the polls even opened. In the end, I won unopposed."

Wolf was unsure of what to say, so he sipped his coffee again.

"My wife flipped out and left. Left her daughter and her husband and went to California or Las Vegas, or somewhere. Who knows?" He looked at Wolf. "Can you believe that? Leaving your daughter high and dry?"

They sat in silence for a beat.

"And ever since, my daughter's blamed me. And now she lives her life trying to hurt me in bigger and better ways. And right now she's stabbed me and she's twisting the knife."

Wolf was stuck on thinking about how Sarah had checked out of his and Jack's lives for years. "Was your wife on drugs?"

Shumway looked at Wolf for a long time. "You know what? You're the first person to ever ask me that." He took a sip of his coffee with a quivering lip. "Thanks."

They watched Jet half-assed chase a squirrel outside.

"What was the second file on your desk?" Wolf asked.

"What?"

"When I first came up here yesterday morning, you had a second file on your desk. You and Etzel had something else going on."

"Oh, yeah. I was ... just checking on some of the local men. The whole my-daughter-screwing-Steven-Kennedy thing."

"How were you checking on them? Why?"

"Financial records. Looking for specific charges, ATM withdrawals."

Wolf narrowed his eyes. "Explain."

Shumway stood up and went to the coffee-maker. "There's a little more to the whole Steven-and-Megan story, I'm afraid."

Wolf set down his coffee. "Oh?"

Shumway took his time stirring some sugar into his cup and sat back down. "Megan was pregnant, with Steven's baby, and had an abortion."

Wolf blinked.

"I was looking for men who'd paid with a credit card at a clinic, or made an ATM withdrawal for large sums ... I was grasping. That's what that file was—eight men in town and their recent financials."

"You didn't know who it was?"

"I figured out with you yesterday that it was Steven who'd gotten her pregnant."

Wolf stared at his coffee. "I need you to start from the beginning. Why were you looking for this guy now? This weekend?"

Shumway leaned back in his chair and rubbed his eyes with his palms. "I told you Levi Joseph and Bradley Boydell used to be good friends."

"Yeah?"

"Well, I guess Levi came to Bradley the other day and told him a little secret he'd been keeping—that Megan had been pregnant with someone's baby and had gotten an abortion."

"And how did Levi know about this?"

"Levi took her down to the clinic in Grand Junction for the procedure."

"And Levi didn't know who had gotten her pregnant?"

"No."

"And Levi told Bradley?"

"Yeah."

"You were looking into the men yesterday. Did Bradley tell you recently?"

"Yeah, a few days ago."

Wolf set down his coffee. "And you didn't think of telling me this yesterday, when we were looking at Levi's corpse?"

"Why? What would that have to do with anything?"

Wolf thought for a moment. "When did this pregnancy and procedure happen?"

Shumway shrugged. "I guess it was a couple of months ago. I don't know when exactly."

"And you learned about it this weekend."

"Yeah. Why? What?"

"What did Megan say about the whole thing?"

Shumway sipped his coffee.

"You haven't talked to her about it?"

"Hell, no. It's not a conversation I'm looking to have with my daughter. It's enough that I learned about it and know the bastard who did it. I don't need to hash it out with her, get in a big ol' fight and have her hate me more."

Wolf thought about Jack and Cassidy's camping trip and how he needed to get a handle on that before this exact situation became a possibility. With a shake of his head he erased the thought and stood up to pour some more coffee.

"What was that?" Shumway's voice was low. "Was that judgment? You judging me?"

"No, I'm not. Like you said, it's tough raising a kid by yourself."

"I'm sick of people looking at me like I'm a shit father."

Wolf swirled the final sip of coffee in his mug and thought better of refilling it. "Maybe I'll head up to the university myself this morning. It'll give us—"

"Sounds like a fuck of an idea." Shumway cradled his mug to his lips and stared out the window.

Wolf set down his mug in the sink and walked out of the kitchen. "Call me the second you get those DNA-match test results."

Shumway held his gaze with the eastern sky and grunted in response.

CHAPTER 37

WOLF WALKED to the SUV and put Jet in the back seat. The air was warm and the light breeze carrying the scent of juniper did little to dry the sweat already building in his armpits. He wondered whether Rocky Points would be getting relief from the heat today.

He felt bad for steering the conversation with Shumway into a brick wall like that, but he also felt the insatiable desire to catch Ryan Frost's killer, so if some people got their feelings hurt in the pursuit of truth, so be it.

And he needed food—enough to fill a garbage-can lid.

He started the engine and tried to remember which way to go, then consulted the GPS and drove down the road, looking forward to a plate of eggs and bacon before he started on the road to the university.

He'd yet to get in touch with Talbot and was eager to discover what the head of the paleontology knew about Dig 2's specimen, or *specimens*.

Because it was a good question that Mathis had raised last night: How had Green hidden that second skeleton from Talbot?

"What the hell?"

A pickup truck with the DOI logo painted on it passed him and pulled in front, then jammed the brakes. A slender hand waved out the open driver's window, and he realized it was Megan.

Wolf steadied his breath and pulled behind her.

After a few turns to the right and left, she finally pulled over.

Jet poked his head out the window and whined.

Wolf got out and Megan met him at his bumper.

"What's going on?" Wolf asked.

She looked spooked, averting eye contact and clutching a cell phone in a white-knuckle fist. "I talked to Bradley Boydell and Deputy Etzel last night about what happened to Levi."

"Yeah?"

"And I heard that you guys are thinking it was Steven."

"How did you hear that?"

She folded her arms. "I just saw Deputy Etzel this morning in town. He told me about all the evidence you and my dad found."

Deputies discussing open murder cases with civilians? It didn't say much for Shumway's training.

"I have a piece of evidence that proves he didn't do it," she said.

Wolf raised his eyebrows.

She was staring at her cell phone, twisting it in her hands. "It's on here."

"What is?"

Her breath quickened and she rubbed her lips together. "Just get inside, okay?"

Wolf walked to the passenger door and opened it. Coconut oil scent spilled out as he climbed onto the leather bench seat. He left the door open and stared at her expectantly.

She cradled her phone and stared at it, as if she were waiting for an update from the SS *Enterprise*. Checking her mirrors, she pointed at the door. "Can you please close that?"

He closed the door and the cab went silent except for her labored breathing.

She was shaking, all the while holding up her cell.

All that staring at a phone reminded Wolf Patterson was going to send him a video clip first thing. He let the urge to pull out his own device pass and asked, "What's on the phone, Megan?"

She tapped the screen and thrust it into Wolf's lap, like she'd just pulled the pin on a grenade.

She put her hand over her mouth, slid over to the driver's-side window, and stared outside.

"Hey, baby," a male voice cooed from her phone's speakers.

Wolf looked at the screen. His skin prickled hotly. In front of him was a video of Megan's naked, spread-eagled body.

She was smiling and reaching forward, her skin illuminated by a yellow light. The recording was shaky. The camera hovered over her, pushing close to her face and then her breasts, before pulling back to reveal her entire form again.

Megan giggled on the video.

"You ready for this?"

Wolf recognized the voice of Steven Kennedy.

Wolf tapped the screen and set the phone on the bench seat between them. "Oh, I wish I could un-see that."

Megan reached over and took the phone. She pressed some side buttons and muted it, then studied the footage, tapping and sliding her fingers on the screen. "Here. Look again. I won't press play."

He closed his eyes for a breath and then opened them.

Megan was holding up a still shot of Steven's face twisted in pleasure. "It's Steven. With me."

"Yeah, I get it."

"Look at the time stamp. On the top of the video."

Wolf blinked. "Saturday, 9:37 p.m." He looked at her, then back at the time stamp. "You were with Steven on Saturday night?"

She nodded. "Yes."

"Where?"

"In the back of my truck."

"Where, exactly?"

"Just out in the sticks. He met me."

"He drove? You drove?"

"We both drove. We have a secret spot where we meet."

The blood was draining from his face now, but he had to blink to remove the image of Megan's naked body from his retinas. "Wait a minute. That said Saturday. How do I know it wasn't some other Saturday?"

She picked up the phone and tapped the screen. "Here, see? Saturday, August 11th. 9:37 p.m. Satisfied?"

Wolf sat in silence for a beat. "You could doctor the time stamps."

She made a face and shook her head. "How the hell would I do that?"

"You could have been anywhere. You could have just shown me proof that you were with Steven just after the murders."

Megan looked horrified. "No ... we were just up the road, toward the quarry. You take a left on—"

Wolf held up a hand. "I can check the location of your phone through the GPS in it."

She nodded. "Yes. Exactly. You'll see that we were up the road."

Wolf looked at her. "Send me the file."

He gave her his number and she texted the video to him.

Wolf stared at the side of her face as he waited for the file to reach his phone.

Counterintelligence training in the army had introduced Wolf to the subtleties of telling lies convincingly and how to spot liars. And with a decade and a half's experience as a cop, he'd met his fair share of lying people. Megan was not one of them. She was troubled—betrayed by a mother who'd ditched her, and a father who'd made it all happen. She had a whole lot of associated problems going on there, but she was telling the truth about her Saturday night.

His phone beeped, and he forwarded the file to Patterson.

"I just sent this to my deputy. So, if there's nothing more, I need to leave and call her as soon as possible to explain. I'm going to have her check the file to see if you've tampered with it in any way. I think they call that stuff meta-data or something. My deputy knows. And if you've messed with it, she'll know."

"I didn't mess with it." She glared at him. "I'm not lying."

Wolf held out his hand. "And I'll need to take your phone."

She handed it over.

He opened the door.

"I think this is going to be it for me and him," Megan said.

"You and Steven?"

"No." A tear slid down her cheek. "Me and my dad. He's already pretty much done with me. This video's going to be the final straw."

Wolf watched her cry for a few seconds.

His phone chimed and a message from Patterson read "?!".

Wolf typed, *I'll explain in one minute*, and pressed send. Then he pocketed the phone. "Your dad knows about your pregnancy with Steven and your procedure. Did you know that?"

Megan looked down and a fresh tear slid down her face. "I figured. And what's he going to think about me now? Jesus ..."

Wolf watched her sob. "It's tough being a father, you know?

You try your best for your family, and sometimes you're misunderstood. Sometimes you're blamed for things, for hurting your kids, but you're just trying to do your best."

"I know it's tough being my father." She shook her head and whispered with a thick throat. "I know that."

Wolf slid off the seat and placed her phone in his pocket. He stopped himself from closing the door and ducked back inside. "Megan, when was your procedure at Grand Junction?"

She wiped her eyes. "June 3rd."

"June 3rd?"

"Yeah."

He slid back up onto the seat. "Two months ago?"

She nodded.

"Is that why Steven sleeps up the wash from the rest of the dig members? Because his wife found out about this?"

She nodded.

"How did she find out?"

"It was Levi." Megan sniffed and shook her head. "Levi told Felicia. After the procedure, he brought me back to my quarters up at the visitors' center and then I guess he went down to the Dig 2 camp and jumped Steven. Picked up a shovel and hit him with it. I guess Mo and Professor Green had to wrestle him away."

"Steven told you about this?"

"Yeah. He said Levi came in yelling and screaming about getting me pregnant and told everyone about taking me to Grand Junction and about the clinic. Levi kind of had a thing for me, and he was mad that Steven had put me through all of that. But Levi got it wrong. I didn't blame Steven for anything. He wasn't doing anything wrong because I never even told him. He didn't even know about my pregnancy until Levi barged in and started hitting him with a shovel." She shook her head. "I'm such an idiot. I've caused so much pain for these people. And Levi? Poor Levi ..."

Wolf stared at her. "So, Levi went down to that camp on June 3rd? You're sure?"

She nodded and looked at him. "Yeah, after we got back from Grand Junction, like I said. And Steven told me later that week. It was the third. And I saw Levi up at Mr. Boydell's yurt that same night. I was resting in my camp chair outside and saw him walk up. I could tell he'd been crying and he looked messed up. I called out to him and he glared at me and wouldn't talk. Just passed me by. And then he went into Mr. Boydell's."

Megan's eyes glazed over.

A text chimed on Wolf's phone, but he ignored it. "All this happened June 3rd."

She frowned now and looked up at him. "Yes. Why are you asking?"

"Does Bradley Boydell have a landline in his quarters?"

She nodded. "Yes. Why?"

"Thank you." Wolf slid out and stood on the road shoulder.

"Are you going to show that video to my dad?" Megan asked.

Wolf pulled his lips into a hard line. "I don't really have a choice here, Megan."

She looked away fast, like she'd been slapped, and then with a face devoid of emotion she nodded and started the car.

He shut the door and walked back to his SUV with his phone pressed to his ear.

"Uhhhhh, hello?" Patterson said.

"Hi."

"Interesting video."

"Yes. Sorry about that ... are you at work yet?"

"Yeah. Didn't you just get my message? I just sent you the

video from the gas station. It's only a thirty-second clip, but it shows all the footage we have of the guy."

"I need you to check the time stamp on that video I sent you and make sure it hasn't been tampered with."

"If I can pull it away from Rachette, I'll get right on it. Is that all?"

Wolf climbed behind the wheel.

"Actually, no," he said. "I'm just getting started with what I need from you."

"Okay."

"First of all, how do I check where a cell phone's been in recent days, preferably at a specific time?"

"It's actually pretty simple. First of all, do you have access to the phone?"

Wolf watched Megan pull away ahead of him. "Shit, just a second."

Pulling out her phone, he pushed the button and the screen lit up. She hadn't set up a password or touch ID.

"Yeah," he said with relief.

"Good. And how about a computer? You in front of one?"

Wolf said nothing.

"Never mind. I am."

"Atta girl."

CHAPTER 38

Two HOURS and ten minutes later, Wolf drove into the Windfield County Sheriff's Department parking lot.

His tires squealed as he came to a stop and Jet bumped into the seat behind him.

"Sorry, boy."

He let Jet out and marched to the front door.

"Stay here," Wolf said.

Jet walked to the front of the building and lifted a leg.

Shumway was standing inside talking with Deputy Etzel. "What are you doing here? I thought you were going to Utah?"

"I need to talk to you."

Shumway waved a piece of paper in front of Wolf's face. "Well, good, because I need to talk to you."

Wolf took the paper. A heading read Nordicran DNA Labs, Grand Junction, Colorado. Four horizontal graphs were printed on the page. The first two graph lines were identical, with the same peaks and valleys. The second two were not.

"DNA inside the bloody glove matches our man Steven Kennedy." Shumway flicked the page.

Wolf frowned. "And the second two graphs?"

"Not quite as reliable. They found two different profiles in the shoes—Steven and unknown."

Wolf nodded. "Of course they did."

"Of course they did?"

Wolf pulled out his phone and showed Shumway and Etzel the video clip of the perp filling the gas can south of Brushing.

When the video was over, Shumway and Etzel looked at one another.

Wolf stared expectantly.

Shumway blinked slowly. "All right, you have my attention. That wasn't Steven in the video. It was someone wearing his shoes. That doesn't change the fact that his DNA was in these gloves."

"Was there an anomaly with the gloves? Some sort of foreign substance they couldn't account for?"

Etzel and Shumway looked at one another.

"Well?"

Shumway hitched up his belt. "The lab tech told us there were traces of ..." he picked up another sheet of paper from Etzel's desk and read it. "Na, Mg, K, Ca ... hell, whatever these letters are. They said there were some traces of the powder from our crime-scene techs' latex gloves."

Deputy Etzel nodded.

"Did you talk to your crime-scene techs about this yet?" Wolf asked.

"Well, no. We just got this back a few minutes ago. Why?"

Wolf nodded. "Because there are a lot of types of latex gloves. Our CSU in Rocky Points uses powder-free gloves. The lab could probably test conclusively if they were gloves worn by the crime-scene techs or the assailant."

"The assailant?" Shumway asked.

Wolf nodded. "That's residue from the killer wearing latex gloves and the leather gloves over them."

"How are you so sure?"

"I need to speak to Steven. Right now. Then I'll let you know."

———

A minute later, Wolf stood over Steven's bed and slapped him on the leg.

Steven snorted awake, wiped drool from his lip, and sat up straight. When he saw the three men standing in front of him he pushed himself back on the bed.

"What's going on?"

"Tell me about the day when Levi Joseph jumped you at the camp," Wolf said.

Steven smacked his lips and rubbed his forehead. "You know about that ... why?"

"Just answer."

"Um, okay. I was lying there, just doing some work, and he came up and attacked me. He hit me on the back with a shovel."

"Steven, we know about the two skeletons," Wolf said. "We figured that out last night with Dr. Mathis's help."

Steven closed his eyes and shook his head. "I don't want to talk to you. I ... know I'm just going to implicate myself. I've talked to my lawyer, and I've taken law classes, guys."

"Just listen." Wolf squatted down and looked up at him. "I know the three of you are spooked about what you agreed to do with Professor Green. You found the extra skeleton and you guys were in the process of selling it when all this happened, and now you're freaked. I get it. Because the bottom line is, we'll easily prove the skeleton Green was selling came from that hole, and you'll be in a heap of trouble. You didn't report the skeleton to your university or the owner of the private land you were digging on. You four were engaging in criminal activity. You're gonna have to face the music on that. But I know you're not murderers.

"Someone else is, though. Someone else who knew about this sale. Someone who went down to Rocky Points, killed the fossil dealer, Professor Green, and Levi Joseph, and is now making it look like *you* did it." Wolf pointed at him. "I need you to answer these questions or else you're probably gonna get locked up without a key on this one."

Steven said nothing.

"Why don't you tell him about the shoes, the bag of money, the pistol, and the shovel we found last night, Wolf?" Shumway said.

Steven looked between them and shook his head.

"And the DNA we found matching him," Shumway said.

Wolf nodded. "We found your shoes, the same ones that left all sorts of prints at the scene of three murders. The one's you claim were stolen by a desert animal. We found murder weapons linked to you. We found your DNA on leather gloves caked with blood. And we also found two hundred thousand dollars in cash. It's not looking good for you."

Steven bit his lip and his knee bounced. "What're your questions?"

"Did Levi see the second skeleton the day he attacked you?"

Steven deliberated for a few seconds. "No."

"No? That didn't sound too sure."

"Probably not."

Wolf blinked.

"He jumped me in the pit. And there were two skulls in there at the time. Couldn't have been more obvious. So we suspected that he had. But he never told anyone, so then we decided he probably hadn't noticed, you know, in the heat of the moment."

Wolf nodded. "Dr. Talbot came and visited after that.

When was his visit?"

"I don't know. Like a week later."

"Unannounced?" Wolf asked.

"No. Green knew he was coming."

"And did Talbot see the second skeleton?"

"No. We'd learned our lesson from Levi. We'd kept it covered before, but we took further precautions for Dr. Talbot's visit. Green rented a garage near a farmhouse and we started moving everything there as fast as possible. Then we started keeping everything covered even while we were working."

"And when Dr. Talbot came to see your dig you had everything out and moved?"

"No. Not even close. Just ... better covered. We even put dirt over it."

"And how did that visit go down exactly? Was he fooled?"

Steven shrugged. "Professor Green kind of worked his magic on the whole thing. Got him out of there without even looking."

Wolf pulled his eyebrows together. "Dr. Talbot didn't even look at your dig?"

Steven shrugged. "He did, but not under the tarps. Just kind of nodded at them and left."

Wolf looked at Shumway.

Shumway shrugged.

"Thanks," Wolf said, and he left the holding cell.

Out in the hall, Wolf turned to Shumway. "Sheriff, you need to call your daughter and tell her to leave work right now."

Shumway blew air through his lips. "Why?"

"Because I have reason to believe she's with the killer right now."

"What? Explain."

"I will, on the way." He turned and ran. "Get everyone you have. We have to go now!"

CHAPTER 39

"BOYDELL? No."

"And Talbot." Wolf jammed his foot on the gas. His SUV's engine hesitated and caught and they sucked back in their seat.

"Talbot? Don't know the guy. But Boydell? Nope. I don't believe it." Shumway made a sour face and sneezed into a handkerchief. "Not the killing type. Jesus, that's what you've been doing all morning? Coming up with this? Pull over. I'm allergic to this smelly dog of yours and you're wasting my time."

Wolf turned a corner and hit the gas again. "Before we get up into a place where cell phone coverage is bad, call your daughter at the visitor's center and get her out of there. Tell her to drive back down into town right now."

"Explain yourself," Shumway said, heat rising in his voice as he grabbed the ceiling bar.

"Now!" Wolf matched his tone.

Shumway shook his head and produced an ancient cell phone from his pocket. He flipped it open, pressed a button, and put it to his ear. "No answer. She's not answering."

"Don't call her cell phone. Call the visitor's center."

"Why would I do that? She has her phone on her."

"I have her phone."

Shumway looked at him. "You have her phone? Why the hell do you have her phone? You'd better start doing some explaining, or it's about to get ugly in here."

"Call the visitor's center. I'll explain, but call first."

Shumway exhaled. "Shit ... where's that number ... here." He put the phone to his ear and checked his watch. "Nobody's answering. The place doesn't usually open for another fifteen minutes. They don't get to work early. There's no answer." He snapped the phone shut. "So talk, damn it. Don't make me pull this gun."

Wolf pushed the gas harder as they came onto a straight-away. The speedometer climbed to sixty-five miles per hour and their seats vibrated as the engine roared, almost completely drowning out Wolf's roof siren.

"This morning, when I left your house, my deputy in Rocky Points and I checked some phone and financial records, and we figured out Boydell is behind all of this."

"Yeah, yeah. You said that. And Talbot, the head of paleontology up at U of U. Now tell me why you think that, and then tell me why the hell you have my daughter's phone."

"Talbot's wife filed a missing-person's report yesterday. The Salt Lake PD found him this morning buried in his back-yard garden."

Wolf turned a corner and passed by a vehicle like it was standing still.

"You kiddin' me?"

Wolf shook his head.

"Shit." Shumway eyed him. "And you're telling me Boydell did it?"

"Okay, listen," Wolf said. "Those students, Felicia, Mo, and Steven, and Green found the two skeletons, and instead of reporting the second skeleton to the university, they decided to sell the bones. They wanted a payday. Green had contacts in the business. He'd done a lot of selling of bones around the world before, according to what we've learned. So Green contacted Ryan Frost down in Rocky Points, and Frost found a buyer."

Shumway nodded. "I get that. Boydell. Why Boydell?"

Wolf gripped the wheel and pumped the brakes as he came into a corner too fast. "Boydell's involvement has to do with Megan and Steven. As you know, the two of them were having an affair, and then Megan got pregnant. She got Levi's help to have the abortion down in Grand Junction. Levi was in love with your daughter and he was obliged to help her. But he got angry about what Steven had done to Megan, so right after taking Megan to the clinic, Levi brought her back to her yurt, went down to the Dig 2 camp and attacked Steven. Hit him in the back with a shovel. And in the process of rolling around in that hole, Levi saw the second skeleton."

They came onto a straightaway and Wolf gunned it again. The transition from pavement to dirt approached fast but Wolf kept his foot on the gas.

"Levi came back up to the visitors' center and told Boydell that night about the second skeleton. June 3rd."

"How do you know that?" Shumway asked.

"I talked to Megan this morning and she told me."

"You saw Megan this morning?"

Wolf held up a hand. "Let me finish. Megan said she saw Levi come up to Boydell's quarters later the afternoon of June third. I had my deputy check Boydell's and Levi's phone records for June third, and the records show that Boydell made a forty-five-minute phone call to Talbot up at the University of Utah."

Shumway said nothing.

"According to the phone records, for the next month, Boydell and the head of the paleontology department talked multiple times, and then, they stopped. It looks like Boydell bought a throwaway phone and started using that to call Talbot's office instead."

Shumway was blinking rapidly.

Wolf chopped a hand in the air. "Levi saw the skeleton, told Boydell, and Boydell got in touch with the head of paleontology and they started concocting a plan. I don't know what the plan was, exactly. Only Boydell knows the specifics, because he's the only one still alive."

Shumway looked out his window, shaking his head.

Wolf continued. "Boydell, Levi, and Talbot got together with the knowledge of the second skeleton in that hole. They were seeing dollar signs. They wanted in on the deal.

"Think about it. Dr. Talbot visited Dig 2 a week after Levi found out about the second skeleton—Steven told us that just now, and Dig 1 told us about that visit. Remember?"

Shumway nodded.

"Steven told us just now that when Talbot visited, he didn't even *look* under those tarps. He barely looked at the dig. Isn't that a little strange? He comes all the way down from Salt Lake City, and just gives the dig a cursory glance? Because the truth is, he wasn't there to see it. He was there for different reasons. He already knew what was under those tarps from talking to Boydell. He was there to tell Green the jig was up, and if he didn't get a cut after they sold that second skeleton then they were all ruined."

Shumway stared out the window with a skeptical look. "Why not just uncover the tarp and say, 'Aha! I caught you! I want a cut of the sale of this skeleton?'"

"If he did that, then he lets the students know that he knows. He lets them realize he's as corrupt as them. More importantly, he wanted to cut them out, without them knowing."

Shumway looked at Wolf. After a lengthy silence, he exhaled, as if resigned to go along with Wolf's explanation, for now. "Okay. So, from that point on, the deal was Green working with Boydell, Talbot, and Levi. The students were getting used for labor?"

"Yes," Wolf said. "Exactly. They'd been cut out. But there's more. Because after Green was approached by Talbot, Green got greedy. Or maybe nobody knew who they were dealing with, and Green had this plan all along, who knows ... but, he wasn't going to share with anyone. He bought a plane ticket to Argentina. He was going to take the money after the sale and run."

Wolf looked at Shumway.

Shumway narrowed his eyes and nodded slowly.

"And *that's* where Boydell's killing spree begins," Wolf said. "Boydell and Talbot must have figured out Green was going to ditch on them. So, rather than wait for Green to go get the money from Rocky Points and leave them high and dry, they followed him down, killed Frost, killed Green, leaving a bunch of evidence that made it look like it was Steven, and came back with the money for themselves.

"It was Talbot's vehicle in Rocky Points that night. He has the same make and model tire we're looking for from the crime scene. Salt Lake PD confirmed this morning."

"Shit," Shumway said.

Wolf nodded. "My deputy looked at Talbot's credit-card transactions. He bought gas in Windfield Saturday afternoon. He stayed in a local motel, using his Visa card. He used his cell phone to call the visitors' center twice."

Shumway shook his head. "That's dumb. Why leave a trail coming down here into Colorado?"

"I don't think Talbot knew what was really coming. I don't think he came into the situation thinking they were going to kill people, or else he wouldn't have left such a clear trail. I think it was Boydell who learned about Green's plan to leave and decided to start killing. He had a whole plan that he was following, stealing Steven's shoes a month ago, the revolver from Green's camp, the shovel, the leather gloves, snuffing out Levi to take his cut of the money, and then Talbot."

Shumway scratched his chin and stared into nothing. "Steven and who? Who was supposed to be the second set of prints?"

Wolf smiled grimly. "I don't think Boydell thought that far ahead. Or maybe he didn't even care. He just assumed we'd pin it on one of the other students. He was just worried about covering his own tracks. Literally. He got Talbot to come pick him up from the visitors' center so he could leave his truck there and claim he'd stayed there that whole Saturday night. He wore Steven's shoes to make it look like it was Steven. He wore a big cowboy hat to shield his face when he needed to. He burned the UrMover truck because he knew forensic evidence would be found inside—hairs, fibers. He killed Levi with Steven's shovel, wearing Steven's shoes and leather gloves with latex ones underneath. Buried Levi shallow in the direction of Steven's camp— a subtle reminder of who we were supposed to be blaming for all of it. And he was even there to remind us in person."

Shumway turned to Wolf but stared past him. "This is just ... so crazy."

"He's slipped up in so many ways it would be comical if it wasn't so sick."

"But why? Why go psycho and start killing over this? For money? That doesn't seem like Boydell."

"I think he's extremely desperate. The SLC FBI field office went to Boydell's daughter-in-law's house this morning. She said Boydell was in the process of inheriting a lot of money from an obscure relative she'd never heard of and he was going to help her pay for her son's blood treatment in Scotland."

Shumway nodded. "His grandson has a rare disease. He sold his house a couple of years ago and moved into that yurt to help pay for treatment."

Wolf eyed the rearview mirror. A line of flashing deputy trucks kept a close follow, despite swimming in stream of dust kicked up by his SUV.

"But Steven still doesn't have an alibi. In my time, I've learned that usually it's the simplest explanation, and all that evidence last night points right to him. He could be in on this, too. Couldn't he?"

Wolf shook his head. "Steven does have an alibi. It's on your daughter's phone. A video with a time stamp and a phone GPS location that puts him out here in the sticks at the time of the murder."

Shumway rubbed his forehead. "A video with my daughter and Steven?"

Wolf nodded.

"Do I want to see what's on that phone?"

"No. You don't. Call her again."

Shumway flipped open his cell. "Shit. No reception."

Wolf handed over his. "Try mine."

"No service either." Shumway set the phone in the center console and eyed the side-view mirror. "Shit. Okay. It's Boydell. My daughter's up there. We're gonna spook him if we roll up on him like this. It'll just make things worse."

Wolf eyed the rearview again. "You're right."

"So what do we do? What's our plan?"

"We don't roll up on him like this. Get on the radio with your guys."

CHAPTER 40

BRADLEY BOYDELL WALKED between the wind-twisted junipers and stopped at the pinnacle of the hill. Grains of sand hissed against his pants and dust swirled against his face. As he dug his knuckles into his eyes, giving them a good massage, a fresh vision of a man's head jerking forward, accompanied by a spray of blood, filled his mind.

He sucked in a breath and opened his eyes. The haunting reminders of what he'd done were relentless.

Back in another lifetime, he'd killed while serving in the army. But only with the pull of a trigger, and from a distance. He'd never looked into the eyes of someone who knew it was coming. He'd never seen the job through to the end. Back in battle, some of his kills could have been wounds for all he knew. He never had to stand over the men as they died to make sure the job was done. He'd never had to put them out of their misery with a shot to the head, or a shovel to the neck.

The ping of the metal as it entered Levi's flesh still echoed in his head. It was as if it happened moments ago. The tears in his eyes. The way his jaw clenched as he brought the shovel up for the tenth time.

"No," Boydell looked to the sky and sucked in a breath.

After a minute of slow breathing, Levi's image dissipated and his sanity returned.

He felt like a walking zombie—a corrupted, diseased version of his former self, wandering through the motions of life in a world where he didn't belong. Killing these people had done it.

No, it had been eleven years ago, looking into the eyes of his son as he had taken his last breath. That had done it. That changed a man. That made every pliable thing in a man hard. Frozen. Brittle.

And when Jeremy had contracted the disease he had cracked.

Boydell was fractured like those bones in the ground down on that plateau. The only thing keeping him from falling into a million pieces was his grandson's heroic fight.

He wiped his eyes and sucked in a cleansing breath.

The good night's sleep had served him well and so had this hike. He always liked getting his blood pumping, his lungs heaving.

Standing on a rounded hilltop, he looked down at the shining windows of the visitors' center below. It had been a week since he'd been here, where he could always count on getting some peaceful time with himself, away from the cluttered minds of the two young people he was stuck with every day in his dead-end job.

With that in mind, he checked his wrist and saw he had ten minutes until the 9 a.m. opening. It was time to unlock the place, make his excuse to the two kids, and head out.

He had a long day ahead of him. He had some shady individuals he'd have to do business with to help launder the cash and send it to Scotland via some means he still didn't quite understand. Some way of manipulating online bank accounts and sending electronic payments.

He clenched a fist, thinking about the day, because he knew these men would be younger. They would think him a soft old coot and be out to steal his money, using electronic jargon to confuse him out of thousands of dollars.

Hitching up his belt, he felt the Beretta M9 he'd acquired in the army wedged against the waistband of his pants and his freshly showered skin. He pulled it closer to the tight spot next to his hipbone and began walking.

He paused, because a line of cars was already kicking up a plume of dust in the distance. He could scarcely remember the last time they'd had three visitors right at opening. And why were they following so close to one another? They were like a caravan, clearly together.

He squinted and brought up his hand to shield the sun. They were far away, but Boydell's vision had always been sharp, and even in his old age he could clearly see that the three vehicles were identical.

Trucks.

With flashing lights.

Everything inside of Boydell's body moved at once.

For five seconds he watched with constricted breath. His heart pumped wildly in his chest.

But it was strange. Because the trucks were all slowing down. Yes, he was sure of it. The three trucks were inching close to one another as they slowed.

The tension in his body melted as he saw them pull to a complete stop and the drivers' doors open. They were at least a mile away, but Boydell could see the tiny dots of men milling about next to their trucks.

Maybe they were doing a search of the desert in that spot. But why? There was nothing there.

The hairs on his neck began crawling. They were convening, preparing something. The three stick-figure forms walked to one another and stood in a tight cluster in the middle of the road.

They were waiting for something.

Why were they standing like that? Were they blocking people from coming up, and waiting to move on him?

He came to his own conclusion and took off at a run down the hill.

Slipping every few steps, he landed on his ass and felt the gun dig into his hip.

"Damn it," he muttered.

He forced himself to slow down to a manageable speed, which was tough because his thoughts were racing.

He needed to escape. He needed to get in his truck and drive. He knew this country better than all three of those deputies combined. There was more than one way to get off this plateau without passing along that road. He had the money stashed in his truck. He could get through, and he could get to Salt Lake City.

Out of breath, his feet stomping the ground with hurried steps, he reached the bottom of the hill behind the visitors' center and began jogging.

"Mr. Boydell?"

He froze at the sound of Megan's voice, and reached back for his gun, but stopped himself short of pulling it.

He forced a smile. "Hi, Megan."

"Everything okay?" she asked.

She was standing near the rear door to the visitors' center, and only then did Boydell realize she was waiting for him to unlock the door and begin the day inside the building.

"Are you going to open up?" she asked.

Boydell stared at her, trying to gauge her expression. Was she messing with him? He looked toward Phil's yurt. It flapped gently in the breeze. The door was still closed.

"Where's Phil?"

She smirked. "It's Tuesday, remember? He'll probably sleep another five hours."

Was she in on this whole thing? Was she trying to trap him? It would've been dumb to think otherwise, so he pulled out his pistol and pointed it at her.

She held up her hands and backed into the wall of the building. "What are you doing?"

"You are," he said. She *was* trapping him.

"What?"

"You're in on it, aren't you?"

"In on what? Mr. Boydell, I don't know what you're talking about. Please. Don't."

He walked to her and waved the pistol to the left. "Let's go. We're going to take a drive."

She stood frozen like a dumb deer.

"Move!"

Stumbling, she thrust her hands up and walked around the building, all the while whimpering.

"Into my truck. You're driving," he said.

CHAPTER 41

WOLF SLID to a stop next to the scarred ring of earth that used to be Levi Joseph's campfire and shut off the engine.

Levi's tent and the table with his personal effects were still there; in fact, the whole campsite looked unchanged, despite the law-enforcement activity the night before. The only indications they'd been there were the new footprints and yellow crime-scene tape around the perimeter, which was fastened to poles and bouncing in the wind.

"Etzel, come in," Shumway said into his radio as he climbed out.

Wolf let Jet out the back of the truck and ducked underneath the tape.

"Go ahead."

Shumway followed Wolf and Jet. "We're at the camp."

"Copy that. Let us know when to move."

"Will do."

Shumway put the radio back on his duty belt and jogged up next to Wolf.

They trudged up the path out the rear of the camp to the

top of the plateau in silence. Shumway hadn't said much on the way up the two-track road, and neither had Wolf as he concentrated on avoiding boulders, trees, and cacti.

The plan was simple: sneak in from the rear and get into position, making sure neither Megan nor Phil were in harm's path, then bring in the cavalry and move on Boydell.

Still silent, Shumway was already breathing hard halfway up the sandy rise that flanked the rear of Levi's camp.

"You all right?" Wolf asked.

Shumway picked up his pace and passed him.

Wolf felt the strain in his lungs and legs. He'd let himself get too soft over the past year, and he vowed then and there to change that. Adrenaline helped power him forward, though, and he kept the new pace easily enough.

At the top, the slope leveled and they entered a maze of juniper trees and man-sized sage bushes. Though the land was flat as a pancake, the foliage obscured their view as they walked. But despite the plants and trees, they could see the top of the visitors' center jutting above it all in the distance, giving them a bearing.

Wolf estimated the distance at a half-mile, and checked his watch. "Can you pick up the pace?"

Shumway shot him a hard glance and grunted in response. Then he upped his speed to a labored jog.

Jet trotted behind them, happily stopping at holes and bushes of interest, then running briefly to catch up before doing it all again.

They swerved between bushes and trees for five minutes, catching glimpses of the building as it grew closer, and all that time their crunching footsteps and huffing breath were the only sounds. Until there was something else.

"Wait," Wolf said pulling to a stop. "Stop."

Shumway ignored him for a few steps than stopped and

turned. He put his hands on his hips and bared his teeth. "What?"

"Hear that?"

A car engine revved and there was a squeak, then another staccato burst of gas followed by more squeaking.

"Someone's driving toward us."

Shumway turned away from Wolf and walked around a juniper to get a look. Just as he reached a clearing, he stopped and hurried back to Wolf. "There."

After a long squeak the engine revved and then shut off.

"Shit," Shumway said. "It was a quarry truck. I think it was Boydell. Fifty yards that way, coming straight at us."

Wolf pulled his pistol and Shumway did the same.

Peering through the gaps in the foliage, they heard the thump of a car door.

"He's out," Wolf said. "You go left, I'll go right."

Wolf skated right, keeping his gaze focused through the branches of the nearest juniper. He saw a shiny bumper, and then the front of a quarry pickup truck, and then the whole vehicle. Wolf paused, because both doors were ajar.

"Come out, Shumway! I saw you! I know you're with Wolf, too! Come on out!"

Wolf and Shumway locked eyes and held still.

"Daddy!"

Wolf's stomach dropped and so did Shumway's face.

"Got your daughter here, Shumway. You have five seconds to come out in the open or I shoot her in the head. Five, four, three ..." Boydell counted with barely a second's pause between numbers. "Two."

"Okay, okay! Hold up, Bradley!" Shumway held his hands high in the air and ran out into the clearing. "Please, Bradley. Don't hurt her."

"Drop the gun."

Shumway lowered his gun and dropped it with deliberate, slow movements. "Now your buddy. I know he's with you."

Wolf clenched his teeth. *Damn it.* He wondered if Shumway was bluffing.

Jet appeared from behind a sage and trotted toward Wolf, oblivious to the gravity of the situation. He stopped and jammed his nose into an animal hole.

"I'll give you three seconds! Three, two—"

Wolf ran into the clearing with his arms up, pistol aimed at the sky.

"Okay. There you are," Boydell said. "Drop it."

Wolf dropped the pistol on the sand.

Boydell had Megan in a headlock, a pistol to her temple.

Her head was tilted to the side as the barrel of the gun pushed hard against it, and she was on her tiptoes, held that way by Boydell's wiry-armed chokehold.

"I'll give the other deputies three seconds to show themselves now." Boydell's eyes darted from bush to bush.

"There aren't any, Bradley," Shumway said.

Boydell narrowed his eyes. "Three! Two!"

"There aren't any! It's just us!"

"There's no one else!" Wolf said at the same time.

"One!"

Wolf closed his eyes and held his breath. The few seconds of silence that followed were the deepest he'd ever witnessed.

"Okay then," Boydell said.

Megan began to sob.

"You," he pulled on Megan's neck, "shut up. You two, turn around slow and show me your belt-lines," Boydell said.

Shumway turned, keeping his arms high.

Boydell kept his pistol against Megan's head.

"You too." Boydell aimed his gun at Wolf.

Wolf turned slowly and lifted his own arms, half expecting the punch of hot lead in his back at any moment.

None came, and he turned full circle.

"Now, walk toward me. Slowly." Boydell's voice shook.

Wolf and Shumway exchanged a glance and inched forward, one foot in front of the other, like they were approaching a cornered bear.

"Please. You don't want to do this, Bradley," Shumway said.

"Walk!"

They were forty yards from Boydell.

Wolf kept his eyes on Boydell's as they walked ten paces forward. The man was alternating between steely resolve and ultimate despair, all the while keeping his hold on Megan.

Her face was dark red, trending purple, and she hung her hands on Boydell's arm.

Shumway held his hands out. "Bradley, please. We know why you're doing this. We know you just want to help your grandson. But it's over now. Don't take away my daughter."

"And what? That would be a fair trade? This alive hooker for my dead grandson?" Boydell's lips glistened with saliva. "Walk at me, boys. Keep coming."

They continued their slow steps toward Boydell.

Wolf's muscles were tense, because Boydell had a crazed look in his eye and he seemed to be rehearsing something very bad in his mind. And as Wolf got nearer, with no weapon at his disposal, he was coming up with no plan other than to dodge if the bullets started flying.

"It's over, Bradley," Wolf said. "Let Megan go."

Boydell lifted his gun and Wolf froze mid-step.

Then Boydell slammed the butt of the gun onto the top of Megan's head.

There was a dull thud and she dropped instantly to her side

without using her arms to break her fall. As she lay motionless in the dirt, blood streamed across her forehead like a red lightning bolt.

"No." Shumway stepped forward and stopped as Boydell aimed his pistol at him.

Boydell tracked his pistol to the side and aimed at Wolf's chest.

"What do you think we're going to do, Bradley?" Wolf said. "Get you a helicopter? A jet to take you to Canada? You know that's not gonna work."

The pistol quivered in Boydell's hand.

There was movement to Wolf's right, and without looking directly he could see it was Jet. The big German Shepherd loped through the bushes and sat a few yards away, resting in the shade of a juniper.

"There's no way out of this," Wolf said. "You don't have to kill more people. The FBI is talking to your sister right now. They know you killed Talbot. They found him in his back yard. We know everything, Bradley. Let's not make this even worse."

Boydell's eyes whirled for an instant and his face slackened. He brought the Beretta to his own temple and screwed his eyes shut, then scratched his head with it and lowered it to his side.

Wolf glanced at Shumway.

Shumway looked preoccupied with Jet. "Drop it!" he yelled out of nowhere.

Wolf watched in disbelief as Shumway walked toward Boydell.

"Whoa." Shumway stopped just as suddenly as he'd started. "Look what Jet has. Just put down the gun, Bradley."

"What?" Boydell said annoyed. "Look what Jet has?" Boydell aimed the gun at Wolf. "Where's that huge dog of yours?"

Wolf shook his head. "He's not here. He's back at the station."

Boydell stared at Shumway and blinked. "Are you messing with me?"

Wolf stole a glance toward the shade of the Juniper.

Jet panted, sitting on his haunches, staring at Wolf and Shumway like he wanted to know what game they were playing but didn't quite have the energy to join in yet. Jet closed his mouth and lowered his head, and finally Wolf saw it. Sitting in the sand near his paws lay a slobbery Glock 17.

Boydell wavered his aim, looking tormented by thoughts.

"Just say when," Shumway said, gesturing to Boydell with his hands.

"What? Why are you messing with me?" Boydell aimed at Shumway, seemingly ready to fire.

"Now!"

Wolf lunged toward Jet. Boydell's gun popped an instant later. A bullet zipped through the air above him as he ran.

"Ahhhhh! Over here! Over here!" Shumway screamed like a crazy man.

Wolf reached Jet and dropped to a knee. He grabbed the Glock, throwing up a cloud of warm dirt as he raised it, and aimed for the center of Boydell's chest.

Boydell took his second shot, this time at Shumway. The sheriff was already running at him, arms flailing, hell-bent on taking him down.

Wolf fired just as Boydell's hand kicked from the shot.

Boydell spun and dropped. Shumway stumbled forward and landed on top of him.

Jet joined the mayhem, bounding toward the two downed men with thunderous barks.

"Heel!" Wolf yelled, and Jet looked thoroughly dejected as he obeyed the command.

Both men lay motionless, heaped on top of one another.

Wolf rushed to the two men heaped on top of one another and pried a Beretta from Boydell's hand. Tucking the pistol in his waistband, Wolf bent over Megan, pulled aside her blood-soaked hair and felt her neck for a pulse. It was strong.

"Is she all right?"

Wolf turned and raised his Glock.

Shumway rose to his hands and knees.

"Yeah," Wolf said, holstering his gun. "She's just knocked out."

"Sir!" Etzel's voice was frantic over the crackling radio. "Sheriff, come in! We heard shots fired."

Shumway got to his knees and pulled his radio. "Yeah. We got Boydell. We need an ambulance. My daughter's been injured."

"Yes, sir," Etzel said. "Is she shot?"

"Negative. Just send the ambulance."

"Copy that. And we're on our way."

Shumway turned down his radio. He checked Boydell's pulse and stood on shaky legs. "This asshole's still alive."

He pressed his hand to his side, then pulled it away. His palm was slick with blood. "Shit."

"You're hit."

"Grazed." Shumway bent down and put the back of his hand on Megan's face. "Poor girl."

"She'll be all right. Probably just a couple stitches."

Boydell whimpered and writhed on the ground, like a child having a nightmare.

"And what about him?" Shumway asked.

"I hit him in the shoulder. It was a hollow point, but by the amount of blood looks like he'll live. I'll take him home and they'll throw away the key."

Shumway looked at Wolf. "You so sure about that? He'll go to trial, and your son's girlfriend and her family will spend those countless months on pins and needles, hoping this psycho gets what he deserves." Shumway stood up, baring his teeth as he pushed his palm on his wound again. "And maybe he's just crazy enough to plead not guilty. Maybe he gets some public defender who'll pick apart our procedures over the last few days."

"He just shot the sheriff of Windfield County. If the rest of it falls through the cracks, at least he'll rot for that."

Megan's eyelids fluttered.

Wolf squeezed her shoulder. "Megan, you—"

Before he could react, he felt Boydell's Beretta slip from his waistband.

Shumway stood over Boydell and aimed down.

"Don't do it, Shumway." Wolf held out his hand. "You shoot him, I've gotta report the truth of what you did. You're going to be put in jail along with him. You want to put your daughter through that?"

"You're gonna take away my chance to make my daughter proud?" Shumway looked at Wolf. "I wrestled with Boydell. I took the gun away and shot him in the heat of the moment. It was pure self-defense. I saved my daughter's life."

"Daddy, don't do it."

Shumway flinched at the sound of his daughter's voice. "Honey."

"I'm sorry about the video, Daddy." Tears streamed down her face, mixing with the blood.

Shumway closed his eyes. "What video, honey?"

Wolf held out his hand. "Come on. It's over. Let me take him back. That family needs this man to face justice. Your family needs you."

Shumway lowered the gun and collapsed to his knees. He studied the blossoming red spot on his side and then fell over.

"Daddy!"

Wolf cuffed Boydell and got to work on plugging Shumway's wound.

CHAPTER 42

MARGARET HITCHENS SNIFFED and put her head on Wolf's shoulder. "My God, it's so beautiful," she whispered with all the awe and reverence in the universe. Not bothering to wait for Wolf's reply, she clasped her hands to her chest and stood straight.

Wolf had to admit, it was an impressive setting for a wedding.

A never-ending sea of peaks with light-green swaths of aspens cutting through a carpet of pines surrounded them on all sides.

The air was crisp and cool, and still—not a breath of wind—which was about as rare as finding a nugget of gold on the ground for the top of Rocky Points Ski Resort. The sun shone bright, with low clouds lazily floating past now and again, painting the mountaintops and valleys with their shadows.

It was at times like this when he renewed his vow to Rocky Points that he'd never leave her.

"You seeing the knockers on the third bridesmaid?" Rachette spoke out the side of his mouth in Wolf's ear.

Wolf gave him a sideways glance.

Charlotte Munford was next to Rachette, smiling and nodding at Wolf. "Beautiful, huh?" she said.

Wolf contemplated her question.

"It is." Margaret leaned across Wolf's lap. "Oh my God, they did such a good job with the decorations."

"Shhhhhh."

Margaret turned and glared at someone behind them.

Jack sat alone next to Margaret, sharing a roll of his eyes with Wolf. Cassidy had stayed away from the festivities, having just put her father in the ground the day before.

If the setting was beautiful, then Patterson was a goddess. She was dressed in a tasteful white dress that displayed her lean shoulders and slim waist. Her auburn hair was pulled back with flowers that framed her glowing, freckled face.

She looked up at Scott Reed and beamed with a toothy smile that kicked off more energy than the sun. In fact, it was such a happy, contented expression that Wolf couldn't help but envy Scott.

Scott seemed struck by the moment too, and though he towered over Patterson, standing at least six foot four to her five foot one, he looked humbled by her huge presence.

Wolf slid his gaze to the shiny brown hair of Special Agent Kristen Luke, who sat in the front row next to a muscular man whom Wolf had met just before the ceremony. He'd been introduced as Gestad, which Wolf guessed was Swedish for muscles. Kristen leaned close and with a conspiratorial smile whispered something into the man's ear, then started laughing uncontrollably.

Margaret reached over and grabbed Wolf's hand, and Wolf gave her a toothless smile.

The ceremony continued without a hitch, and when the officiant pronounced them man and wife, Wolf wondered whether they'd be calling her Deputy Reed now.

After a heartfelt round of applause from Wolf and the guests, a considerable crowd by any wedding's standards, the bride and groom wandered off along the mountain top with the photographer toward a wildflower-covered ski run.

Everyone else walked and mingled, making their way along the ridgeline to the Antler Creek Lodge.

Wolf put his arm around Jack and steered him to a spot devoid of people.

"What's up?" Jack asked.

"I want to talk to you."

"Okay."

Wolf stared at an eagle circling in the sky.

"Dad?"

"Yeah. Listen, I want to talk to you about sex."

Jack's eyes widened and his face went red. "Uh, okay. You think this is the place to have this conversation? Kind of a bad place, Dad."

"I don't care. We need to have this talk."

Jack looked down at his feet.

"I know about you and Cassidy camping together, alone, last weekend. You want to talk about a bad place? Think about where you'll be if Cassidy gets pregnant and you aren't even old enough to drive yet."

Jack huffed and kicked at a piece of grass.

"Look at me," Wolf said.

Jack did.

"I want you using protection. I want you two acting responsible."

"We haven't had sex yet."

"Hey, there you two are." Margaret came up and looked at both of them. "But ... this is a bad time ... so I'll talk to you later." She walked away and warned someone else to stay clear as she disappeared into the crowd.

Wolf could think of nothing else to say, so he put his hands on his son's shoulders and gave him a meaningful nod. When they were done understanding one another telepathically, he ruffled Jack's hair and began walking.

"How's she doing?"

Jack stepped next to him. "She's sad. They all are. I'm not sure what to do for her."

"Well, you know how it is. It'll take time, and even then, it still sucks. And takes more time."

Wolf and Jack walked to Rachette and Munford, who were standing and talking on the trail.

"'Sup, dude?" Rachette asked Jack, giving him a mock uppercut to the stomach.

Wolf and Munford stood shaking their heads as Jack and Rachette wrestled for another few seconds, and then Jack spotted a friend named Chip, whom Wolf had once heard was a "bomb" skier.

"I'll see you guys in there," Jack said and ran to his friend.

"I don't know about you guys, but tonight I'm gonna get housed." Rachette looked at Wolf. "Of course, I'm off work tomorrow, so you're fine with that."

"Just don't fall off the gondola on the way down."

Rachette's face dropped. "How would I fall off? Those doors are locked tight, aren't they?"

Wolf smiled and checked his watch.

"What? You have somewhere better to be?" Munford asked.

Wolf shrugged and made a noncommittal noise.

They walked in silence for a beat, and then Munford bubbled over. "Oh, I'm so excited. I've never been here."

"That's because it's five hundred bucks for a meal," Rachette said. "When Wolf decides to double my salary, I'll bring you here. How about that?"

"Oh, I wasn't hinting you needed to take me, Tom. How about you, sir? Have you eaten here?"

Wolf remembered the last time he'd been inside the restaurant. It had been with Sarah. "A couple of times."

Munford whistled. "Five hundred bucks for a meal? There's gotta be over two hundred people here. Apparently, Mr. Patterson is well-to-do."

"Entertainment lawyer in Aspen," Rachette said. "I'm gonna get on his good side tonight. The guy knows TC personally."

Munford frowned at him. "And what? He's going to introduce you?"

"Never know, babe. Maybe he has some extra memorabilia lying around."

Munford laughed and then looked like she remembered Wolf was still there. "So, you thought she was beautiful?"

Wolf was taken aback by the phrasing of the question. "Yeah, she looked really beautiful. Scott's a lucky man."

"No, I mean the bridesmaid Tom pointed out."

He looked at her, thoroughly confused.

Rachette bounced his eyebrows. "Charlotte knows her pretty well. Small world, eh? We can introduce you if you want. She knows who you are."

"She thinks you're hot," Munford said, flashing a mischievous smile.

Wolf tried on a few facial expressions, and ended up mumbling something incoherent.

"David!" Margaret yelled behind them.

"I'll see you guys," Wolf said, dropping out of the procession.

"Wait up." Margaret jogged up and stopped, twisting an ankle. "Ah, dammit."

"Why'd you wear those shoes?"

"Why did I wear these shoes? Have you seen them?" She pointed down.

"Oh, yes. Those are great shoes, Margaret."

"Ha. Thanks."

He checked his watch again.

"Why do you keep checking your watch? You're not thinking of leaving, are you?"

Wolf nodded. "I've got a thing."

"You've got a thing? This is Heather's wedding. That's your thing for the night."

A woman stared at Wolf as she passed by, leaving behind a cloud of perfume that choked his nostrils. A little behind the nameless woman, Kristen Luke and Gestad strolled arm in arm.

Kristen was cuddled close to the man's ample pectorals and laughing, and then her face dropped as she saw Wolf.

They smiled and nodded at one another as she passed.

"Anyway, I've gotta go."

"Heather will be devastated."

Wolf caught a glimpse of Patterson and Scott through the throngs of people. They were laughing and holding one another in front of the photographer. Wolf looked at the gondola terminal and then back at the bride and groom and felt a wave of guilt wash over him.

"I'll talk to you later."

Wolf walked away from the throngs of people, out among the long grass of the mountaintop toward the bride and groom. He waited patiently with his hands in his pockets, ruining a couple of shots as Patterson broke her pose and looked at him.

"Just a second," she said to Scott and walked over.

"Sorry. I just have to leave and I wanted to say congratulations."

"You have to leave?" She looked heartbroken, but tried to play it off. "Okay, yeah. No problem. Thanks for coming."

He nodded. "I'm sorry."

They stood in silence for a moment, and he waved to Scott.

"Congratulations, Scott."

Scott smiled. "Thanks, Dave."

"Sir?" Patterson stared up at Wolf with a troubled expression.

"Yeah?"

"What happens if I have a kid?"

He frowned. "What happens if you have a kid?"

"If I decide to have children, am I screwed?"

"Yes."

She frowned.

"Because anyone who has a child is screwed."

She rolled her eyes.

"Are you talking about your job?"

"Yeah. I mean, I can't hold my job and have kids, can I?"

"I have a kid, and I hold my job."

She gave him a look that said she was seconds from killing him.

He put a hand on her shoulder. "You're the sharpest detective I have. I'll never let you go as long as you want the job. If you decide to have children, then we'll work around it."

She instantly burst into tears, and then she lunged forward and hugged him tightly, dropping her flower bouquet on the ground next to them.

Wolf stared at Scott with wide eyes and patted her back.

She pushed away and smiled so brightly he couldn't help but return one of his own.

"Thanks. I hate that you have to leave, but thanks." She turned and walked back to the photographer and Scott.

The photographer's jaw dropped and he looked at Wolf with naked contempt.

CHAPTER 43

WOLF WALKED INTO THE STEAMY, beer-vapor-infused restaurant and searched the pine booths lining the windows.

"Table for one?" A disheveled looking hostess grabbed a menu and looked at him.

"No, thanks. I'm meeting that man over there."

She dropped the menu back in its slot and left, disappearing into the sea of loud drinkers in the bar area.

Wolf walked over, loosening and removing his tie and shoving it in his jacket pocket. Stopping at the table, he slid onto the creaky pine bench opposite the man.

"You're late." Senator Levenworth didn't bother looking up as he sawed into a steak that looked like a burnt hockey puck.

Wolf nodded.

"Can I get you something to drink, David?" a female voice said next to him.

"No thanks, Kim."

She smiled warmly and looked at Levenworth.

Levenworth pointed his steak knife at the half-drunk glass of golden liquid. "Another Dewar's. Less water this time, more Dewar's."

She nodded and left.

"This food is shit. This is the best place you could come up with to meet? And you're not even getting anything?" Levenworth shook his head and took another bite.

"I saw the bones weren't in the back of your truck," Wolf said. "I thought you already picked them up from the building."

"My assistant is driving them back in a rented truck." Levenworth set down his knife and fork, then took a long pull of his Scotch and eyed Wolf over the rim of the glass. When he was done, he exhaled and put down the glass with a clank. "I don't have any obligation to help you with your request."

They stared at one another until Kim came over and slid another glass of Scotch in front of Levenworth.

"But I like you," Levenworth said as he looked around the room. "And I like kids. Don't have any of my own, but I find them tolerable." His eyes came back to Wolf. "I sent the money via my personal foundation to the medical clinic in Scotland. Wasn't cheap. Three hundred forty-five thousand American dollars."

Wolf nodded.

Levenworth gripped his Scotch. "The kid and his mom have a first-class plane ticket that leaves tomorrow morning from Salt Lake City, and he'll be under the knife, or whatever they use, in two days."

Wolf nodded.

Levenworth finished his almost empty Scotch and pulled over the new one. "I know you think I knew about the illegal nature of those bones, but I didn't."

Wolf nodded.

Levenworth stared at him for a few seconds and then shook his head. "I've been looking at those procedures they do up there. That treatment has a sixty-five-percent success rate. There's no guarantee this is even going to work for the kid."

Wolf looked at his watch. 6:54 p.m. "I've gotta go." He slid to the edge of the booth and stood up. "See ya."

"That's it?" Levenworth looked up with an incredulous smile.

"That's it."

Wolf walked through the loud bar area of Stan's Pub and Grill and out through the side entrance. The door creaked and slapped shut behind him, and the bar noise was muted to almost nothing.

He crunched his way on top of the downed pine needles, through the twenty yards of forest and out onto the community-center parking lot.

His dress shoes crackled as he stepped on the pebble-strewn asphalt, and he walked to the front door and went inside.

Immediately, Wolf felt like he'd been punched in the stomach, because Sarah was right there to greet him. Her smile was bright, her eyes radiant, a gleaming orb in the center of each of her pupils from the picture flash. Underneath her photo, a brass engraving read her name.

"David?" a woman's voice said.

Wolf turned. "Hi, Carol."

Carol Fitzsimmons was short and squat, with a puffy wave of white hair and thick glasses. She was in her seventies, but moved like a woman twenty years younger. She got up from the desk and hurried over to him with a tiny outstretched hand.

Wolf shook it and smiled, noting a sign with press-on letters on the wall that said, Tonight @ 7 pm: Grief Counseling Group.

"What brings you to the Old Bank?" she asked, referring to the nickname of the community building, as it had been the bank of Rocky Points over a hundred years prior.

He eyed Sarah's photo again. "I'm here for the meeting tonight."

Carol looked at Sarah's photograph and back at him. "Oh, I

see." She gave Wolf the most compassionate smile he'd ever seen in his life and took his hand again. "Come. It was a good thing to come here. It's a good thing to seek help."

Wolf nodded. "So I hear."

"This way."

She led him around the corner and down the hall.

He was bombarded with memories, and swore he could still smell Sarah's perfume as he passed by her old office. With every step the floor squeaked underneath his feet, just like the last time he'd been here. With her.

And now he was here alone, smelling her perfume, and looking at her face hanging on the wall. As he followed Carol into the room, he felt a surge of something—not quite panic or regret, but something close to both. Like he was a fraud, like he really didn't mean it, because he probably didn't really need the help, and he was being disrespectful to these people who were here for a real reason.

There were seven of them sitting in a circle, sipping coffee and happily chatting: four men, ranging from younger than Wolf to twice his age, and three women, all much older.

They hushed at the sight of him and stood up from their chairs.

"Everyone, this is David Wolf."

He swallowed and approached, and shook each of their hands. And with each new greeting, he felt a tiny surge of strength well up inside, like he was standing much taller by the time the introductions were done. And as he finally sat down the apprehension was gone, replaced by the unrelenting vision of a smug, knowing smirk plastered on Margaret Hitchens's face.

ACKNOWLEDGMENTS

Thank you for reading To the Bone. I hope you enjoyed the story, and if you did, thank you for taking a few moments to leave a review. As an independent author, exposure is everything. If you'd consider leaving a review and helping me with that exposure, I'd be very grateful.

CLICK HERE TO LEAVE A REVIEW

I love interacting with readers so please feel free to email me at jeff@jeffcarson.co so I can thank you personally. Otherwise, thanks for your support via other means, such as sharing the books with your friends/family/book clubs/the weird guy who wears tight women's yoga pants at the gas station, or anyone else you think might be interested in reading the David Wolf series. Thanks again for spending time in Wolf's world.

Would you like to know about future David Wolf books the moment they are published? You can visit my blog and sign up for the New Release Newsletter at this link – http://www.jeffcarson.co/p/newsletter.html.

As a gift for signing up you'll receive a complimentary copy of Gut Decision—A David Wolf Short Story, which is a harrowing tale that takes place years ago during David Wolf's first days in the Sluice County Sheriff's Department.

.

PREVIEW OF DIRE (DAVID WOLF
BOOK 8)

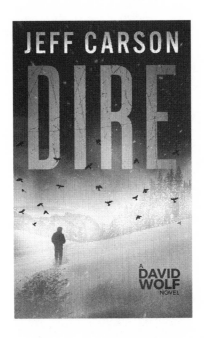

"DID YOU SEE THAT?" Chief Detective David Wolf of the
Sluice–Byron County Sheriff's Department twisted in his seat
and looked through the tinted rear window of the SUV.

"Whoa, you're gonna slide off the mountain!" Detective Sergeant Barker reached a meaty hand toward the wheel.

Wolf corrected his steering and pumped the brakes, sliding to a stop in a foot of snow on the shoulder.

A pickup truck honked and slowed on the way by, the driver's middle finger extended in the window.

They were driving in an unmarked department SUV, a dark-maroon Ford Explorer specially ordered for Wolf and his detective squad, which meant sometimes they received less than the normal law-enforcement respect afforded other cops with rooftop turret lights and fancy paint jobs.

"Move on, asshole!" Barker pointed out the windshield with teeth bared.

With tires spitting snow, Wolf ignored the blossoming road-rage incident and reversed up the shoulder. As they bounced in their seats, the front end fishtailed side to side.

Barker eyed the steep drop-off to the right that sloped down to the icy Chautauqua River. "I didn't see anything, and you know we have a Situation in ten, right?"

Greg Barker was talking about the impending meeting in the Situation Room. It was the third time he'd mentioned it on their otherwise silent drive back from the resort, where they'd been at a Colorado State law-enforcement conference for most of the morning. Wolf had stayed late to speak to an old acquaintance from Glenwood Springs with whom he'd worked a case, and Barker had been left behind by his partner. And now they were stuck together, an occurrence made rare by mutual design.

"Christ." Barker shook his head and pulled out his cell phone, probably preparing a text message to cover his ass.

Wolf jammed the SUV in park and stepped out just as an eighteen-wheeler rounded the curve behind them. Behind the oversized windshield, the driver's eyes widened and he over-steered the wheel to avoid them, sending the truck into a sideways slide. Wolf tensed, watching the wheels catch on an exposed piece of blacktop, providing just enough traction to avoid a collision.

"Shit," Wolf muttered as exhaust-laden wind whipped against him.

He jogged to the two slide marks and edged up to the crest of the ravine, seeing what he'd dreaded—an upside-down vehicle in the river below.

Wolf popped the rear hatch. "There's a vehicle in the water." He grabbed the Life Hammer out of his emergency kit, a twin-steel-point head designed to shatter car windows and a hook blade on the handle to cut seatbelts.

Barker twisted around. "What?"

"We have a vehicle down in the water!" Wolf slammed shut the hatch and went back to the side of the road.

Barker stepped out slowly and craned his neck over the edge, cell phone still in hand.

"Call it in!"

Wolf tucked the hammer into his jacket pocket and stood for a moment, picking the best line down. It was steep, with rocks and bushes covered by a few months of snowfall. There was no best line, just a fifty-degree slope that would've been designated double black diamond at the ski resort. Crouching and planting a hand in the frigid snow, he leaped over the side and slid down on his left hip.

It was soft for a few feet and then turned to pure ice. His legs kicked up and wind whistled past his ears. Twisting onto his stomach, he tried to dig his toes in and grab with his hands to slow himself, but the ice was impenetrable. The rock-solid nooks and bumps hit his kneecaps and scraped the skin off his hands, and then he hit the water and stopped instantly with a splash.

Shocking cold replaced the horror of the uncontrolled

descent, because now he stood thigh deep in the rushing water of the Chautauqua. In late January. Not that there was ever a month when the water ran warm.

"You all right?" Barker yelled from above.

Wolf took stock of himself. He was fine from the waist up, and anything below that was too cold to feel.

He nodded. "Yeah!"

The car was a new-model SUV, upside down and pointing upstream, the passenger side completely submerged, the driver's side angled out of the water. Inside, a male driver was hanging upside down in the seat, his bloody head tilted and bobbing with the movement of the vehicle itself. The top of the man's head was submerged—if he was alive he was losing body heat fast.

There was no one in the seat directly behind the driver, and Wolf prayed that the front and rear passenger sides were empty too—they were completely submerged and any occupants had likely already drowned.

The vehicle moved with a scraping sound.

He waded forward, then stumbled as he stepped up onto an unexpected rock and splashed his arms up to his elbows into the icy flow. Straightening himself, he continued wading through shallow water until he reached a deep pool between himself and the SUV.

Hesitating, he looked left and right. The pool extended up and downriver, and there was no going around it without adding on several minutes of wading.

Barker was still up on the road, standing with a radio in his hand and watching with wide-eyed interest.

"Bring my sleeping bag and extra clothing in the back!"

Barker raised a hand to his ear and then shook his head. Then he shrugged and put the radio to his lips.

What the hell was he doing?

Wolf pulled his radio from his belt. Pressing the button, he said, "Do you hear me?" Wolf twisted the knob back and forth, getting nothing. Close inspection showed water streaming out of the speaker holes.

Barker clearly couldn't hear him. The radio was close to his lips and he spoke excitedly, but he was looking away from Wolf, so it was probably something along the lines of "Get the Fire Department up here quick!"

Wolf chucked the radio to shore, fumbled in his jacket pocket, and took out the Life Hammer. Crouching down, he jumped as far as he could toward the upturned truck.

It was then, just barely over the biting, freezing numbness, that he felt the first shooting pain in his ankle.

A second later he was submerged completely, the water gurgling over his head. He resisted the overwhelming urge to inhale as the cold hit him like an electrocution.

His head popped out of the water and he sucked in a breath, grabbing for the roof of the car. He whiffed, then went back under. The angle of the car was such that the edge of the window was a few feet above the water. Bobbing back up, he kicked hard, his boots lead weights on his feet, and barely caught hold where the upper edge of the window met the top of the door.

The water cascaded off his face and stung his eyes as he pulled and brought up his other hand, ready to slam one of the needle-point steel tips into the corner of the window, but he slipped and submerging again.

He kicked harder, and then whiffed his hand-hold again, because this time the current had brought him downstream.

This is ridiculous! he thought as he went back under. He was going about it the wrong way. He needed to go around the car, climb up on the underside of it, then over the edge and to the driver's side door.

He kicked and paddled, keeping a numb fist around the hammer. The current helped him to the edge of the deep pool and he scrabbled up a slick, algae-covered rock to shallower water.

Panting, he got to his hands and knees and stood.

He paused and did a double take when he noticed Barker still standing on the road. His red hair was like a flame against the snow-covered mountaintop behind him. His eyes were unblinking, his expression flat.

"I could use some help!" Wolf screamed at the top of his lungs.

Barker started descending the hill.

"Bring the sleeping bag in back!"

Barker stopped, nodded, and made his way back to the SUV. Taking his sweet time with every movement.

"And the extra clothes! Move!"

Barker moved.

"Shit." Wolf was shivering uncontrollably now. Hypothermia's first signs were coming on strong.

Moving on unsteady feet to the upturned guts of the car, he yelled, "Sir! Can you hear me?"

There was only the sound of rippling water and now Barker's scraping footfalls finally coming down the incline.

Dropping to his belly, Wolf hung over the door and slammed the hammer into the window. It instantly shattered and the glass fell away. At the same time, the car creaked and dropped a few inches.

With relief, Wolf noticed there was nobody else in the car, but following the shift, the guy's upside-down head was now submerged to his mouth.

He hooked the blade of the emergency hammer on the seatbelt and pulled back, cutting through the tough fabric and a piece of the man's shoulder. With the seatbelt no longer holding the man up, his head dunked under the water completely.

Wolf dropped the hammer, grabbed hold of the man by his sweatshirt, and tipped himself over the side. His legs up to his torso splashed back in the water, but he had purchase on the man and wasn't letting go.

"I gotcha," Wolf said, his voice shaky from the cold.

Hooking his foot into the window, he did a push–pull–grunt ballet and finally got the man free. He rolled onto his back and balanced the reclined man on his chest. Thankfully the victim was young and slim, but Wolf's limbs were slow now, and it seemed to take an age to swim the few feet back to the other side.

Wolf kept expecting Barker to appear with his strong arms, but the detective sergeant never came.

He continued his labored ascent over the rocks, collapsing in the shallow water, then hauling the man a little further.

"Get down here!" Barker was just a few yards away, on the shore of the river and yelling into his radio. "He's out! Let's go!"

With clenched teeth, Wolf dug deep to find his remaining strength and heaved the man up onto his shoulder. Staggering on the slick rocks, he watched in confusion as Barker stood up from the water, soaking wet.

Had he fallen? What the hell was he doing now?

With mouth wide, water dripping off his face, Barker came rushing over. "Careful, be gentle with him."

The weight lifted from Wolf's shoulders as Barker took the man and carried him to the sleeping bag at the side of the river. Wolf saw Barker had brought the dry exercise clothing, too.

The sirens were right above them now, and a line of rescue workers appeared at the edge of the ravine, springing into action.

Wolf unraveled the sleeping bag and watched Barker put

his large muscles to use, ripping the guy's clothing off like it was made of tissue paper.

Wolf stood hunched over, hands on his knees, still trying to catch his breath. If he moved, his wet clothing lapped against his skin, worsening his distress, so he tried to remain still, despite the wracking shivers making it all but impossible.

"He's got a pulse," Barker said, zipping up the bag to the man's head.

Wolf nodded. He heard footsteps and yells behind him, and then there was a man crouching in front of him and looking up.

"Hey, Dave. You all right?"

Wolf tried to nod.

━━

Living in the mountains of Colorado made one realize why people had worshipped the sun for millennia. Life-threatening cold was always an inopportune moment away. A broken-down car, an injured leg, a drink too many, a wrong turn on the walk home—people had died for all these reasons and more in the mountains of Colorado.

Wolf sat in the back seat of a fire truck and wondered whether there were any cultures that worshipped rapid-deployment heat packs. There should be because they were doing the trick right about now. He had six taped to his back, a further six on his chest, one for each foot, and one more balanced on his head. He was naked under two wool blankets, knees drawn in a cannonball position.

The diesel engine of the fire truck rattled underneath him while the vents howled, pumping out heat like dragon's breath. He'd started out as a numb block of ice; then there had been a stinging sensation as his body had regained sensation; now the heat was almost unbearable. He also needed to take the biggest leak of his life, but that was going to be a whole other logistical problem without shoes or clothing, parked on the busy road with passersby slowing to a crawl and gawking at the flurry of activity.

A young firefighter came to the window and looked in.

Wolf nodded at him, giving him the okay to open the door.

The firefighter opened it, letting in a blast of cold air, and climbed inside. "The victim is stable and on his way to County."

Wolf nodded.

"We need to get you in now. We have another ambulance on the way."

Wolf shook his head. He had stopped shivering a few minutes ago and concentrated on keeping it that way as the cold from the open door bit into his face. "No need. I just need some dry clothes."

"You sure? Give me your arm."

Wolf stuck out an arm and the cold burrowed into the opening of the blankets, caressing his exposed skin. "I'm starting to sweat."

There was no way he was spending the next thirty hours in a hospital bed for observation.

The firefighter ignored him, concentrating on his watch and Wolf's pulse. After another few seconds of staring into Wolf's eyes he said, "All right. You're okay."

"Damn right I am. I've got my exercise gear in the back of my SUV. You mind grabbing it? And I could use something to take a leak in."

The firefighter nodded and left, and Wolf assumed his huddle position under the blanket.

Barker climbed out of the truck parked in front of Wolf's current warming hut, looking refreshed and toasty in his stocking cap, fireman's coat, boots, and sweatpants. He exchanged a few words with a fireman, shaking his head and thumbing over his shoulder.

The rescue worker, a guy Wolf recognized as Tim Dunlop, and one of Barker's friends by the looks of it, stole a glance towards the fire truck Wolf was sitting in and shook his head.

Wolf narrowed his eyes, wondering what Barker had to bitch about, and why he was pointing toward Wolf.

Greg Barker was the only member of the detective squad that Wolf would've liked to see the back of. The other three— Rachette, Patterson, and Hernandez—were good deputies who had proven themselves good detectives over the past year and a half since the inception of Wolf's team. Barker had not.

Not only that, but Barker hadn't been appointed by Wolf, but rather by Sheriff MacLean as a favor to Barker's father, a man who lived south of Williams Pass and owned one of the biggest cattle ranches in Colorado—by far the biggest in Sluice–Byron. Upon his appointment, MacLean had immediately promoted Barker to sergeant, presumably for the same reason.

Barker was the type of deputy Wolf despised: a ladder climber with aspirations of sitting in Sheriff MacLean's office chair one day, stepping on any and everyone who was in his chosen path.

Which made the hesitation in Barker's actions today even more puzzling. Normally, Barker showed over-the-top aggression during these types of scenarios, trying to outshine everyone —promotions, medals, and commendations first and foremost on his mind.

Wolf had never detected fear in the man, but Barker's actions, if not motivated by crippling fear, had made no sense.

Once again, the door opened and cold air came in.

"Here you go." The firefighter handed Wolf his clothing and an empty Gatorade bottle.

"Thanks. Hey, what's your name?"

"Grenning, sir."

"Thanks, Grenning."

Grenning nodded and shut the door, then went to Barker and Tim Dunlop and joined in the conversation, like a freshman sidling up to the seniors in the high-school halls.

He, too, snuck a glance toward Wolf and shook his head.

Click here to download DIRE (David Wolf Book 8) and continue the adventure!

DAVID WOLF SERIES IN ORDER

Gut Decision (A David Wolf Short Story)– Sign up for the new release newsletter at http://www.jeffcarson.co/p/newsletter.html and receive a complimentary copy.

Made in the USA
Coppell, TX
25 October 2023